$\frac{1}{22}$

MESSAGE FROM A STRANGER

A NOVEL BY MARYA MANNES

Message
from a Stranger

NEW YORK · THE VIKING PRESS · 1948

Acknowledgment is made to The Macmillan Company, publishers of James Stephens' Collected
Poems, for the lines from "Deirdre."

PRINTED IN THE UNITED STATES OF AMERICA
AMERICAN BOOK—STRATFORD PRESS, INC., NEW YORK

"The dead can live only with the exact intensity and quality of the life imparted to them by the living."

—Joseph Conrad: *Under Western Eyes*

To My Mother and Father

Contents

MESSAGE FROM A STRANGER

The first days . . .   I died on November 12,
1946, in New York City,
after a brief illness. I do not remember much pain, although
the violence of the infection that caused my death must have
brought acute discomfort and consuming fever. I do remember,
though, exactly when I knew I would not live. The doctors
had given me an injection and I felt suddenly quite pure
and without substance. More than that, I saw my room, the
nurse, the doctor, from an angle not at all relative to the position
of my bed. They seemed farther and lower, as if I myself were
slightly levitated. Then I saw myself, with one arm hanging
over the edge of the bed and Whitney, my husband, holding
on to my hand. He was sitting on a chair, bent toward me.
My head was turned on the pillow toward him.

It was confusing, for although I seemed above and out of
myself, I could still feel the warmth of Whitney's hand and see
the look in his eye. I must have been like an image that splits
in two when your eyes, fixed on it, are out of focus: a candle
flame that becomes two identical flames. Like a faint voice on a
telephone, Whitney's was saying: "You're doing fine, Livvy.
You're doing fine . . ." He looked gray with fatigue, and his
mouth, usually so firm, seemed to have difficulty forming the
words; but his eyes were the reflections of my knowledge: they
said, She is dying.

I could not speak but I matched the dishonesty of his words
by smiling. It must have been a poor smile, because Whitney's

3

head sagged on my arm and the nurse turned her face away.

Then it happened. I remember one final spasm, not unlike the birth of Philip. And I remember thinking to myself, this must be the delivery of my soul; and I saw then a primitive Italian painting in reds and blues where, from the prostrated body of a noble lord, escapes the white puff of his spirit, freed. But there was this strange addition: I was for a time both the bearer and the born, the issuant and the issue. I was at the same moment creating and being created, and I could not tell which was the more arduous: the black hot fighting up into light, or the more familiar expulsion of my burden.

But that is only part of the story. So much happened in what must have been so short a time that any ordered description is misleading. And yet the only way I can convey the overwhelming simultaneous rush of sensations is to tell of each of them one after another, although they are no more separate than the separate colors that go to make up white. And I shall have to use the world's arbitrary measurements of time—days, weeks, months—to parcel out this chronicle of space.

First, with a fearful roar and clanging as if a thousand metal hearts were beating against their walls, I was whirled into an emptiness as crowded with substance as are certain silences with sound. It was a wild and headlong flight, where I spun and reeled and palpitated like a leaf in a hurricane. In all this roaring and palpitating there was music—phrases, voices, instruments engaged in some gigantic cosmic tuning-up; a perpetual prelude—to what symphony? And there were words—phrases, fragments of poems; and through them all I myself screaming—to whom?—"Hold me! Hold me! Hold me!"—for the loneliness was terrible.

And Whitney held me. Or rather, he held a shell, for I had slipped out of it, as a hand out of a glove. My body lay there, completely still; but it had no more to do with me than the

starched white cap of the nurse. She went to Whitney and
gently tried to pull back his shoulders and take him away from
the bed. Whitney raised his head slowly and looked with blind
eyes at the doctor in the doorway. The doctor lowered his head.

The headlong rush, the wheeling and roaring, then stopped,
and a great silence came. I seemed to be quivering like a seis-
mographic needle; suspended in a stationary dance as a part of
some microscopic palpitation. This dance took place in an electric and impalpable space that had no boundaries. The nearest
likening to the visual quality of this void is the queer light that
one can see when the eyes are tightly shut against the sun:
white-violet, indigo, sometimes crimson; speckled and shifting.

I was not alone. In this featureless state there was a definite
pattern, of which I was only one point of many. I remember
once seeing, in motion pictures, a "model" of an atom—several
white billiard balls jiggling and palpitating around a central
billiard ball. This, presumably, was the final breakdown of
matter.

A great peace settled over me. I had not realized until this
moment how heavy was the burden of identity. This is the
end, thank God, of Olivia Baird; the end of this terrible and
vigilant consciousness; the end of doubt, of pain, of error; the
end, even, of emotion, and the beginning of freedom.

As usual, I was a fool.

I was a fool to think that any such drastic transition could
be completed all at once; any more than an adolescent can
become wholly mature overnight. Like every growth, it was a
slow process. And it was to be a long time before I could really
leave my life, before the severance from the world I knew
was final.

I should not have been surprised, therefore, to find myself
present at my funeral. The few times Whitney and I had talked
of death, I had inveighed against funerals. "For heaven's sake,
don't give me one if I die," I said. "I think funerals are

barbaric and miserable. Everything connected with them—the black, the casket, the shiny hearse, the sepulchral tones of the preacher—is destructive to true memory."

Whitney laughed at me as if I had been a willful child. "Okay, dear—we'll just dump you into the nearest ditch."

I was dumped, instead, into a Presbyterian church on Madison Avenue, in a very elaborate casket. The church was crowded, which surprised me. Whitney, Philip, and Auriol were in the first pew, of course. Behind them were assorted cousins, aunts, and uncles; Whitney's brother and sister and their children; Anna, my cook of so many years. I recognized many friends, but there were many more whom I did not recognize. In the back pew of the chapel sat Brian. The cavernous shadows under his brow made it seem as if his eyes had been torn out, like the eyes of Oedipus.

The altar was covered with flowers. At the right of it, the organist waited at his keyboard, his head turned to watch for the cortege. At a signal from the head usher, he began to play the choral prelude *Ich ruf' zu dir*. Philip must have arranged that, for we had heard it together when he was fourteen, and at the end I had asked him what he thought of it. After a pause he had said, "Gosh! I guess that's religion." I told him it was mine; then added, half to myself, "I'd like to die listening to it."

The pallbearers were carrying my body slowly up the aisle. Brian did not look at the coffin. Neither did Philip. The boy was fixing his eyes, enlarged but dry, on an organ pipe. The only movement I could see was his collar working up and down on his thin neck. His hands were closed so tightly into fists, hanging at his sides, that the knuckles were white. His inaudible voice kept saying, over and over, This isn't Mother. This isn't Mother. This isn't Mother.

Whitney, correct and grave, followed the cortege with his eyes, and so did Auriol. Mourning became my husband: it refined his usually florid face and gave his bearing dignity. I think he was too tired to feel much, except a kind of incredulity. Over and over, he said, My wife is dead, my wife is dead— as if to convince himself of something he doubted. As for Auriol, my daughter, his stepdaughter, tears were streaming down her face. But they were not tears of uncontrollable grief. As clearly as if she were speaking above the crowd in her girl's voice, the words came out: This is a tragic moment. My mother is dead. I have no mother. She was great and famous and everybody is here and everybody is looking at me. I look like her. I am all in black and very pale and everybody is saying, "Poor child, how like her mother." My mother was famous and she is dead. This is Sorrow.

All that Brian whispered was, Stay with me.

I suppose, in spite of my aversion to funerals, mine could have been called a simple and unpretentious one. With few exceptions, these people had come to grieve for and honor me; with few exceptions, they loved me in their own separate ways. The dissonant notes (and I heard them as clearly as if the organist had struck them) came from three others besides Auriol, my daughter. There was Elizabeth, who wondered how long she must wait after this day before presenting herself as consolation to Whitney. There was Whitney's sister, Eleanor, whose abiding reaction was, Thank God, Whit's free of that woman. And there was Agnes, my cousin, who considered my early death as a sort of fitting answer to what she had always believed an amoral and indulgent life. When the three of them got together in the vestibule after the service was over and muttered to each other about the "tragic loss," it was a wonder that a gigantic projection of my smile did not alarm them into silence.

I must explain that this extra-terrestrial eavesdropping of mine was accompanied by a complete absence of emotion. As far as I can see, this was a sort of compensation for total

vision, which in life would have been unbearable. It was as
though I were looking down at a borderless oriental rug of
infinitely complex design. I could see each part in relation to
every other part. I could see the deer stepping delicately through
flowers and, at the same time, the man raising his bow to shoot
at it. I could see the arrow speed and the deer stricken. I could
see the river winding among the hills and the woman drinking
at its source. I could see two men fighting and one of them
dead. The light was the same over all; nothing was in shadow.

There was, of course, no element of time. Or rather, perhaps,
past, present, and future co-existed exactly as they do in the
word "today."

In these early stages of seeing without feeling, I thought to
myself, this is Heaven. Later on I said, this is Hell. Whereas in
life I had so constantly yearned for passivity, for immunity, for
non-feeling, now I knew a faint prick of nostalgia for the tem-
pestuous reactions of my life; much as one feels pain in an
amputated limb.

Will had died with my body. I was now totally at the beck
and call of those who remembered, needed, and wanted me.
They re-created me in their own wills, they conjured up my
presence, they plucked me out of my crowded electric void and
gave me shape, if not substance. How long this slavery to the
living (for that was what it was) would last, I could not know.
I was often in three or four places at once, especially in the
weeks immediately following my death. The continuity of this
record is therefore an arbitrary one.

I came to Max soon after the funeral. It was like him not to
be there. Not only had he an abhorrence of even the most
innocent social conventions; but he had been trying for the
last fifteen years to put me out of his mind.

I married Max Aronson about twenty years ago. I was nineteen at the time and in a state of violent rebellion against my good, decent bourgeois family (or so I called them after I knew Max). For even then, Max had all the Marxist patter, using the word "bourgeois" for everything that was comfortable, conventional, static, or even polite; and the word "worker" for everything that was honest, strong, noble, and fearless. He spoke constantly of the masses, although at twenty I doubt whether he knew more than a few dozen people at most. Like so many of his friends, he was conventional to the point of fanaticism in his avoidance of convention. By making a fetish of sloppiness—of the crumpled collar, the soiled sweater, the unclean nails—he bestowed far more importance on his appearance than the "bourgeois" husband who took a shower and dressed for dinner as a matter of course.

You may wonder then why I loved him and married him. In the first place, Max was beautiful, in a strictly masculine sense. He looked something like an El Greco figure—gaunt, attenuated, long-wristed; with brown eyes that burned in their sockets with some kind of insatiable thirst. His hair was appropriately long, and fell in a black shock over one side of his really magnificent forehead. His intensity was frightening and yet attractive; he set up about him an immediate tension that I mistook—and continued for a long time to mistake—for warmth.

Again, there was great attraction in the idea that he lived "dangerously" as against the even safety of my family's world. After the dark and comfortable upholstery of our living room, after the thick rugs and heavy green portieres; after the curtained sunny windows and the warm smell of German cooking coming from the kitchen, the disordered bareness of Max's room in the Village had a most romantic austerity. Here was a boy who had and needed no money, who scorned dependence on material things, who nourished himself on the hard roots of thought and warmed himself on the ardor of human striving.

I was already writing poetry at the time: bad little quatrains peppered with "thees" and "thous" and imbued with a kind of exaltation that was sincere enough at source but actually derived more from a current worship of Keats and Shelley than from my own convictions. Even so, one of them—printed in a "little" magazine of verse—had apparently made its editor, Alida Morris, consider me worthy of cultivation. She called me one day at my home.

"I want you to meet some interesting people, Olivia—people who really think." I did not take this as implying that my own environment was thoughtless, although this was what Miss Morris meant. So I accepted eagerly.

Miss Morris picked me up in the lobby of my apartment house. On the way down to Greenwich Village in a taxi (it was a cold, rainy night), she described the party.

"We're going to Max Aronson's—he's a brilliant political thinker—he writes, but only for magazines who have the courage to print him. Then there'll be Bertram Weber, the sculptor—you know, he takes a boulder and lets it evolve itself; and his mistress, she's a Wigman dancer."

The word "mistress" entranced me. It was so much more attractive than wife. I could hardly wait to get there.

We stopped at a doorway on Perry Street, a low red house with small-paned windows, and walked up a narrow stairway which smelled of paint, urine, and stew. On the top floor Max Aronson was leaning over the rail. He had on a gray turtleneck sweater, slightly spotted, and red sailcloth pants. He had a glass in his hand and he was smiling.

"Max, I brought Olivia Baird—you know, I told you about her."

"Hello, Alida." He took her hand, said "Hello" to me, and ushered us into his room. On the one couch and on the floor were a number of people in various attitudes of relaxation. The dim air was full of smoke, and what light there was picked out glasses, bookshelves, bare feet in sandals and the half-bare breast of one girl sprawling on the couch. I felt wrong in my new green dress and silly because I had washed my hair. They would think I was snobbish.

The others raised their heads briefly to look at me, but nobody introduced anybody. Alida, who seemed to know them all, squatted down to talk to a man on the floor, and I went to sit on the edge of the sofa.

Max brought me a drink—the usual Prohibition drink of home-made gin and ginger ale. Even my family drank it, although Mother apologized to her guests each time she served it. I took it eagerly and started to sip.

"So you write poetry?" said Max.

"Yes—now and then."

"What for?"

I didn't know whether he was teasing or serious. I decided to be flippant. "The usual reasons."

"You mean you're bored and lonely and unhappy," said Max. "Nice girls only write poetry then."

I was annoyed. "I'm not nice and that isn't why I write poetry."

"Why then?" asked Max, looking at me obliquely, with amusement.

"Because I want to say something—in a special way."

"What do you want to say?"

"Oh, lots of things . . ."

"Flowers and birds and rain?"

"Yes. Sometimes." My tone was defiant.

"What about people?"

Unaccountably I felt like crying. "I hate people!"

Max smiled. "At least you're not afraid of emotion." I said nothing and looked down at my glass, angry because my eyes were filling with tears. "Bring some of your stuff down some time," said Max—"and I'll give you some new things to write about. Real things."

I steadied my voice as well as I could. "What do you call real?"

"Ideas. Action. Revolution," said Max. "Anything but the outworn symbols of bourgeois romanticism."

The man next to me on the sofa had put his hand down the front of the girl's dress—the girl with the half-bared breast. He was holding it and nuzzling the back of her shingled head. I had never seen love-making before. Although I was shocked, the sight of it and the heat of the room and the drink and the presence of Max all combined to excite me. The word "orgy" came to my mind: this was probably what it meant. In the far corner of the room, under the bookshelf, another couple were fondling each other, the man stretched out on the floor, the woman seated and bending over him, stroking his face.

"I don't suppose this sort of thing happens in your chaste drawing room," said Max, with an indication of his hand.

"No," I snapped. "Bourgeois lovers like to be alone."

"Bourgeois lovers can afford to be alone. They have the money to set themselves up in nice little apartments or stroll down the leafy lanes of big country estates or take a trip to Sorrento."

"There's always Central Park," I said, and knew that it was a cheap remark.

Max took me by the shoulders and shook me. His fingers were hard and his black hair shook as he did it. "My God, I'll wake you up one of these days!" he said. Then he let me go abruptly, walked away, and slumped down on the floor next to Alida Morris and the sculptor.

I don't remember much else about the party. There was a violent discussion as to whether Jefferson had a bourgeois mentality, more intensive love-making on the part of the two couples, and a great deal of drinking.

Everything was beginning to blur when Alida, the sculptor, and his mistress rose and offered to take me uptown with them. I was going out of the door when Max pulled me back and kissed me on the mouth. I had been kissed by a man only once before, and that was soft and gentle. This was hard and I felt his teeth against mine and I pushed him away.

But that was the last time I pushed him away. Within a month we had become lovers and within a year we were married.

Two days after the funeral I was in Max's study, for the first time. I was surprised to see how comfortable, how almost cozy, the room seemed; until I remembered that Max was now a lecturer in Political Economy at N.Y.U. and had a Russian wife who had supplied him not only with two male children but with plenty of bourgeois attentions. The wife was not there, but Max was with a young man who looked as if he might be one of his students. He had the intense and avid look of a bright Jewish law student, but from the content of the conversation that followed he appeared to be a writer.

"Too bad about Olivia Baird," said the young man. "Funny thing, we were studying her stuff in class just last week."

"What do you think of it?" asked Max.

"Pretty exciting. Sort of a more relaxed Emily Dickinson. No, I guess it's not austere like that. She's more like a female Donne. Do you know her stuff?"

"Quite well. I was married to her for five years."

The young man sat up in his chair. "My God! I didn't know that!"

"Not many people do. It happened pretty long ago and wasn't much of a success anyway."

"What was she like—as a woman?"

Max rose, went over to a side table and poured himself a glass of beer; came back to his chair and sat down again.

"Complicated as hell. All mixed up inside. Like all women, incapable of being objective."

"What busted it up? Or don't you want to talk about it—"

"Hell, George, I don't mind. It seems a thousand years ago anyway. I was a kid and she was a kid, and there was something fresh and exciting about her—sort of open to everything. Had a good mind too, if it hadn't been so crammed with romantic illusions. She thought she'd be a sort of George Sand to my Chopin, but instead of that I was working on labor committees all day and most of the night, you know, organizing and planning, and the kids came too soon and pretty soon she didn't have any time to write. So after about four years she couldn't take it and went back to her mother with the children—"

"What was her family like?"

"Nice, middle-class conventional. Her father called himself a sculptor because he designed birdbaths for tycoons' estates —but he was about as creative as a Pekinese. Her mother had some money from the family paper business, so they lived comfortably enough and with a simple-minded kind of morality. You know, right is right, and wrong is wrong. Mrs. Baird was always patting cushions . . ."

The young man laughed. "Doesn't sound like your meat."

"It wasn't. They hated my guts. The father always looked at me with that 'You're-not-doing-right-by-my-Annie' look."

"Well, were you, Max?"

Max took a long swallow of beer and tilted his head back, speculatively. He had not changed much in the last years: his hair, though thinning, was still black, his face and body lean, and the only real change I could see was in his mouth, which was more hard-bitten.

"I treated her as a partner—not as a child-bride. The main trouble was, she was hipped on personal relationships, like most women; and I couldn't drive it into her that they were profoundly unimportant compared to the major human issues."

You're right there, my lad, I said to myself. I had wondered, even then, how you could love the human race if you didn't love the human being, but Max seemed to be able to manage it. At least, he loved part of the human race. His love was very restrictive. He would not bestow it on anyone who had more than five thousand a year; who read the *New York Times*; who wore good clothes; who—and this was much more important—did not have either a manual or an intellectual job. He could not love employers, no matter how benevolent; or brokers; or shopkeepers. He had enormous contempt for my mother because she drew a small income from her father's paper factory. He thought exclusively in labels and categories.

For a time I, loving him so, adopted these labels and categories. I was ashamed of my father for catering to Long Island tastes and money. I was ashamed of Uncle Fred for belonging to the Manufacturers' Club. I was ashamed of my pretty ex-school friends who cared about clothes and worried about their hair. That this was a colossal form of snobbery I did not realize. I had thought snobbery confined to the upper classes. But no set on Long Island was more exclusive than Max's group. They were the elite: sole custodians of courage, integrity, and truth.

"Do you see much of your kids?" asked George.

"Only the boy, Phil. I'm trying to stir him up a bit. But the girl's beyond repair. Complete little parasite, with all the fixings."

I hardly heard the last of this sentence because I was already on my way—out of Max's mind.

I had only a brief interlude in the featureless and electric condition which was my home before I was brought to places

which were completely strange to me, among people whom
I at first did not recognize.

In one instance I was surrounded with grocery baskets, some
filled with cans and vegetables, with slips sticking out, others
empty and in the process of being filled by a clerk. When
I saw the face of the clerk, I recognized Joe, who had always
waited on me at the local market. This must have been the
back room where they loaded. The delivery boy was waiting
around, watching. I recognized him too.

"Hear about the Corning dame?" said the delivery boy.

"No, what about her?" said Joe, tearing the green feathers off
a bunch of carrots and dropping them in a box.

"She's dead. Died a couple days ago."

Joe looked up. "What? How do you know?"

"Well, last week I took some orders to 929 and the porter
told me. Then I seen it in the papers today."

"Holy smoke—" said Joe. He seemed genuinely distressed.
"Why, she came in here 'bout a week ago. Looked okay to me.
What happened?"

"Dunno. Papers just said 'brief illness.' They was a whole
column about her—you know, how famous she was and all."

Joe leaned back against the shelves, his salesbook hanging
from his hand. "Jees—gives you a kinda shock. She was always
kidding—here."

"She didn't look like forty. I seen her once in a negligeay—
didn't look like a dame who works—"

"I can't get over it," said Joe. "It don't make sense. Why,
the other night I had a dream about her. I dreamed I was
married to her . . ."

The delivery boy leered. "How was it, Joe . . . ?"

The clerk turned on him, his mouth pinched with anger.
"Stop hangin' round here, for crissake, and get some of these
loaded!" I had not expected to find in Joe a shield and a
lance.

Nor had I expected to be in a furnished room, watching Miss Furman cry. Miss Furman had charge of the lending library around the corner from our apartment, and I used to get in there every ten days or so to get a book to read; usually something trivial and escapist, as I had never been able to read anything serious while I was writing. I don't suppose Miss Furman and I ever spoke more than three minutes together at one time. She was middle-aged, had cropped gray hair, and always wore a bit of Navajo jewelry: a silver necklace hanging on her flat chest or a silver thunderbird clip or a big turquoise ring. She had gone to Taos for a vacation once and never got over it.

And here she was at home, at night, alone. On a mantelpiece with no fireplace to justify it stood a copper bowl with some bittersweet in it. That and the Navajo rug and the East Indian print spread on the day bed and the photograph of a man with a white beard were what I first noticed. Then I saw a large framed photograph of myself, autographed, on her night-table.

Miss Furman was sitting in a mission chair under a wrought-iron bridge lamp, reading. Or rather, she had a book in her lap and was not looking at it because she was crying. The book was my first collection of sonnets, called *Intimations*.

Like most writers, I was embarrassed by earlier work, thinking always how much better I could have written this or that poem now. The page was open at a sonnet called "Choice," which began: "If you decide to barricade your heart By building walls between yourself and pain—" A tight, pedantic poem, somehow without true melody, but here was Miss Furman crying, and I was glad I was incapable of tears, because what I heard in her mind was nothing short of idolatrous grief—a woe so crushing and immense that one would have thought her own child dead instead of a woman seldom seen and barely known. What was I to this lonely woman, then? Was I something that she longed to be? Was I her unfettered spirit? Was I the projection of a dream, the woman with everything?

What had I done for Miss Furman, ever, but speak to her kindly?

But there was a more imperious summons, a voice so well known—saying, "Olivia—Olivia—Olivia—Olivia," and nothing else. I had been with Brian most of the time since the funeral, but always with him alone; and we talked together exactly as we had always done. At night I was with him in his bed, with his arms around me. Sometimes he must even have felt the weight of my head, for he shifted his arm, smiling, as he slept. Sometimes he would wake in the night, thinking I had gone away; and once he groaned out loud, "Olivia!" and lay there staring into the darkness, his body rigid, his arms so aware of their emptiness that even I, who lived in him, could feel their ache.

I was with him in the mornings when he dressed; and sometimes when he stood before his tie-rack, debating, he asked, This?—or shall I wear that? No, you don't like me in stripes, do you?

I was with him when he was reading manuscripts, at home at night, and he would say, This fellow's got something, hasn't he? Needs tightening up, but he hasn't got that constipated style that so many young authors think is Hemingway. Or, God, what tripe. Another one of these costume novels with two eyes on Hollywood. You always said that no one could write good prose if they thought of pictures first. It's up to the writer to make pictures himself—not leave it to the cameramen.

But the particular summons that took me from Miss Furman's room that night brought me not to Brian's apartment but to a party in a place I did not recognize. There were eight or ten people there, but the only familiar faces belonged to an English publisher and his wife, friends of Brian, called Betteridge. The group around Brian and Betteridge were discussing my death.

"Quite a loss, Brian, quite a loss," said Betteridge, highball in hand.

"Yes," said Brian, "she was a very good poet."

"She was almost too good to be true, wasn't she?" said an older woman. "Happy home life, attractive children, and then all that talent."

"Couldn't see what she saw in her husband, could you, Brian?" said Betteridge. "A crashing bore, I always thought . . ."

"He gave her what she needed," said Brian, "security."

"You knew her quite well, didn't you, Brian?" said Mrs. Betteridge.

"Yes. After all I was her editor. Although in the last years she hardly needed one—she edited herself."

A man said, "She didn't strike me as a particularly domestic type. Her poems don't exactly suggest the happy housewife."

"Oh, but she was, wasn't she, Brian?" said Mrs. Betteridge. "You could hardly tear her away from her home these last years."

Betteridge said, dryly, "I think Olivia's wild oats had been amply sown. From what I gather she ran through a pack of men, didn't she, Brian?"

Brian said, I love you, Olivia. I love you. I love you. He looked up from his highball at Betteridge, smiled, and said, "I gather she did."

"She couldn't have been very successful at it," said a handsome young woman, smartly dressed. "Women who are good in bed don't have to express themselves."

Brian was about to speak, but stopped himself. Betteridge laughed, saying, "I don't think any of us are qualified to judge —are we, Brian?"

"No," said Brian, looking at the young woman. "But I think we are qualified to call Miss Ransom's statement nonsense." He turned abruptly and went to the sideboard to pour himself another drink. Betteridge looked after him, quizzically.

Miss Ransom laughed. "As a matter of fact, I have evidence

for that statement. A man I know said she was cold as ice."

"Gallant type," said Betteridge. "Did he provide you with all the details?"

The young woman flushed, angrily. "I don't see why one has to idolize people just because they're dead."

Another man joined the group. "I gather you're talking about Olivia Baird."

"Yes," said Betteridge. "Her aptitudes as a lover are under discussion."

"Too thin for my taste," said the man, "but plenty of fire in the eye."

"Fire was the substance of Olivia Baird," said Betteridge. "She warmed others with it, but she burnt herself out in the end. I personally find the phrase 'good in bed' misleading and trivial. It implies an absolute technical standard which does not exist. A woman is good or bad in bed entirely according to her understanding of the man she is in bed with. It is a sensitiveness which is as much a part of intelligence as the ability to listen to music; a sensitiveness which can be born only of love—whether that love be transient or lasting."

Brian raised his head and looked at Betteridge with profound gratitude. I too would have felt that gratitude; no one knew, not even Brian, that fifteen years ago I had spent a night with Betteridge in London; a night without passion but with a tenderness that had colored our friendship from that time forward.

In the early time after my death I was, of course, a great deal with Philip; not in my home but in his room at college and sometimes in his classes. It was evident from the pull he exerted on me that he missed me intensely. But the tone and direction of his thinking made me believe that my death may have brought him a certain peace.

Philip had plenty of reasons for not being at peace. For

one thing, he was still at the tormented age. For another, he was living *in* a tormented age; in which the values by which one might achieve some kind of balance were either distorted or negated. For a third, Philip had a great deal of his father, Max, in him; a kind of purity of motive, a kind of ruthless exclusion of "inessentials" which was at constant war with the over-vulnerability he had inherited from me. Philip would pursue an idea so long as it was in a purely abstract form. The moment it became involved with humans, his heart became the dominant arbiter. Finally, Philip was not particularly happy in our home. Outwardly, the home was harmonious, for Whitney and I both worked at making it so. But the boy was far too aware of the conflict that underlay this harmony: to him, his stepfather was the living symbol of reaction, of the profitless past; while I, his mother, was the elusive image of freedom.

So often, Whitney would interrupt the boy's rambling specu-lations on socialism or "the ideal state" by saying, "Phil, you've simply got to get down to fundamentals. A man won't work without incentive—and the incentive that activates everyone is money." And I would say, "Phil, one of the worst fallacies of this age is a thing called 'a high standard of living.' So long as human beings continue to think that refrigerators, television sets, and a new perfume are guarantees of happiness they're riding for a fall. A high standard of living is usually accompanied by a low standard of thinking." Yet, who was I to talk? I, who had married Whitney for "security." I, who loved comfort and grace and ease and breakfast in bed. My words were fine enough, but was it not Whitney and his kind who supported the sick and housed the poor? What did his words matter, when each day brought forth an act of kindness or of ordinary human decency? What was the boy to believe?

I suppose, also, that Philip was jealous of me. I had tried very hard, particularly after leaving Max, to avoid imposing my personality as a mother on my son, having seen too often the

effects of "mother-love" in our country and the feeble men it
produced. I gave him love but I also gave him liberty. And
whenever I tried to teach him anything I would say, "This is
what I believe, Phil, but a lot of people don't. You'll just have
to make your own choice."

In spite of this he was, in the way of a great many perfectly
normal adolescents, half in love with me. And as I grew to
work harder and harder and spend less and less time with him,
jealousy of this work and later of my external success took hold
of him. Philip used to throw at me that I saw too many people,
that I was a public and no longer a private person. And when
I told him that I spent, as he well knew, at least four or five
hours a day entirely alone in my workroom, thinking or writing
or trying to write, he would say, "You're just as far off then
as you are with a lot of people."

Auriol, on the other hand, thrived on my prominence, caring
for me far less as a human being than as a foundation for her
pride, since she worshiped success. But Auriol comes later.
Now, while all these reflections of my son flashed through my
memory (or whatever it is that allows the dead to recall), I was
with Philip in his room in Hollis Hall in Cambridge.

It was four in the morning and Philip was sprawling face
downward on his bed. He was dressed, the bed had not been
turned down, the bed-lamp lit up his black straight hair, so
like Max's, his thin long wrists hanging out of their too-short
sleeves, the pile of books on his work-table, the open notebook
with Physics II printed on it, and a snapshot of me on the
mantel over the fireplace. It was taken of me on a beach near
Portofino many years ago, and I looked quite young and smiling.

Philip moved his head and groaned and then put his hands
to the back of his head, pressing on it, and all the while he was
saying, Mother, I'm so drunk, I'm so cockeyed drunk, I want
to die. I'm glad you're dead and can't see me—or can you?
Pretty, isn't it? You should have been here an hour ago, I was

sick all over, God what a feeling, what a godawful feeling,
Christ why does one have to do that, Christ, I want to die. . . .

Mother, the room's still heaving, what shall I do? For God's
sake what shall I do? I feel so cockeyed sick.

It isn't only that I'm drunk. I went to bed with a girl I
didn't want; well I guess I must have wanted her but when I
got in bed with her I didn't want her, I hated her face, it was
all mushed up, and I hated the way she took me, and she was
drunk too, and hell, it was dirty and I feel dirty and I don't
ever want to go to bed with that girl again—

Phil tried to raise himself from his bed. He half sat up,
but his head went down in his hands again and he fell cross-
ways on the bed.

I think I got drunk to forget the funeral, Mother. That
was the big idea. The funeral was awful and I couldn't take it.
So I went drinking and whoring, or is wenching a nicer word?
I guess you'd like wenching better. Mother, please put your
hand on my head, I feel so goddamned sick. . . .

I put my hand on his forehead and he gave a deep sigh and
in a few minutes he was sound asleep.

It seemed strange to me that I was not more with Whitney,
in my own home. Actually I did revisit the apartment often
but it was always in a haze, out of focus. I saw Whitney and
I saw Auriol and I saw all the familiar furniture, but never
clearly. Nor did I hear clearly; the voices of Whitney and
Auriol were distant and muffled, with some of their words
blown away as if by a high wind. I finally came to the con-
clusion that this dimness, this diffusion, was created by the
living themselves. Because Whitney did not feel or see my
image clearly I was never brought close to him; I was merely
a blur in his mind. And then it dawned upon me, with brilliant clarity, that this had existed while I was alive and was the
root of all our trouble together. Whitney never saw me as I

was. He saw only his own projection of me. Perhaps this is why
it is possible for two people to live together for years and still
be strangers.

The reverse of this was just as startling and just as evocative,
for I was constantly being summoned by human beings who
were complete strangers. Not like Miss Furman, or Joe, the
grocery clerk, for we had met; but people thousands of miles
away who had never laid eyes on me. These were the ones who
read, and understood, my writing. I remember particularly a
student in Prague who had come across a book of mine in the
National Library. For some reason the words, laboriously read
in a tongue alien to him, lit a spark, and he got my true image.
It was while he was reading a long poem called "The Dis-
possessed" that I came to him in the library, in Prague.

I remember, too, sharply, a girl in an English boarding school.
Someone had lent her an anthology of modern verse, and she
found in it a group of my love sonnets. There was music in her
head as she read, and I could literally see her mind flowering.
She laid down the book after reading them and gazed out of
the window, across the rolling Sussex downs. Her roommate
blustered in in hockey-clothes, slamming the door behind her.
"What's up, ducky, seen a ghost?"

The girl turned slowly round, smiling, and said, "Yes—!"

The second week . . . What I did see of Whitney through the haze engendered by his false image of me should have moved me, had I been capable of being moved. For the first days he was entirely alone, except for Auriol. He went to his business in Wall Street but he ate alone in his office. He went nowhere at night, but sat in his favorite chair in the living room, sometimes reading, more often doing nothing. I had never known him to drink alone before, but whenever I saw him now he had a highball next to him. Once, when I saw him a little more clearly than usual, he was standing in my study and staring at my desk. On it in a silver frame was a photograph of Whitney in his colonel's uniform, looking like the perfect American staff officer. Whitney walked over, took the picture and brought it to the bedroom, setting it on his dresser.

The first time Whitney came into sharp focus was not in our home but in Elizabeth's apartment. Elizabeth Warren was the widow of one of Whitney's associates, killed in 1942 in the African campaign. We had seen a great deal of Elizabeth in the following years, not purely out of sympathy but because Whitney admired her. She was beautiful in a static, magazine-cover way; perfectly groomed and dressed, and very good at small talk. Like many women of her type, she could speak fluently of everything from Picasso to U.N. without being in possession of a single fact. Although she bored me, she was a useful and decorative single woman; and I kept inviting her as a sort of

atonement to Whitney for filling our house with the people I
liked instead of people who could be useful to him.

Elizabeth was pouring tea out of a beautiful Georgian silver
pot. She was in a long black velvet hostess gown, full skirted
and tight bodiced, with Holbein collar and cuffs of fine and
immaculate linen, stiffly starched. Her yellow hair was piled on
her head in a complicated but becoming manner: her face
was serious and sympathetic, and it seemed to me that she
wore less make-up than usual in deference to my death.

"You take cream, don't you?" she asked.

"Yes, please," said Whitney. He, too, was grave, but he
glanced around the room with obvious admiration. It was a
page out of *House and Garden;* soft and restrained, with con-
trasting textures (the satin upholstery against the rough pile
rug) and complementing colors (the dark green walls, the
shell-pink curtains). Over the fireplace hung a portrait of
Elizabeth by a successful young artist who salved his bad
conscience at giving all his sitters technicolor prettiness by
painting them against a surrealist background of beaches and
strange shells, with sometimes a bleached bone for drama. The
only other pictures were Victorian flower prints; and, on the
piano, a photograph of Jim Warren in his Army Air Forces
uniform.

"I'm so glad you decided to come, after all," said Elizabeth.
"I've been so worried about you."

"It was a fine idea," said Whitney. "I haven't been out
at all—"

"I know," said Elizabeth, lowering her voice and her eyes.

"People have been wonderful, of course," Whitney went on,
"the place is overflowing with flowers and letters—but Auriol
attends to all that—"

"Poor little thing. She must feel so lost."

"Auriol's got a head on her shoulders. She's doing a fine job."

"She's not very like her mother, is she? I often noticed

how different they were." Elizabeth held out a plate of buttered muffins, and Whitney took one.

"Olivia was very critical of Auriol. Philip's always been her special pet. You know, women always seem to like the weaker ones."

"What's the matter with Philip? I thought he was doing so well at college, Whitney?"

"Oh, his brain's all right—but he's full of cockeyed ideas. I guess it's his father's blood."

"It must be terribly difficult for a woman to be famous and bring up children too—"

"Well, Olivia spent quite a lot of time on them. She worried about them a lot."

There was a pause, while both of them drank their tea. Then Elizabeth looked at him, her face a picture of tender sympathy.

"Whitney—I know what it's like. It's terribly, terribly hard at first, but somehow one just goes on living—"

Whitney returned her gaze. "You're a brave girl, Elizabeth."

"Not brave," she said with a little smile. "It's just a question of facing reality—"

"The worst thing about it," said Whitney through his teeth, his eyes closed, "is that I can't seem to remember her face. I remember how she looked when she was—dying—but I can't remember how she used to look—"

Very softly Elizabeth said, "Why do you try?"

Whitney opened his eyes and looked at her. "What do you mean?"

"Whitney—are you sure you really knew Olivia at all?"

"Knew her? My God, I've been married to her for three years!"

Elizabeth said nothing as Whitney got up and began to walk around the room, obviously upset.

"I'm sorry, Whitney—"

Whitney wheeled around and faced her. "Sorry for what?

Sorry because you hit the nail on the head? Hell, what's driving
me nuts now is the feeling I never had her at all!"

Elizabeth rose to her full handsome height and went over to
the fireplace next to Whitney. "I was sorry, Whitney, because
I asked you over here today to try and make you forget a little.
Instead, I just make it worse."

Whitney took her hand. "No. No, you haven't made it
worse. You've made me feel sane for the first time since—
since—"

"I'm so happy, Whitney," said Elizabeth. "I did so want
to help—" And she drew him back to his chair by the table
and gently made him sit down.

Brian was sitting at his desk going through a pile of letters.
They were mine, and there must have been at least a hundred
of them, for separate piles, tied with string, were on the floor.

Brian was taking out each one and reading it. Some he tore
up and threw away, others he put aside in a separate heap.
Finally he came to a thick one—it looked about six pages long—
read the first page, then took it over to his big red leather
armchair and sat down. He was smoking his walnut pipe, and
his face showed no particular emotion. I looked over his shoulder
and saw that the letter was dated February 16, 1943.

"Brian," it said, "it's so hard for this to make any sense.
I have rephrased it twenty times and it still doesn't make
sense. Here it is, anyway: I'm going to marry. His name is
Whitney Corning—a colonel now, normally an investment
banker. He's a very good person—brave, kind, dependable; the
type of man Max would sneer at but whom I find increasingly
valuable in the sort of world we live in.

"This doesn't make much sense, does it? But I have to go on,
anyway. I couldn't stand it any longer. Being alone, without
you, I mean. It's been four years, you know. And not hearing

from you for over six months. And imagining, anyway, that you
and Mary have more or less found each other.

"I was all right until about a year ago, and then I began to fall
apart, except for the job. I was losing direction without you, and
the children had begun to suffer from it. The war is dreadful
enough without adding destruction to the one center of sanity,
which should be home.

"I need Whitney, Brian. So do the children. I've tried to give
them a sense of stability these last two years, but it's wearing
thin. I suppose you must know whether I love him, and I can't
tell you. I am profoundly fond of him and need him. I think he
loves me and needs me.

"How can I say now that I shall always love you? What sense
will that make, even if it is the truth?

"Brian—Brian—what else can I say but your name?—over
and over. Pray for me, please. I am trying so hard to see clearly,
to do right. It's no time now to run after private dreams of
happiness. You didn't, did you?

"Bless you. . . ."

Brian laid the letter on his lap. He looked at the photograph
of me on his side-table—one taken about seven years ago for
the jacket of *Anonymous*—then closed his eyes and covered
them with his hands in order to see me better.

You crazy thing, said Brian, you crazy tortured misbegotten
woman. You and your black hair and your wide gray eyes and
your little body and your enormous and impossible thoughts.
Why didn't you wait, for Christ's sake? Why didn't you wait?

Forget the letter, forget the time, forget what happened,
said Brian savagely. I want the indulgence of the old, I want
the further past, the bright dream. I want to think of the day
we met. That's always a lover's game, isn't it? Do you remember
the day we met? Do you remember what you had on, what I
said, what you said? Do you remember what we felt?

And so Brian and I—he living and I dead—together conjured up the hour, fixed in our personal history and now in time, when we first met. I started:

It was in 1937—nearly ten years ago—

In New York, in May, said Brian. I remember, walking to my office, the little yellow shoots on the trees in the park—and the people sitting on benches with their sightless faces turned to the sun. I remember everything that day.

You had written me a letter, Brian—on the firm's stationery: Howe and Littleton, Publishers, New York and London. It said: "Dear Miss Baird: We have heard that you are contemplating a change of publishers for your next book, which we understand is to be a narrative poem. As long-standing admirers of your writing, whether prose or poetry, we wonder whether you would care to come and see us to talk over possibilities of publishing your subsequent work."

"Very sincerely yours," added Brian.

I knew of your house, of course. It had a reputation for distinguished, if not profitable, books. So I called you and we made an appointment. You suggested my coming to your office first, then going to lunch. Your voice was nice. Cool but nice.

Your voice sounded blurred, said Brian. Hangover, I said to myself. They say she drinks like a fish, anyway.

It was a hangover. I felt awful. I didn't care how I looked, I put on an old tweed coat and a beret and I said, "To hell with Howe and Littleton. They can take me or leave me."

You were late. You were due at twelve-thirty but you didn't turn up till one.

I stopped to listen to a barrel organ. I felt tired and dim from the night, but open to everything. The thin smell of spring was wonderful.

And then you came in—

You forgot the elevator. I went up fifteen flights in your

building and the elevator swooping made me sick to my stomach—almost.

My secretary announced you. "Miss Olivia Baird." Then you came in. You looked pretty terrible—little and forlorn, like a child dressed up in its mother's skirts on Thanksgiving Day. First I saw nothing but your eyes—as I see them now—light and enormous, with long lashes and an almost uncanny innocence.

Deceptive, weren't they?

No. I've always told you you were innocent—even when you were sluttish. After the eyes, I noticed your hands and legs—how delicately they were made.

I didn't see you looking. You're one of these men who can see everything in a woman without seeming to look.

We sat down and I said, "Well, Miss Baird, how about it?"

And you said, "You mean, about publishing my next book?"

And then it happened. I was looking at your face—hard. I was looking at that fine bent thin nose and at the high forehead and at the way your dry sandy-gray hair sprung from it; and the deep shadow where your eyes were, and then at your mouth—

Go on—

And I saw that it was sensual. Not loose-sensual, but controlled-sensual. Not thick, but well articulated. And then I forced myself to look away—into your eyes. But that was no help.

We sat there staring and saying nothing at all for a while.

And then you took me to lunch at Gino's. It was dark and shabby and smelled warm and Italian. Do you remember, Brian, we ordered whiskey sours?

We talked business for a while but I don't remember what we said, do you?

No. It didn't matter. I couldn't take my eyes away from yours.

Nor I. I drowned in them.

I felt weak, and as if I couldn't breathe; a tree of fire was growing inside me.

You had taken off your hat, and in the dim orange light I could see how white and fragile your forehead was, and the lines under your eyes, and the wide, mobile mouth, the under-lip sticking out a little and curling over. Your hair looked damp, as if it had been blown against your face by a wind from the sea.

And then you reached out your hand and laid it palm upward on the table, saying nothing.

Saying nothing, you bent forward and put your hand in mine, and I held it there. I could feel a separate small heart beating in it.

That was yours!

And then you said, "I love you."

There was no flirtation about it. No game.

I even told you you were not beautiful. I said, "You are too thin and your forehead's too high and your mouth is too restless."

I said, "I was whistled at once by a truck driver!"

You wanted to be a sultry bitch—all women do.

Wasn't I—sometimes?

You were everything. You were a slut and you were a puritan, you were right and you were wrong, you were a good mother and a bad mother, you were homely and you were too beautiful to be whistled at, much too beautiful for Hollywood or for the tape-measured dreams of college boys.

You made me beautiful.

Olivia—so much parted us. Work, illness, people, war. Can we stay together now?

I don't know, Brian. That would be a kind of death for you.

But I'm only half alive.

You've lived without me all these years.

It was easier then. The ocean, Whitney, Mary—were between us. Our own integrity—and our own insignificance in the face of the world's sorrow. Now there is nothing between us—but the substance and the shadow of my own body.

I love you, Brian.

Stay with me—

Brian, his eyes still closed, lifted his hand a little in a gesture of pleading. The clock on the mantel said nine. The telephone rang. Startled, Brian rose and went to his bedroom to answer it. I looked at the familiar dark red spread, at the night-table piled with books, at the series of Goya prints across one wall—"The Caprices of War"—and at the small green bronze Cambodian head smiling secretly on the top of the bookcase. For three years this room had been my refuge. A woman's voice, high, strong, and gay, came over the phone.

"What's the matter, did I wake you, Brian?" it said.

"God, no. I was just reading something."

"You sounded half asleep. Look, why don't you drop around here tonight. The Betteridges are clamoring for you and I have a beauteous girl for you."

"You sound like a Madam. What's the matter with yourself, Nora?"

"I was wondering about that. You have a ghastly way of making a woman feel inadequate."

"Sorry. I'll try not to do it again."

"Then you'll come over tonight? Please!"

"I'm sorry, Nora—I think I'd better beg off this time."

"Oh, come on—everyone's saying you're getting too serious lately."

"Blame it on the state of the Union. Or on bad writers. Seriously, Nora, I wish I could come, but I have to wade through about ten manuscripts tonight, so give me a rain check."

"Lunch Wednesday?"

"Yes—fine. I think I'm clear then."

They said good-by and hung up. I did not know who the woman was. Whoever she was, she had broken our communication for the moment. As I felt myself slowly withdrawing from his world, Brian was picking up a pile of typewritten sheets from the top of his desk and settling down, pipe in mouth, to read them through.

The third week . . . Whitney, Auriol, and Philip were in our living room discussing mourning. I saw them and heard them clearly because Philip was there. Their conversation was extremely interesting to me.

"Whitney," Philip was saying, "I'd rather take off this band, if you don't mind." He touched the black strip on his left arm.

"Take it off?" cried Auriol, horror in her voice. "Why, Phil, how can you!"

"It's been barely three weeks," said Whitney to Philip. "I find it hard to understand why you find that small mark of respect too much to show."

"That's not the point, Whitney. I just think it's exhibitionism. Anyway, I'm sure Mother wouldn't like it."

"You know, Phil, if we all acted on individual impulse there wouldn't be any human society left. There's a reason for the conventions—they mean something."

"Whitney's perfectly right," said Auriol. "It's the least one can do." Auriol had on a very neat black jersey dress with a small white collar and she looked at herself with pleasure in a mirror across the room. Philip watched her with undisguised scorn.

"You may like people to feel sorry for you," he said, "but I don't. People act as if I had a disease, or something. They even speak in low voices. As far as I'm concerned, the sooner I forget the funeral the better."

35

Whitney looked sternly at his stepson, and his voice was cold. "I always suspected they were teaching you some sort of anarchy at Harvard, and now I'm sure. Either that or you've been seeing your father again—"

Philip turned and left the room. Auriol went up to her stepfather and took hold of his lapels. "Daddy Whit," she said in a soft voice (in life I shuddered when she called him that). "Daddy Whit, I'm so glad you made me a Corning!" He put his arm around the girl and rubbed his chin on her curly dark red hair. "I'm glad too, Sis. You're really mine, aren't you?" And they rocked together back and forth playfully, until Auriol broke away, took a comb out of the pocket of her dress and combed through her hair.

I should explain here that in the first year of our marriage Whitney said he wanted to adopt the children and give them his name. At first I told him it was out of the question, feeling there was implicit dishonesty in it. But later I thought that if Max had no strong objections and the children were willing, there was no good reason against it.

I hadn't spoken to Max for years, although Philip saw him from time to time; and his reactions, when I called him up about the adoption, were quite characteristic.

"What's the idea—want to save them from the taint of the race? Or are you embarrassed at having procreated with a dangerous radical?"

"It wasn't my idea," I said, "but Whitney seems very set on it and as you haven't been overly paternal these last four years and as you have two new Aronsons, I—"

"Oh, stop the humbug. The name's a handicap for kids who live on Park Avenue, and Auriol'll make a better marriage if she's a Corning."

"Call it anything you want. For my part it may simplify life considerably. What with being a Baird, having Aronson

children and marrying a Corning, I'm developing schizo-
phrenia—"

"You always had it anyway."

"Then, you have no objection to the adoption?"

"None at all. Except that Philip should have his choice.
The boy's entitled to be a Jew if he wants."

"I agree. But you'll abide by his choice?"

"Certainly."

"Thanks, Max."

"The pleasure is all mine. Let me know who wins." We
hung up our receivers.

I was secretly very pleased when Philip flew into a rage at
the thought of adoption.

"Gosh," he said, running his fingers through his stiff black
hair over and over, "I don't want to change! My name's Aronson, it isn't Corning, what's the idea giving me a phony label?
Mother, I tell you I don't want to change my name, I want to
be Aronson!"

I tried to calm him down. "Nobody says you have to, Philip.
Whitney just wanted to make you part of his family—along
with me. You see, he's always wanted children and—"

"Well, why doesn't he make 'em himself, then?" cried
Philip.

"Look, Philip. You can do exactly as you please, but you
must know the reasons behind this idea. It's purely kindness
on Whitney's part. He thinks it will make things easier for
you—"

Philip shot me a strange look; old and canny. "You mean
he's ashamed of us being half-Jew—isn't that it?"

"It has nothing to do with being ashamed."

"But it has to do with being Jewish, hasn't it?"

I put my hand on his shoulders. "Look, Phil, if I thought
for one moment that there was any sense of shame on Whit-

ney's part, I could never have married him. It *is* true that he
feels your father has forfeited certain rights—he's never felt
any particular responsibility toward you and Auriol. And
Whitney wants to make us a homogeneous family. I personally
think that names are unimportant; or, rather, that they're only
what you make of them."

Philip was silent for a moment. Then, "What about Auriol?"

"Auriol was delighted. She's been getting a snub complex
at school."

"Yes, I know," said Philip. "She was blubbering about it the
other night."

"Shall I tell Whitney that you'll stay the way you are?"

Philip looked up at me, his face composed and shining.
"Yes! Tell him that— Please!"

"And you won't mind if people wonder why your mother
is called Baird and your sister is called Corning and your father
is called Aronson?"

"I don't mind." And then suddenly, "Do you?"

"No, I don't mind. I'm rather proud of you, Philip Aronson!"
And I kissed him lightly on the cheek.

Not long after the scene between Whitney and the children
about mourning took place in our home, Whitney had a talk
with Philip the night he was to catch the train back to Cambridge.

"Philip, have you made up your mind yet about what to do
with your life?"

"I'm beginning to."

"Well, what is it?"

"I think I want to go into the Foreign Service."

Whitney showed his surprise. "The *Foreign Service?*"

"Yes. You see, I've been majoring in languages and economics, and I'd like to pull out of this country for a while."

"What's the matter with it?"

"A hell of a lot. But that's not why I want to go. I think somebody ought to try to make sense with the rest of the world."

"It's not a highly profitable profession, you know. You'll have to be a minor clerk in godforsaken spots for years before you get anywhere."

"I know that. But somebody's got to do it."

Whitney reached for a cigarette and lit it. "I don't think the State Department will take kindly to some of your views, Philip."

Philip said in an aside to me, It's all right, Mother, don't worry, I'll keep my temper. He smiled at Whitney and said, "You mean because I believe in a planned economy?"

"That and a number of other theories."

"I don't believe in the overthrow by violence of the American government," said Philip happily.

"That's a comfort, I'm sure," said Whitney dryly. "But beyond that, you'll have to change certain habits of yours. I've heard that you've been drinking hard lately."

Not looking at his stepfather, Philip said, "That's true."

"Also, that you've been hanging around with a pretty tough bunch of veterans."

"That's true, too. But they've got a lot to say, and I wanted to hear it."

Whitney changed his tactics. "Did you ever talk to your mother about this Foreign Service idea?"

"Yes—vaguely. I said I wanted to get out and see the world—before it was blown up."

"What were her reactions?"

"She said I wouldn't look convincing in striped pants."

Whitney did not smile. He was putting out his stub with an air of profound concentration.

"Philip," he began finally. "I suppose it's no use suggesting

that some practical business experience might be a good foundation for any profession you choose later on—"

"You mean, going into your office?"

"Yes. If people knew more about a free economy they might
not be so enamored of a planned one."

Philip grinned. "The trouble is I *want* to be enamored!"
He got up and leaned against the fireplace. "It's nice of you to
offer that, Whitney. Most people would jump at it, but I guess
I'm born screwy."

Whitney rose too and sighed. "I dunno, Phil. We just don't
see eye to eye."

"I've been pretty much of a heel around here," said Philip.
"I know that. You've had to take a lot. I'm sorry." He walked
back and forth, his hands in his pockets, his head bent and his
long shock of hair falling down over his forehead. I saw that
his trousers were too short and one of his socks had a big hole
in the heel; his shoes (he had enormous feet, like all the young)
were scuffed and dull. I tried to visualize him being charming
to a Bolivian colonel at an Embassy party, but with little
success.

"I want to do what I can for you—for your mother's sake,"
said Whitney. "I'd like you to feel free to come to me if you
need any help."

"Thanks," said Philip. He was looking at his shoes with
disfavor.

"If you'd like me to speak to Coyle about you—he's in the
State Department, you know—he might be of use."

"Thanks a lot," said Philip, "but I think I'll manage the
regular way." He looked at his wristwatch. "Hell, I better get
going. I've got twenty minutes before train time." He went
up to Whitney and shook his hand. "So long. Thanks—" And
he rushed out, grabbing his bag and his coat with one sweep of
his long arm. As usual, and although the weather was freezing,
he wore no hat.

In most concepts of after-life judgment plays a dominating part. Many believe that the one who dies is submitted to an examination by higher powers, who determine whether his soul shall be condemned to the fires of hell, admitted to the glory of heaven, or put through a special sort of protracted trial of atonement in purgatory.

Although there were no judges in this state of molecular suspension, I felt increasingly sure that my compulsory visits to the living world constituted, in fact, this trial of the spirit before its final release.

I have said before that I felt no emotions during these visits; but that is not entirely true. If one were to consider the severance of spirit from body as a kind of amputation, then I continued to have sensations in this non-existent entity that was Olivia Baird; a form of reflex, I suppose.

One emotion was anxiety for those whom I loved; an insistent desire to help them; to guide them, to put in them the distillation of what had been best in me.

The other emotion—or perhaps reaction—was that of anyone confronted with the evidences of his own guilt. The introspection of the living is only a mild rehearsal for the merciless examination of after-death. Here I was confronted, whether I liked it or not, with the complete pattern of my own life. I remember once saying to Whitney, apropos of a court proceeding in which a man's most intimate life had been pieced together in public by a series of witnesses, that not one of us could survive such exposure with his reputation intact. I see now how true that was, and how merciful was the half-blindness and half-deafness of the living. How merciful, too, was the illusion we create, the rationalization we make, to prove to ourselves that we are really better than we are. In this way do people compose their faces before they look into the mirror. In this way are people shocked when they are confronted, unprepared, by their image in a window or in an unexpected mirror. "That is a stranger," is their first thought; and only later, "My God, that is *Me!*"

And so, in the words and thoughts of the living and in the still-adhesive memories of my life, these self-illusions, so carefully maintained, dissolved into thin air; and there stood the full, illuminated image, without shadow or nimbus, of a woman bearing my name.

The fourth week... The first time that I came really close to my daughter Auriol was in trivial enough circumstances. She was in a department store buying an evening dress; confronted, at this precise moment, with the choice of a black one, strapless and naked—and a green one, simpler and modest. She was thinking of me very hard because she knew exactly which of the dresses I would have urged on her. With this clarification in her mind, but with a very discernible twinge of conscience, she chose the black.

Auriol, at seventeen, was a very beautiful girl. Her electric copper hair, her green eyes, her fully developed breasts, and her blue-white skin were already incitements to desire. Only her rather heavy legs and her big feet and wrists—so typical of that vitamin-fed and exercised generation—retained any of the clumsy innocence of youth. She certainly did not look either like Max or me, although some claimed her mouth (now darkly red) was reminiscent of mine and the carriage of her head like Max.

Auriol was one, and Philip three, when I left Max. I felt a great responsibility toward them, determined—in spite of my own confused and erratic life—to give them stability and peace. Since Max was too poor to contribute to their support, and my salary as reader in a publishing house far too meager for the three of us, my parents paid for their nursing and later their schooling until I myself was in a position to do so.

I saw them little in the daytime, but spent at least an hour in the later afternoon, after work, to read to them, play with them, talk to them. In contrast to Philip's nervousness and excitability, Auriol was a placid, happy child, easy to raise. It was not until she was seven or eight that I began to worry about her.

Like most pretty young females, Auriol knew her charms. She spent a great deal of time before the mirror, cared deeply what she wore, and was greedy about everything, from food to possessions. According to current American standards, all this could be classified as "cute." In a country where special fashion magazines are published for adolescents, where cosmetics for children are advertised and four-year-old girls have manicures, anything is possible. But I found this precocious materialism in Auriol distressing.

I proceeded to implement this distress in exactly the wrong way. I read aloud Shakespeare to her, I took her to symphony concerts, to ballet, to plays. I lectured her on the unimportance of externals. "Because you are pretty means nothing at all, Auriol," I said. "It's what's inside that counts."

But Auriol saw only too easily that this was not so. The outside was very important indeed. People were nice to her because she was pretty; at school, in the park, among friends, everything was easy, everything came to her. The world about her refuted me daily. The beautiful were queens; no one cared what was inside so long as the physical elements qualified. So Auriol set her chin and decided early to devote herself to the national cult, where woman is a priestess worshipping tirelessly at the temple of her own image.

I know now I was wrong to try to force her. I know also that in the last years I grew jealous of her beauty. I suppose it is characteristic of all but the most assured women to want to be other than what they are; and Auriol's fresh voluptuousness was exactly what I lacked and wanted.

The more it flowered, the more I played it down. At twelve, at thirteen, and at fourteen, I refused—with almost fanatic intensity—to allow her any cosmetics, although all her school friends were wearing them. I insisted that she dress with almost puritanical modesty, even for parties. Once, when I found in her bureau drawer a black slip edged with the cheapest lace, I flew in rage at her and tore it up. "If you want to be a vulgar little chippy, Auriol, at least wait until you've learned the technique."

How stupid, how futile were these tactics I know now, well. But my feeling toward Auriol was part and parcel of my feeling toward this American century; a prescience of suffocation, where, on the spiritual desert of a mechanized civilization, a sandstorm of consumer goods and second-hand words were choking the breath out of the human being. I wanted to save her from this suffocation; instead, I had made it infinitely desirable.

My next contact with Auriol was in the nature of a revelation. She was riding home from a dance in a taxi; her first social evening since my death, it appeared. She had on a white fur jacket over the new black dress, and the texture and color of her long red hair against the fur were, among other things, too much for the young man beside her. He leaned over to kiss her, putting his arms around her. She pulled away. "No! Please! Please don't!" she said, in a small, muffled voice.

"Yes—please, Auriol—please—"

Out of my sultry daughter came the voice of a frightened child. "But I don't want to—please let me go—please—"

The young man, saying nothing, relinquished her. Taking a handkerchief out of his pocket, he wiped off the lipstick of his abortive kiss. Auriol shrank in her corner and cried out to me, Mother, I'm scared, what does one do? I don't want him to kiss me, I feel queer all over, what shall I do? Did you start at seven-

teen, Mother? You knew a lot of men—you knew what to do—
I'm frightened, Mother, I don't want to know yet.

The young man finally found his voice. It had a slight edge
of rancor.

"My mistake, Auriol," he said. "The way you look—"

"I'm sorry," she said, "I didn't think—"

"No—you just danced. I can't make you out, Auriol. You
look as if you were burning up, but every time I try to get close
to you, you freeze—"

Auriol was looking out of the cab window, saying nothing.
Two large tears were sliding very slowly down her cheeks.
Mother, she said, I don't know what to do. I don't know what
to do.

The boy turned to look at her, but Auriol kept her face
turned away.

"I don't know what's the matter with you. If you're that
cold why don't you stay home and play with dolls?"

"I'm not cold—" Auriol's voice was shaky.

"Okay then, prove it!" He put his arms around her and
pulled her face around. He was too excited to notice that her
cheeks were wet. He forced his mouth on hers and this time
she did not seem to push away. When the boy finally broke
away he said, "That's more like it!"

Auriol said nothing. The boy kissed her again, this time
putting his hand inside her coat. Auriol's eyes were closed; her
long red hair fell back as she lifted her chin to his face.

As the taxi approached our house, the boy again wiped his
mouth, and Auriol looked into the mirror of her compact, ar-
ranging her face and hair.

"Can I come up for a sec?" asked the boy.

"No—I'm afraid not, Ted. You see, my stepfather—"

"Okay, okay." He saw her to the door. "Good night, gorgeous.
When are we meeting again?"

"Call me, Ted. I don't exactly remember what my dates . . ."

The boy kissed her again, roughly, on the mouth. "Still don't like it?"

Auriol, in the doorway, gave him a small smile. "Thanks for the party," she said, "and everything," and went inside.

I think this was the first time I felt a close identity with my daughter. I knew how she felt when she was kissed. I remember the first time I was kissed, and it was very much like that. I remember that I was frightened, in some strange way; that I didn't like the male mouth stifling the breath out of mine, the feeling of the tongue between the lips, the sound of the urgent breathing. But I was ashamed to feel that way, for I knew that women should be passionate. And so, before real excitement ever touched me, I kissed back; pretending for the first, but most certainly not the last, time in my life.

For there is a good decent tart in most women, wanting to please a man without necessarily demanding pleasure. The act then is a mixture of generosity and pretense; until that time when a real passion removes the motive of generosity and the need for pretense; or, passion wanting, there grows in women a love of the race of men which endows that pretense with tenderness and warmth. But I at eighteen and Auriol at seventeen knew neither passion nor love of men. They excited us, they flattered our vanity, they were mysterious and full of danger. They meant the end of childhood, and that was both desirable and frightening. And we kissed them because they wanted so much to kiss us.

If Auriol takes after her mother, I thought, it won't be long before her hand encircles the back of the boy's head, without being put there by him; whether she loves him or not.

There were times when the featureless and yet patterned matter of which I was an infinitesimal part was violently dis-

turbed. This phenomenon seemed to occur in those intervals
when I was not bound to any particular living individuals but
"at large" in the world. It was only after several of these intervals
that I realized the nature of these dislocations as being evil.
Or rather, that this state I was now in was highly susceptible to
evil.

It happened first, actually, in the department store where
Auriol was buying her dress. There were hundreds of women
crowding the store (it was close to Christmas) and the emanations of greed that rose out of them were as tangible and
visible as the disease microbes to a biologist's microscope. I
understand now why I was always so sickened by this spectacle
of life, and why crowds in general frightened and depressed me.

I had always believed that the emanations from human beings
which we call "personality," or its components—"charm" or
"aggressiveness" or "dishonesty"—had actual, if not visible,
substance. They pervaded the air about these people, they
penetrated their homes, they were, in fact, atmosphere. It was
felt on entering a strange house, or a familiar room. The
atmosphere was benign or malignant, cold or warm, gloomy or
gay. You felt at ease and at peace, or you felt disturbed and
restless, depending on these emanations thrown out by the
inhabitants.

If you took a thousand people, then, and put them together
in a crowd, their combined emanations would become a thick
miasma. For some reason, this miasma was usually of a base
and anarchic nature. The only "good" crowds I ever saw in life
were those dedicated to music or to certain forms of sport. All
other mass gatherings (and I witnessed a number after death)
threw up a spiritual stench. I remember particularly some
political rallies where hate rose like a black cloud to the sky;
and where the heat generated by the words of some demagogue
consumed what innocence and reason there was in the head
of any single being.

Max could talk reverentially as he might about the "masses";
I found them often the agents of evil. That was the danger of
cities. The poisons generated by the crowds in any one block in
New York were powerful enough to assail and corrode the
spirit of any man, alive or dead. They assailed me, and I was
dead.

The second month ...   Like a voice penetrating through a deep sleep, Brian said, This is a luxury, Olivia: four solid hours with you, and no interruptions—

I found him on a train bound for Washington. He had turned his parlor-car seat toward the window and was looking out at the grayish-ochre wastes of the Jersey flats, particularly melancholy under a light drizzle. And yet these Jersey flats had been the symbol of release and joy for us ever since we had taken this same trip together soon after our first meeting.

I called you up two days later, said Brian, and asked you to come to Washington with me, just for the day. It meant eight hours with you alone, and I had to have them.

I cancelled all my engagements for the day. I have never loved Penn Station so much as on that day.

Or the Jersey flats, said Brian smiling. At that, they have a sordid sort of romanticism. Or a romantic squalor.

In the tube, under the river, we just looked at each other. But I think I was the first to speak, Brian.

You said, "I wish this train were going three thousand miles—"

Now, no longer sitting opposite him, no longer touching the side of his leg with mine, no longer speaking out loud, I was still there, beside him, hearing him. Not because I needed confirmation, I examined again those outward things for which

I loved him; the noble shape of his head, the short crisp sandy hair now mostly gray; the generous ears set close; the high forehead with the frontal lobes jutting above the bridge of the articulated nose; the thick tangled reddish brows; and that long vertical groove cutting down his cheek—the mark, I had often found, of the virile and knowledgeable man. His hazel eyes were focused at infinity. Although he was looking at the Jersey flats, I am reasonably sure that they were not the image on his retina.

On that trip, said Brian, we got the lover's game out of our system.

Yes, I said—the Story of My Life.

How urgent that is, said Brian, to explain to the other what one is, how one came to be; to unfold, to present one's identity on a platter, saying: Here I am.

I don't think I was very honest, Brian. As I remember it, I told a touching story of myself.

You presented the picture of a harassed young woman—and something of a fool. Now, now, Olivia, you know it was the fool in you that I loved. You were carried away by your illusions, which were always superior to your acts.

Aren't they always?

Not always. We weren't an illusion.

I had told Brian, on that first ride together in '37, of my life with Max and of how I had left him after nearly four years of tension, bewilderment, and disillusion. Of my own childishness, of my own egotism, of my over-vulnerability, I implied little. Nor—in the wash of self-pity that engulfs most women when they speak of an unhappy marriage—did I mention (then, at least) the qualities which made Max an interesting and potentially valuable man: his detailed classical knowledge, his deep understanding of music, his sharp sense of satire, his wrath against injustice, whether toward state or sparrow. Instead I made him something of a monster: a man whose theoretical absorption in humanity had made him blind to individual human need. I described those moments which had hurt me most, not those which, often enough, had impelled me toward him.

One of the former seemed trivial enough. I was furnishing the walk-up brownstone flat where we lived after our marriage; partly with the meager contents of Max's old room and partly with furniture and hangings given me by my family. Our wedding checks did not go far, and we had to do what we could on my hundred dollars allowance a month and the small sums that Max earned from writing for little reviews. Max left the material side of our life entirely to me: "Go ahead and fix it any way you want. Just so I don't have to waste any time."

Instinctively I proceeded to make the little flat into my current version of "warm and cozy." I found cheap old hooked rugs for the floor, re-covered some of mother's Victorian chairs with a strong red material and our double bed with a candle-wick spread I had bought. I was just hanging some frilled white window curtains in the bedroom when Max walked in and stopped dead in the middle of the room.

"Christ," he said. "This is getting to look more and more like a stuffed bird."

I turned around on the stepladder, holding the curtain in one hand and the rod in the other. "What's wrong with it, Max? It's perfectly simple—" My voice trembled a little.

"Look, Livvy—I didn't marry you to import the family atmosphere. The inside of a tea-cozy may be okay for your father's dubious inspirations, but it would drive me nuts."

I didn't trust myself to speak. My throat ached and my eyes burned.

"What's wrong with a good bare window, anyway?" said Max, and left the room.

I took down the curtains and cried on the bed; and as usual in the first year, Max ended the tears by making love to me. His

brutality as a lover excited me in those days; he wasted no
words and no tenderness, but his ferocity and power made up
for them. He often left me bruised; often unsatisfied but
always in love. I felt that this was primitive and therefore right;
and like most women, exulted in submission.

Brian broke in: You didn't tell me any of these things at
first. Not until months later— Brian's brow was clouded.

No, Brian, I didn't. And the day I did you behaved almost
like Max.

I remember. As a matter of fact, I raped you!

It was mutual, I said.

And Brian must have heard, because he smiled.

Another thing that I told Brian about Max on that first
trip had to do with the birth of Philip. Max was delighted with
my pregnancy: proud and very good to me during the whole
time. He seemed to have acquired a new gentleness, and I
don't think I was ever happier with him than during those nine
months.

But soon after Philip came, a change came over Max. He
was, I think, primarily disappointed in having a boy, preferring
—like some men—to maintain alone the male prerogatives of
the family. But all sorts of things irritated him. He was scornful
at my inability to nurse Philip. "That's what comes of having a
'cultured' background!" he sneered one day while Philip was
pulling at a bottle. He was annoyed at the time it took me to get
my strength back after the birth. He was particularly infuriated
at my parents' obvious adoration of the child and of my own
absorption in him. Philip, in the womb, was part of Max's
primitive man-woman feeling. Philip as a being was an intrusion
and an obstacle to free living.

I know now that if I had had either common sense or
intuition, I would have quietly weathered this storm, taking it
for granted as part of Max's character and biding my time. His
subsequent marriage to Marusia, a woman older than himself,

wide and wise, was evidence enough that he needed the calm
maternal bosom as refuge from his own confusion. But I,
intent as usual on my own needs and unaware that this confusion existed (I had not learned that this was the basic root of
dogmatism) had built up within me the idea of the holy
family trinity—mother, father, and child: seeing in my mind's
eye the classical triad of the father, his arm about the mother,
gazing tenderly down at the infant's crib. Instead, the father
in my real trinity would turn away with a sharp and flippant
word and absent himself as much as possible from the doings
of the nursery.

As I told all this to Brian, he had asked me why I had another
child within two years.

"Oh," I laughed, "that's a long story, Brian. I could say
that I wanted a companion for Philip. I could say that I loved
the bearing of a child. I could say that it was an accident. And
all these reasons would be true. But I think a sense of failure
had much to do with it."

"What kind of failure?" Brian had asked.

"Failure at work, chiefly. When Philip was six months old,
my parents paid for a nurse so that I could go back to writing.
I did—producing a spate of poems which were rejected as fast
as they were sent out. I stopped showing them to Max because
his invariable comment would be, "Why do women always
have to sublimate everything?""

Anyway, a year of this shook most of the faith I had in myself;
and Max, increasingly disinterested except toward his political
work, shook the rest.

"So," Brian had said on that first train ride, "you did the one
thing you knew you could do well—produce a child."

"Yes. For most of us who are fools enough to try to be
artists the making of a baby is the best escape—at least until
the child is born. We tell ourselves that we are performing our

rightful function: all the rest is illusion. The doubts recede, and a great peace settles on us. So long as a woman is bearing she cannot be a failure."

Brian guided me back to my last year with Max. "All right, so you had another baby. But what really made you get up and leave?"

"Max stopped wanting me," I said.

Brian looked at me with incredulity. "What a fool," he murmured, "what a colossal fool."

"No," I said, "Max wasn't a fool. He was never that. But I expected too much. I kept waiting for small, warming things: his hand on mine, a playful affectionate word, a light kiss. Those things mean a great deal to a woman. But Max generated heat in only two ways: love-making and argument. The small amenities, the small tendernesses, he considered inessential. And so I suppose he began to notice that waiting look on me; a sort of pleading expectant eye. And I cried too often—quietly and usually alone; but for no reason that would convince a court. And I was much too humble—almost cringing, like a dog pushing his head under your hand to make you stroke him."

"That still wouldn't have made you leave him," said Brian.

"No—it still wouldn't. But one night we had a party—the usual group of self-conscious young neurotics in love with chaos—and I saw Max bending over one of the girls. I had seen her once before—on the night I first met Max—and I remember how her dress fell open and her long big breasts—the loose and flaccid kind—swung under it. She had the liquid prominent eyes of the Fourteenth Street oriental, a rapacious face, and mobile fleshy lips over large white teeth. She was sprawled on the sofa with her legs up, and you could see where her stockings were rolled and her green-white flesh began. So could Max. They were looking at each other in only one way. Not "Let's do it," but "Let's do it again." Their lust seemed to be sharpened by knowledge. And in a wave of ferocious jealousy I felt like killing them both."

"We had a terrific scene after the party, in which Max said that I had for four years been trying to make us into a *Saturday Evening Post* cover; that I had become the image of my mother; that it was a relief to be with a girl who demanded nothing; and that he had never really wanted to marry me in the first place."

"Did you really believe all that?" said Brian.

"Of course I did. I always believed everything."

"So you went home—to mother—babies and all."

"Yes, I went home to mother—for a while."

That had taken us as far as Philadelphia, on that first ride together. But on this ride, Brian had not yet reached Trenton. He turned his gaze from the window and began to look at the people in the parlor car. They were an unexciting lot.

It's what we said before, Brian mused, talking to the invisible me. These people have no *faces*. That man in seat 18 with his fat body and floral tie is a typical American businessman. That man behind him, heavy and white-haired, with the black eyebrows and the pompous mouth, is a typical American politician. That woman in front of me with her velvet hat and careful white hair is a typical American club-woman. The girl across the way, with her shining blond hair and expensive wool suit, is a typical American teen-age girl. The people in this parlor car, Brian went on, are the most rigid conformists in the world— thanks to the private enterprises which control their thinking, their appearance, and their eating!

Looking at them myself, I thought of the compartment-load in a European train. Good or evil, their faces bore the strong marks of their characters and the stamp of their emotions. They were free from the obliterative patina of money.

But there are fewer and fewer poor in America, said Brian, pursuing my train of thought, and therefore fewer and fewer faces. It won't be long before the ultimate aim of all advertising will have been realized: complete uniformity.

How un-American you are, I teased. Are you really advocating a return to poverty?

No—I'm only advocating freedom from the tyranny of forced demand.

Just then a woman walked down the aisle of the parlor car, toward Brian, then past him on her way, presumably, to the dining car, since others had been filtering past in the last half-hour. Brian looked up at her intently. She was a handsome, rather ravaged woman of thirty-eight or so, with strong features and compelling eyes. She wore a well-cut gray suit and a small beret.

I knew—as I seemed to know too much now—that Brian was looking at her not because she was an interesting woman but because she reminded him of Mary. She did, indeed, bear some generic resemblance to a photograph Brian had shown me, not long after we had met.

It was, actually, on this first train trip we took together, wasn't it, Olivia?

Yes. After I told you so much about myself we said nothing for a long while. We looked out of the window or at the other passengers or at each other. Then suddenly you said:

"You know that I'm married, don't you, Olivia—"

"Yes. Even if I hadn't, I would have guessed it—"

"Why?"

"Simply because I don't think you're the kind of man that lives alone."

"And yet you know that I live alone—in New York?"

"Tell me about her, Brian."

Brian took out his pipe, knocked it out on the window ledge, pressed fresh tobacco in it, lit it, and started to pull. As he did so the grooves in his cheek, pressed inward by suction, deepened, and his upper lip lengthened.

Brian, usually so articulate, told his story haltingly, as if it were some kind of difficult confession. But in retrospect the tale seems coherent enough and entirely reasonable.

He met Mary when he first went to England to establish a branch of his publishing house in London. He was in his middle twenties, had never been abroad before, and was immediately dazzled by the intellectual life of London at that time. "I had heard of people finding their spiritual homes outside their own lands, and I knew now what that meant. London made me completely happy. I liked the fog, I liked the massive dreariness, I liked the smell, and above all I liked the disciplined intelligence of the people. I seemed to have none of the American's instinctive distrust of the British; and never at any time found them cold or difficult. I suppose I was lucky in those early years because my work kept me from the two worst elements of English life—the county families and the smart Mayfair set. The people I met were the poets and the critics and the political writers—and I could not help finding them superior, both in knowledge and in balance, to our own. I reveled in good talk, in the sense of historic continuity that an old city gives you, in the measured rhythm of the English life. We—Americans—are apt to deride this 'slowness' of pace. I came to find it natural: all growth is slow—except malignant growth.

"I met Mary Freemantle one evening at a small gathering of people in Hampstead who were passionate Labourites at a time when Conservatives were wholly in the saddle. Mary was one of these, in spite of her youth. She had already written brilliant satiric pamphlets, and articles for *The New Statesman*; and had graduated with honors from Girton College at Cambridge at a time when proportionately few women were admitted to the university. In addition, she was a fine looking girl—a healthy country type, big-boned and strong, with straight fair hair cut in a bang and the kind of fresh skin only English girls seem to possess. Her eyes were a dark and brilliant blue and grew even darker with the intensity of her speech. I don't think I've ever heard a woman talk so brilliantly—"

Something in my expression then made Brian smile as he looked at me. "No, you're not brilliant, Olivia. Intelligent, yes, but not brilliant. Mary had the kind of forensic talent that great statesmen have, which is rare among either men or women.

"I saw a lot of her then. But it wasn't until my second trip to London, a year later, that she said she would marry me. She was dead against the idea of marriage at the start; in that group, marriage was a horrid bourgeois contrivance, a plot against liberty, an admission of defeat. I finally broke her down—but only after accepting her conditions—"

"I can't imagine putting up any," I said.

Brian grinned. "Pushover!" he said; then grew serious again as he relit his pipe. "Her conditions were typical of the 'advanced' and 'enlightened' thinking of that time. We were to be man and wife but still—and here is one of the most fallacious phrases in history—to 'lead our own lives.' If Mary wanted to go out with someone else, she would; and so should I. If I had friends in that bored her, she would feel free to go out; and vice versa—"

"Wonderful if it works," I remarked.

"Well, I was young enough, and in love enough, to think it might. Mary was as convincing in these arguments as she was on the subject of state socialism. She made it seem the only way for two reasonable and hard-working people to live. At the root of it, of course, was a fierce desire for independence, and an equally violent fear of being, as she put it—with all the arrogance of her twenty-two years—'just a wife.'

"Actually, the scheme did work for quite a while. Largely because we found we didn't really want to go out with other people. We had more fun together. Sometimes Mary and I would force ourselves to go on separate dates, but we were always glad to come home afterward and compare notes—"

I must have betrayed an involuntary sadness at these words, because Brian reached out his hand and put it on my knee. "Olivia—this was ten years ago—"

"I know," I said, "it's just that when you're in love you always hope—against all better knowledge—that there was something missing in past loves—"

"I can't lie—especially to you," said Brian. "We had a happy and stimulating life, Mary and I—"

"Until?"

"Until I came back from my first trip back to New York. I wanted to bring her with me—it was only for two or three months—but she said she couldn't leave her work, and anyway, it was much better for people to be separated once in a while. 'Otherwise,' she said, 'one gets too dependent.'

"When I came back," said Brian, and a shadow of this memory still crossed his face, "a change had come over her. She was reserved and cool, with none of her old buoyancy and assurance. I had been home several days before she told me that she was pregnant. Bitterly she said—'Brian—that wasn't to happen. We said it wasn't to happen.' We *had* said it wasn't to happen—at least for several years—but I thought it was wonderful. I told her so; and told her how happy it made me. But I knew what was eating into her. She saw her freedom go out of the window; her freedom, her work, her Joan-of-Arc inviolability. She was even younger than her twenty-four years. babies to her meant drudgery, sordidness, slavery. Like all spiritual virgins she had a horror of fecundity and all its implications. Nothing I said seemed to comfort her. So we said nothing."

"My God," I said, "how badly things are timed. If only I—"

Brian sighed. "I don't know. There are things one has to go through. Anyway, Mary wasn't burdened with a child. The baby—a boy—died at birth."

"Oh, Brian!" I cried.

"It was pretty bad for both of us. Mary may not have wanted the child but any woman who carries one for nine months and then loses it has lost a part of herself. Mary said only one thing, 'Forgive me.' She wept once from sheer weakness. Otherwise she behaved with magnificent control. That was, I suppose, the trouble. She should have broken down, if only to loosen the terrific knot of defiance and guilt and bewilderment that had formed within her."

"And you?" I asked.

"I wanted the child, of course. I felt somehow that it would have made everything all right."

"Couldn't she—couldn't she have another, eventually?"

"The doctors said she could—with a slight operation. But I waited for Mary to make that move. She never did. We never spoke of the child we had lost, or of children at all. Superficially, after a few months, she seemed to be her old self again— brilliant, gay, productive. We were very seldom alone together; there were always other people, or we were going out—often, separately. I couldn't help feeling that she needed constant distraction from me, and I let her have it—reluctantly, for I still preferred being with her to being with others. You see, Olivia, I'm really a one-woman dog. I would much rather love one woman than sleep with several."

"Thank God," I said.

"But there must be mutual need. I thought the loss of the child would make Mary need me more, but it worked the other way. She liked being with me but she was equally happy without me."

"How do you know?" I asked.

"She told me. And the evidence of my friends confirmed it."

It was hard to get out, but I managed, "Do you still love her?"

Brian looked at the raindrops squirming and joining on the

window pane. It was pouring hard now and the glass was almost opaque. "If I did, I wouldn't be on this train with you now."

We were silent after that. The inevitable question—"Then why are you still married?" formed and expired without sound.

That was ten years ago—on our first trip together. Now I looked upon this man from some other dimension; reliving with him these confessions of the past. I loved Brian for a great many things but I loved him then especially for never belittling Mary. So many men, because they loved you at the time, reduced former bonds to unimportance or in some way distorted their outlines. But Mary emerged through his talk as an extraordinary and compelling woman, whom I would have liked to know. I felt a strange compassion for them both. I remember wondering at that time whether Brian, in spite of his words, really loved her no longer. And of one thing I was quite sure: regardless of what he said and regardless of what she did, Mary was still in love with him. It was inconceivable to me then, looking at his face and hearing his voice, that any woman who had known and lived with Brian could ever reject him. It was one of the few times in my life that I had ever been right about anything.

The train drew into Philadelphia and there was the usual bustle of people getting off, and porters squeezing through the aisles with luggage and then squeezing back again with other luggage, followed by new passengers. A gray-haired man with horn-rimmed glasses who looked like a senator came through and was starting to settle himself in the seat across from Brian when their eyes met.

"Why, hello there, Littleton—"

Brian wheeled around to face him. "Hello, Stacey. What are you doing in Philadelphia?"

"Been to see the *Inquirer* bunch about that campaign they're—" The words became fainter and fainter as I left Brian to the stranger, left the train, and had one final glimpse of it—this time from outside, snaking its way through the Philadelphia suburbs, and into the wet country.

When I next saw Philip, he was walking in Washington Square with a girl. I imagined it must be the mid-term vacation, for otherwise he would have been at college. For January it was a remarkably warm day, and Philip and the girl were strolling along with that relaxed and aimless pace which sun and quiet air induce.

The girl was dark and medium-sized, with olive skin and large dark eyes that slanted up a little. Her shiny hair was braided in coils over each ear, and the center part at the back of her head made her neck seem very young and defenseless. They were walking hand in hand.

"When do you have to be at your father's?" she asked, and there was a slightly foreign intonation to her voice.

"I said I'd be there around three," said Philip. "He's right near here—University Place."

"Do you see him a lot?" asked the girl.

"Not very much. I only go when home starts to suffocate me; or when he happens to remember I exist."

"What a strange kind of father."

"What I've been trying to dope out all these years," said Philip, "is how he and Mother ever got along. They're so different."

The girl looked up at him. "I wish I had known your mother," she said.

"I wish you had too."

"I've read some of her things. I'd like it if you'd read them to me."

"I don't think I could take it yet," said Philip.

The girl took her hand from his and said, "I didn't mean now, Philip."

They said good-by at the door of the apartment house where Max lived.

"Pick you up at seven tomorrow, Micky?"

She smiled, "Yes, Philip. I want you to meet my father," and she walked away, turning back to wave after a few paces, knowing he was watching her.

Max came to the door when Philip rang. "Hello, Phil," he said. He was in pajamas and dressing gown; and seeing Philip look at them, explained, smiling, "Vacation. Luxury not to have to dress. Let's go into my study, Phil—everything else is cluttered with the debris of the young."

"Where are they?" asked Phil.

"Out with Marusia," said his father. "They were curious to see you, but Marusia wanted to get them out while the sun was still warm." He led the boy into the study and they sat down, facing each other.

"Want a drink?" asked Max.

"Three's a little early for me," said Philip, smiling. Max's desk was piled high with what looked like examination papers. On the wall above it was a photo of Pavlov, the Soviet scientist. I noticed also a group picture of rather ragged, unshaven men in odd parts of uniforms, and so did Phil.

"Who are those?" he asked.

"International Brigade," said Max. "Bunch of men I knew."

"Wish I'd been around when that happened," said Philip. "I mean, I wish I'd been old enough."

"I would have been in it myself if I hadn't been told to stay put—"

Philip looked at him curiously. "Told? Who told you?"

"Well, told isn't exactly the word, I guess. But somebody's got to stay around and attend to this end of the fight. The romantic instinct is to go off to the wars, but there's a war here, too."

"Damn it," said Philip, "I got born just at the wrong time.

Every time I talk to one of these guys that's been overseas I feel like a prep-schooler—"

"Well, you were well out of this one, Phil," said his father. "Anyway, it's been lost already—"

"Isn't that rather a sweeping statement?" said Phil.

"I know—you've been reading some of your mother's poetry. According to her, it was the Powers of Light against the Powers of Darkness—"

"Well, wasn't it? Or do you think it would have been better if the Germans had won?" Philip's face was flushed and his voice had an edge.

"The Germans have won, in a sense. Certainly the forces of reaction have won. Would you call this exactly a brave new world, Phil?" Max arched one eyebrow as he looked at his son and watched him struggle with his confusion.

"Mother didn't say this was a brave new world. But she did say it was braver and newer than Belsen!"

"There are worse things than Belsen, Phil."

"Where—in Russia?"

Max got up, went over to the window and looked down into the street six stories below. Then he turned back to Philip. "That sounds like your stepfather—although I've never had the pleasure of meeting him."

"My God," exploded Phil, "why do you always have to make out I can't do my own thinking? I'm not standing up for Whitney, I'm just trying to find things out!"

"I wonder if you really are. Or whether you're trying to force the world into your own comforting little concepts."

"Look, if I had comforting concepts I wouldn't be here. But I wish I could stop feeling like a Red whenever I'm with Whitney and like a reactionary whenever I'm with you. You're so damned sure all the time. How do you get that way?"

"Well some people are born sure, like your stepfather—"

"What about you?"

"I've just read a lot of history—and economics."

"What about people?"

"Aren't economics people?"

Poor Philip! I knew so well what he was feeling: anger and confusion and impotence. For some reason it was as impossible for him as it was for me to argue with Max. He invariably made you feel flustered and undocumented. Feeling thus, you lost your head and said something foolish. Max had an uncanny faculty for double-talk, all the more baffling because of the directness with which he delivered it. He had also the Jesuit's talent for avoiding straight answers to anything. Instead he countered a question with a question, as he had done with Philip.

"Look, Phil, I know what you're up against—after all, I'm with kids of your age all the time at N.Y.U. But the whole thing really boils down to a choice between going forward or going backward. The issues are pretty simple."

"But how can you be sure what will get you forward?"

"A wheel goes forward by turning around, doesn't it?"

"Yes—"

"Well," said Max, "there's a word for that movement: revolution."

"Does it have to be that drastic?"

Max shook his head, with a pitying smile. "God, how that word scares people. Is a turning wheel drastic?"

There it was again: the old superficially reasonable analogies, the playing with words, the question responding to the question. Philip pushed back his front lock of hair with his long stiff fingers, worried and flustered.

"Well, don't worry, Phil—it's a long way off yet!"

"I'm not worried and I'm not scared, I just don't see why you've got to go through a lot of blood and hell to get anywhere—"

"But I thought just a while ago you said a lot of blood and hell *had* got us somewhere—"

"That was war. That's different."

"And yet even your mother—if I remember correctly—once called that war a revolution—against fascism!"

This was too much for Philip. He rose and faced his father and almost wept as he shouted, "Stop it! Stop twisting things around!"

"My dear boy, I'm only quoting," said Max. He came over to Philip and put his hands on the thin high shoulders. "Look, Phil. I just don't want you to get your head full of tragic illusions."

Philip moved away a little so that his father's hands dropped, and spoke without looking at him. "I suppose you think going to work for the government is a 'tragic illusion'—"

"That depends entirely on what you expect to do."

"I wrote you," said Philip. "I said I wanted to get into the State Department—diplomatic service."

"Yes, I know," said Max, a little impatiently. "I mean, how are you going to tackle the job: be a rubber stamp or get something accomplished?"

"Well, I don't suppose I'll be in a position to do much for the first few years." From Philip this was an unexpected remark, and one that was very welcome to me. Like all the young, he expected immediate results, always; and chafed when they were slow in coming. I had been afraid that Philip saw himself Ambassador to France in three years.

"Possibly not, but you'll be in a position to learn," said Max. "And learning is power."

"I don't particularly want power," said Phil.

"How do you expect to do anything without it? Or do you think the State Department is perfect as it is?"

"Nobody thinks the State Department is perfect. But it's

the only way I know of working with the rest of the world."

"Well, God knows the Department needs some new blood—although when they get it, a congressional investigation throws it out."

"They only throw out Communists, don't they?"

Max eyed his son obliquely. "Don't you know yet that Congress calls everybody who doesn't like the National Association of Manufacturers a Communist?"

Philip laughed. "Well, I guess so; but they say the Department's getting much more liberal now. A lot of fellows don't even own a pair of striped pants!"

"Well I hope you're right, Phil. My own informants aren't so optimistic."

"Do you know people there, Father?"

Max's tone was light and casual. "Oh, everybody knows somebody."

"Anyway, I hope I get in. The examinations are supposed to be pretty tough—"

"I wouldn't worry, Phil," said Max. "You'll be okay so long as you keep your sense of proportion. The trouble with most people who go into government is that they start out with a lot of fine new ideas and then get bogged down in bureaucratic apathy and red-tape. What's worse, they end up by defending it all. Don't get the idea that it's loyal to defend it. There's only one valid loyalty and that's to an ideal."

"Isn't democratic government an ideal?"

"If it's democratic—yes. But don't ever obey blindly, Phil. If you get into the government and you find out there's dirty work going on, no matter how trivial, it's up to you to let the outside world know about it—"

"Except that everything's pretty confidential once you're in," said Philip. I could see that he hadn't caught on yet, and I hoped that he wouldn't.

"Top Secret, eh? That's mumbo-jumbo, Phil—meant to

impress officials with their own importance. Just don't forget: you're in there to serve the people—not the government—" The telephone rang and Max went to answer it. Philip's mind was worrying the last phrase: but our government *is* the people, isn't it? He reached for the coat he had thrown on the leather couch and put it on. When Max finished telephoning, Phil was already at the door, standing awkwardly.

"Off already, Phil? What's the rush?"

Philip stammered a little. "I—I told Auriol I'd take her to a four-o'clock show."

"Oh. Well, drop in again before you go back to school. Marusia and I are having some people in Friday night, in case you're free. Jean Welldon'll be there—you know, the playwright—she's just back from Russia and she's talked to all the big boys."

"Thanks. I don't know if I'm free then, but if I am—"

"That's all right, leave it that way. I just thought you'd like a change from the Chase National Bank, or whatever your stepfather owns."

Philip laughed without much conviction, bobbed his long head in farewell, and went out.

He walked all the way from University Place up to Seventieth Street, looking at nothing. His head was whirling with thought and he was trying to find out what it was his father had said that upset him so. As he retraced his conversation, he couldn't put his finger on a single remark that was wrong in itself. And yet the whole talk had disturbed him profoundly; shaken him and filled him with doubt.

I didn't see Philip clearly the whole walk up. There were intervals when he disappeared behind a thin shredding of matter, much as land disappears below a plane when low-flying clouds intervene, only to reappear in patches of clarity. The matter that came between had the same general quality as the state in which I resided most of the time, only the texture was less dense. I suppose that Philip was thinking of the dark girl on this walk, to the exclusion of me; then, when echoes of his father's words came back to plague him, turning again to me for some sort of answer, some definitive sign.

When he got into our apartment, he walked into the living room, calling, "Anybody home?" No one answered, so he hung his coat in the hall closet and started up the corridor toward his bedroom, which was at the end. As he passed the door to what had been my workroom, he saw that it was slightly ajar. He pushed it open a little further and saw Auriol kneeling on the floor before an old steamer trunk. She looked up as she heard the door creak. She had on an old pair of flannel slacks and an over-size sweater in the sloppy-Joe tradition. Her long red hair was tangled and she had no make-up on to speak of. There was a gray smudge on her right cheek, and her hands were dirty. She looked thirteen instead of seventeen, and vulnerable instead of assured.

"Hello," said Phil. "What are you doing?"

"Sorting Mother's stuff," said Auriol. "The trunk just came up from the storeroom."

"Who said you were supposed to do that?" Philip's tone was belligerent and harsh.

"Whitney said I could." On the floor next to the trunk were bundles of manuscript, letters, old magazines, clippings and files. "It's all in the will, anyway."

"Maybe so, but carrying it out is no job for a kid."

Auriol's green eyes narrowed and her mouth turned down. "Look who's talking," she said. "Anyway, you're always off somewhere and somebody's got to sort this out. The will says exactly who's to get what."

Philip squatted down beside the trunk and began reading the writing on some of the big manila envelopes. I was not normally a very tidy person, at least in this room; and I wondered how the contents of the trunk were as well organized as they seemed until I remembered a certain day—it must have been six months before my death—when I did a thorough housecleaning of all the accumulation of years, personal and professional. I went through all the drawers in my desk, all the files and boxes on the lowest shelves of my bookcase; and had this old trunk brought up for weeding out. I don't think I had any special premonition; only a general desire to be unencumbered by this residue. It was Whitney who, amused by this sudden frenzy of clarification, said, "Now all you need is a will, Livvy!"

I laughed at the time and went on with my tidying. But somehow the words stuck; and the next day I called up my lawyer, Jim Fosdick. "Jim—is a letter all you need to make a will?"

Jim said no; to come down to his office and draw one up, a regular will; and I did.

It was a simple document. I wanted Philip to have all the rough drafts of my manuscripts—if only to show him how tough it was to write. Whatever prizes and awards and other marks of success there had been were to go to Auriol, since she would appreciate them most. All other manuscripts were to go to my publisher, Brian Littleton.

"What about your personal correspondence, if any?"

"Oh," I laughed, "that's gone up in smoke!" I remembered the night I'd burned all personal letters; reluctantly in a way, for I had clung to the best of them long after their senders had vanished from my life. Their destruction seemed a sort of exorcism which I did not need, or particularly desire.

"Wise woman," said Jim, approvingly. "What about your personal effects?"

"Oh, whatever jewels I have should go to Auriol. Clothes too. Everything else I leave behind is Whitney's, of course."

I wondered now why I had not been around when the will was read. Surely that would be one moment when thought of me would be intense in at least three people. Then I remem-

bered the legal language. That must have acted as an insulating
barrier. The best way to de-humanize a being, dead or alive, is
to project him in Whereas, Whereat, and first, second, and
third parties. In the will I was the Testator. Olivia Baird was
somewhere else entirely.

But here, in this room where I spent so many hours of
every day brooding, thinking, writing; and where the hands of
my two children were touching things of mine, I was entirely
present. They were both keenly aware of this, for Philip said,
"I feel like a lock-picker. I wish we didn't have to do this."

"But she wanted it," said Auriol. "She said so."

"I know," said Philip. "But this damn place is so full of
her. You'd think she might come in any minute—" He looked
at the door, his voice trailing off.

"She hated anybody looking at her things. Once I was just
looking at the top of her desk and she came in and raised
hell!"

Philip turned to look at her with fraternal contempt. "You
always got on her nerves, that's why—"

"Well, she never understood me!" Auriol burst out. Philip
saw that she was near tears and let the subject drop.

"Put all the manuscripts over here," he said, "and the letters
over there. When it's all sorted, Whitney can look it over and
okay it—"

They were there in that room a long while, Philip and
Auriol, but they didn't get much done. Philip was reading the
manuscripts and so was Auriol.

"Gosh, she's got seven different versions of this poem—you
know, the one about northern lights—"

"Look at all this dialogue," said Auriol, "batches of it. I
didn't know she wrote plays—"

"Let's see," said Philip, reaching over for the manuscript
and taking it from her. "Oh, that's the rough draft of her
radio play—"

"What radio play?"

"Oh, she told me about it once. They never put it on the air—"

"Why?"

"She wrote it before the war and it was all about isolationists and they wouldn't put it on the—"

"Why not?"

"I dunno. Guess it was too hot to handle, or something—"

I remembered the day when Miles Andrews of CBS called me in and said, "This is a fine play, Miss Baird—but we can't do it. You know our policy—"

"Non-intervention, you mean? But this isn't an argument for war. It's an argument against the kind of people who cause wars—the isolationists—"

Andrews smiled tolerantly. "Miss Baird, you're more effective than you know. You've practically indicted a group of Americans here for treason." He slapped the manuscript with the back of his hand. "And they're all too recognizable—"

"But the President himself—"

Andrews interrupted. "My dear Miss Baird, this radio chain is not, thank God, a government organ. What the President says is not necessarily what the nation wants—"

We argued for quite a while, Mr. Andrews and I, but it was no use. He had the familiar defense of all those who wield great power in a popular medium: "We only give the public what it wants—" It is the most useful, and least valid, reason for having no convictions that I know of.

While Philip was reading the play, sprawled on the floor, Auriol was pulling a scroll or certificate out of a big manila envelope. As she did so, some letters fell out on the floor. She ignored them at first and examined the parchment, which was a poetry award I had won in 1938. Then she put it back in the envelope and picked up one of the letters. It had an Italian postmark and was addressed to me in thick black writing. The handwriting I knew. The letters must have slipped into the envelope by accident, for I had been ruthless (I had thought) in my weeding out.

Pulling the letter out, Auriol read: "Olivia carissima! It is now months since you were here but I cannot stop seeing you. I cannot go anywhere without a desperate longing to be near you and hear your voice, and the streets are full of women who, just because they have your kind of hair or walk a little like you, bring pain to my heart. At night when I cannot sleep I keep seeing your face across the table from me, with the golden Piazza Navone behind you and the children playing in the square." There was a paragraph in Italian, and then: "I know that we could never stay together—I am too Italian and you are too American. I need a simple woman to live with—and you—I do not know what you need, but it is not me. Why do I say this? To comfort myself? Carissima—I am a frivolous and selfish man; but when I say I want you with me this night—the whole night—I mean that I want to give and not to take. Ti voglio bene, ti abbraccio—Carlo." Auriol turned back to the first page of the letter; it was dated October, 1935. Slowly she put the letter back into the envelope and the envelope on the floor.

A great deal was going through her mind. One of the latest— and hardest—discoveries of the young is the entity of their parents as men and women, not as mothers and fathers. Acceptance of this fact is part of maturity; and Auriol, in spite of her looks, was far from mature. She was torn now between fascination at this revealing, intimate "find"; and a sharp pang of revulsion. So—my mother is nothing but a tramp, after all. All the while when we were children she was playing around with men. And *she* was telling *me* how to behave! And all that noble poetry—

Auriol picked up the second letter and began to read. There was no date and the letter was written in a small erratic hand that gave Auriol (as it had always given me) trouble to decipher.

"The concert went well enough last night, although the hall was freezing and the acoustics really terrible. What a middlewest you have—so big and so bare! Some elegant lady asked me to stay at her house, but I excused myself and said I was tired. I was tired, but what I really wanted was to be in a hotel room alone and think of you. I do not like mixing music with society anyway, although that seems to be a conductor's life.

"I forgot to tell you. Klingel slipped on the ice outside the hall and hurt his wrist. So he can't continue the tour and Loeb will be concertmaster. I am not very sorry as Klingel gets on my nerves more and more; every time we have a violin soloist he behaves as if it were a personal insult. He has to tap his rack to applaud, of course, but you should see his face when he does it.

"My own sweet love—why should I speak of all these silly unimportant things when all I want is to be back in New York with you. You are music too. My God, if only I were twenty years younger—what joy we could have for years—and years—"

The letter was signed "Eric." I could see Auriol trying to piece the thing together. Conductor—Eric. Heavens, that must be—that must be Eric Steiner. Why, I've been to his concerts. *That* old man—that old famous man—was in *love* with *Mother?* Why, I went to his concert with her once—and all the while . . . Amazement flooded Auriol's mind, as the concept of the old being capable of love upset and disgusted her, although the fact of Steiner's importance helped a little.

Now, compelled in spite of, or perhaps because of, her conflicting emotions, Auriol opened a third. This one was on thick white paper and the letterhead, in raised gold, said

"H.M.S. *Cardiff*, Royal Navy." The letter was dated: Singapore, May, 1936. The writing was extremely even and legible.

"My dearest Olivia—I've wanted to write long before this, but His Majesty's Navy has kept me on the run and I never seemed to have managed either the peace or privacy for writing until now.

"It is fearfully hot, and I'm sitting on the Club verandah imbibing one pink gin after another. Funny thing is, the hazier I get the clearer you become, and I see you the way you were on that last night we were together. You had on a white frock and a sort of star thing on one shoulder and another one in your hair. That's pretty good for an Englishman, isn't it?

"I wish I could write better, like you. There's so much I want to say to you and it's so hard to say it right. Olivia, I've never known anyone like you. I know this sounds like utter tripe, but I mean it. I've had a lot of good times with women and fallen in love and all that sort of thing but you were something else. It was all rather like a dream—a very short dream. I suppose Bermuda is a dream anyway. It was much too good to last—all of it. That night we swam—the water was like black velvet and the sky was black too, and I could hardly see you. Olivia, why can't life always be like that—two people alone, on a beach?"

Auriol turned to the second page: "So many women want to own you—or else they're just in it for the fun and don't really care what man it is. But you didn't seem like either. You didn't put strings on anything and still I felt you cared for me, although God knows why. I haven't any brains to speak of and not much of a character.

"Olivia—darling—could you ever possibly conceive of marrying a sailor? I know it's a rotten sort of life and no money to speak of and I'd have to be away a lot—but I'd take care of you always. I think I could stand almost anything if I knew you were waiting for me somewhere.

"I suppose you think I'm crazy, or drunk, or something to

write like this. But I've been thinking it over for a long time and I've decided that I know what it's all about for the first time in my life.

"I suppose you will throw this letter in the wastebasket, as it probably deserves. But please—please think about it . . . You see,

"I'm frightfully in love with you—the real kind—

"Bless you—"

The letter was signed with the initial "A."

Auriol was still holding it when Philip looked up and said, "Anything interesting?"

Auriol started as if in alarm. "No—nothing—just business things," she said. She then resumed the process of sorting, reaching into the trunk and examining the descriptions on the envelopes and folders, but all the time her mind was on the letters, and forming inside her was the fiery question: What shall I do with them? Shall I keep them, so nobody else can see them? Shall I tear them up and throw them away? Shall I leave them for Whitney to see? And, above all, what am I going to feel about my mother?

Finally Auriol came to a decision: she would leave them where they were, for Whitney's inspection. No one need know she had ever read them. If Whitney asked, she would say no—she had just sorted them.

But what if Whitney read them and confiscated them? Could he do that, when they belonged—whether intentionally or not—in her batch of papers? Auriol was deeply perplexed and troubled. Finally she looked up and her eye caught the traveling clock on my desk.

"Golly—six o'clock; I've got to get dressed—" she said, sprang up, and half-ran to her room.

Philip remained in my room for another half-hour. Finally he picked up a poem called "Stimulant" and read it. The burden of it was the tonic effect of death and disaster on the poet.

Stapled to the back of it was an office memo, written in long-hand and signed "Brian:" "I don't think this ought to go in the book. In the first place, it's not you; it has a sneering, belittling quality; a small kind of satire. The whole premise is false, anyway. Death *should* bring out poets. Any part of life should. Bad poets are bad on any subject.

"Technically, it's not a very good poem either. When you do free verse you're not free enough, so you'd better stay chained to predetermined forms. 'Stimulant' is just a lazy sonnet: you use iambic pentameter and fourteen lines but haven't taken the trouble to rhyme.

"How about lunch tomorrow? Or aren't you speaking?"

Philip smiled. I'd like to know that guy, he said. I wonder why Mother didn't bring him around more . . . ?

I left my children finally as Philip went out to pick up his girl and as Auriol was putting the finishing touches to herself. She had bathed and dressed and was brushing her hair in front of the dressing-table mirror. When she had finished, she opened a drawer and took out a star-shaped pin and fastened it on the low square neckline of her gray wool dress. It was an old jewel, made of a semiprecious paste that looked like aquamarines. Then she took a smaller star out of the drawer and pinned it at the top of the heavy cascade of hair she wore on one side.

They were my pins; "You had on a white frock and a sort of star thing on one shoulder and another in your hair." At that moment, watching her lovely image in the mirror, Auriol was thinking kindly of me.

Soon after that, it must have been, Auriol was entering the lending library which Miss Furman presided over and which I had used so often. She was carrying two books and a square manila envelope.

Miss Furman was attending to a customer when Auriol walked in—marking the date down on a card, putting it back in the file, and handing the customer a book; but she looked up and said, with warmth in her voice, "Miss Corning! I'll be with you in a moment—"

As the customer went out, Auriol went up to Miss Furman and said, "I'm afraid I should have brought these back long ago. I didn't see that they belonged here till yesterday. I guess my mother just forgot—" She laid two detective novels on the table in front of Miss Furman. "I guess there's quite a lot to pay."

Miss Furman looked at the books for a moment but she wasn't seeing them. "No—there's nothing to pay. Nothing at all." She turned to the shelves marked "Mystery" and put the books in their proper place. Before turning back to face Auriol, she said in a queer unsteady voice, "Your mother gave so much—" then stopped abruptly and turned around, a bright smile on her face.

"And how is school going?"

"Oh, all right, thanks," said Auriol, not bothering to explain that school was finished. "Miss Furman, my mother left something for you in her will—"

Miss Furman said nothing, so Auriol went on. "She left this manuscript—it's all the poems that went into the book called *Intimations*. I don't know if you read it—" She handed the envelope to Miss Furman, who slowly took it and held it.

"Anyway," said Auriol, "it's meant for you."

Miss Furman still said nothing, looking down at the envelope.

My God, these queer old maids, thought Auriol. "Well, good-by," she said, and turned to leave.

Miss Furman jerked her head up.

"Good-by!" she said; then, "I can't tell you—" but Auriol was already outside the shop. Miss Furman put the packet down, paused a moment, then began to arrange things for closing time. The clock on her table said six. She put all her sales records in the drawer, picked up loose volumes and inserted them on the shelves. A woman opened the door, came in, and said, "Too early, Emmy?" She might have been anywhere from forty to fifty years old, with dry, short colorless hair sticking out from under a black astrakhan cap. Her features were pinched and without make-up and I had a feeling that under her black coat she wore a dress with peasant embroidery.

"Why, no, no, not at all, Niles," said Miss Furman, looking up from her tasks. "I'm just closing up."

"It's the restaurant problem. You just never get in unless you go early."

"Yes, I know," said Miss Furman. "I'm practically ready." She went to a small closet and took out her coat and hat. The latter she put on without a mirror, and indeed it would not have helped; for it was one of those hats that are bought by women without taste, a cluster of felt flowers on a small felt disk, with veil attached, meant to be worn on the forehead and anchored to the back of the head by a felt clamp. Miss Furman's grizzled hair bunched out behind while the front part served only to obscure the one good feature she had—the shape of her forehead. Around her neck she tucked a flowered scarf before putting on her coat. She took one look about her, pushed back a volume that protruded from one of the "Juvenile" shelves, and said, "All right, Niles. I'll just lock up."

"Where shall we go—Schraffts?" said the woman called Niles as they stepped into the cold street.

"Oh, no," said Miss Furman, "it's always so crowded and noisy. Let's go over to Mary Conklin's." Her friend assented and they walked three blocks down Madison and one block east to a small restaurant with a cake on a pedestal in the window and two brass candlesticks on either side of it. The place was full of women very much like them; of indeterminate age and indeterminate dress, pecking at salads or Southern fried chicken at an hour when other people were either playing with their children or drinking cocktails with their friends.

Miss Furman slipped off her coat but kept the envelope with my manuscript on her lap.

"Niles, I think I'll have a little something to drink," she said. "It's been quite a day and I feel a bit chilled."

Miss Furman ordered a Dubonnet, but Niles refused a drink, saying, as she doubtless always did, that it was poison for her. They talked of books and plays for a while—Niles, it appeared, worked in the theater section of some downtown settlement school—and I was just beginning to recede when Miss Furman, a little flushed with the Dubonnet, picked up her envelope and placed it on the table.

"Niles," she said, "I want to show you something." She pulled the poem manuscripts out of the envelope and handed them across the table.

"What is it?" said Niles.

"It's something I still can't believe. It happened this afternoon. Look at them."

"Olivia Baird—but these look like original manuscripts."

"They are," said Miss Furman, "and they're mine. She gave them to me in her will."

"But how extraordinary, Emmy. I know you saw her now and then, but this—why this is quite extraordinary." Niles examined several pages with her long bony fingers. "I imagine these are worth quite a lot—"

"That is hardly the point," said Miss Furman, with an edge to her voice.

Oblivious of the intonation, her friend continued to examine the titles of the poems. "Mostly about love, aren't they—I remember all these sonnets in the White Nights series made quite a stir when they came out."

"She always made a literary stir!"

"I don't mean that kind," said Niles. "I mean they shocked

an awful lot of people—she was so frank. As a matter of fact, I couldn't help agreeing with some of the attacks, I did think she showed a certain lack of taste—"

Miss Furman reached across the table and started pulling the sheets from Niles' hands. "Give them back to me," she said harshly.

"Good gracious, Emmy, don't act that way about it. I think it's wonderful having those manuscripts—why, it's almost historic—"

Miss Furman put the sheets back into the envelope, her hands trembling a little and her cheeks still quite flushed. The felt flowers on her hat shook a little.

"No one's going to argue about her importance as a poet," said Niles, "but that apparently hasn't anything to do with a person's character. Look at Wagner, for instance—"

Miss Furman broke in. "And just what is wrong about her character?"

"Now look here, Emmy, don't pretend you don't know. I don't doubt she was completely charming when she came in to borrow a book, but it's common knowledge that she led a fearfully promiscuous life—"

"Don't you use that word," Miss Furman almost shouted. "Don't you dare use that word!"

Niles looked up from her sugar-cured ham with amazement. "Why, Emmy Furman! You're always the first one to be disgusted by all this sex stuff in modern literature, I—"

"So I am," cried Miss Furman, "because it's cheap and vulgar and sensational, and if you think those poems of Olivia Baird are anything like that we might just as well stop talking altogether!"

Niles was upset. "Now, Emmy, for heaven's sake calm down, I didn't mean anything like that, but I simply don't understand your sudden change of attitude, why, you've always been terribly hard on women who keep having affairs—"

Miss Furman was twisting her Navajo necklace in between her fingers, and the cords in her thin dry neck stood out.

"Why, once, Emmy, you remember that girl who used to work for you who always had a string of men coming to visit her in the shop and you found out what she was up to, why, you told me you felt absolutely contaminated by her, *infected*— those were the exact words you used."

In a low, cracked voice and not looking up, Miss Furman said, "Are you intimating that Olivia Baird was like that?"

"I'm intimating nothing," said Niles tartly. "She does all the intimating in those poems. You'd think she spent half of her life in bed with someone."

"Well, if she did, what of it? I wish to God I had," said Miss Furman, looking Niles straight in the eye this time and raising her voice. "What have we saved ourselves for, I'd like to know?"

"Please, Emmy," said her friend, "not so loud!"

"What do you think I think about half the time, day in and day out, night after night—books and plays and things of the spirit? And does that make me happy or any man happy or do anything but eat out my insides until I hate every last gray hair on my head and all this dry and unused skin and this flat chest that never rose to any touch?"

"Emmy, please!" Niles looked about her nervously, for already several women were eavesdropping, and Miss Furman's voice was now highly audible.

"These were the only things that helped," she cried, pressing the envelope with the manuscripts against herself. "These poems by that promiscuous woman, because I know now the quality of love and I know that millions of women have never had it but all of them want it and the only way they'll ever get it is to give themselves, freely, the way she did. And if that's promiscuous, I wish to God I were a whore, myself!"

The people who had been eavesdropping bent their heads

over their food in consternation. Niles was speechless. Altogether there was that awful hush that always seems to leave the surrounding air to one lonely speech, leaving it naked, outrageously stripped of its accompaniment of sounds. Everyone in the room must have heard the last sentence.

Miss Furman, bent over the fricassee that she had barely touched, recovered herself, now aware of the scene she had made and of the atmosphere about her, reduced to a clatter of knives and forks and the kitchen sounds and the thudding of the waitresses in their flat shoes.

She made a pretense of eating but remained silent. So did Niles, afraid of saying anything that might rouse her to words, afraid of breakdown, afraid of God knows what.

Finally Miss Furman spoke. "There's a very good French film, they say, at the Little Carnegie. If we skip dessert we can catch the seven o'clock showing . . ."

I left them there asking for the check.

Promiscuous. Until Brian went back to Mary, and I lost direction for nearly two years, that was a word I had never applied to myself. Possibly no one ever does, for it is a sordid word, reducing many valuable moments to nothing more than doglike copulation.

And yet, soon after Miss Furman's scene, the word revolved and echoed in my void again and I was drawn down its sibilant spiral to Whitney, who was now using it.

"Promiscuous . . . letters . . . Auriol . . . promiscuous mother—" For a while I could hear only isolated words that Whitney spoke, and I saw him and Elizabeth unclearly and sporadically, as on an old and flickering film that is streaked and blurred with use; or more, even, like reflections on troubled water. Finally this form of emotional static that almost always came between me and Whitney died down and I could see the two sitting in Elizabeth's drawing room. Whitney looked extremely disturbed, and he was pacing back and forth, high-ball in hand.

"But can you imagine, Liz, can you imagine leaving letters like that around for a young kid to read? Why, it's incredible . . . it's . . . it's wicked!"

"But Whitney, dear," said Elizabeth quietly, "you haven't told me what they were all about, what they were like—"

"God, what more do you have to know than that they're love letters—three of them, mind you—lousy, corny, sickening love letters from every damn place on earth. And she leaves *that* to Auriol!"

"But are you sure she's read them—she said she didn't, didn't she?"

"Sure she did. But how do I know she's telling the truth?"

"Well, she's a pretty honest girl, isn't she? And anyway, you've destroyed them, so the only thing to do is to put them out of your mind and pretend they never existed."

Whitney sank down in a deep armchair and took another swallow of his highball.

"I can't get them out of my mind," he said.

There was a considerable silence. Then Elizabeth, looking at him steadily and speaking in a soft, even voice, said, "Whitney —you didn't ever think that Olivia was a saint, did you?"

His eyes on the floor, Whitney said, "No. I didn't think she was a saint!" Then, a little later, "I didn't stop to think."

I noticed then that the portrait of Whitney in uniform was now on Elizabeth's piano instead of on Whitney's dresser. It might have been a copy, but I rather imagined that Elizabeth had asked for it. Whitney was not the kind of man who hands out photographs of himself without demand; even on demand, he demurred.

But he was definitely the kind of man who looked his best in uniform. I saw him again as he first walked into the War

Department office in lower Manhattan where I was working in 1942. The office was pretty busy during the six months before the African landing, and a great many officers came through the department for background material and documentation in general. One of these was Whitney, then a major attached to a motorized corps.

I saw him only twice in the office and once for lunch in the fall of '42, but from the first I was impressed by his handsomeness, his efficiency, and his economy of speech. Our meetings in the office were of necessity impersonal, and although he told me at lunch that his wife had died several years ago, and although I told him that I had two children and used to be a writer, the conversation could hardly have been called intimate. The contact was there, though: I found myself appreciating (more than intellectually) his fresh virility, his bigness of stature, and a quality of simplicity, almost naïveté, that balanced his fundamental shrewdness of mind.

"I saw her only a couple of times, then," Whitney was saying to Elizabeth, "but I couldn't get her out of mind. She was so damned smart, but she was feminine, too, and she seemed sort of unprotected. I didn't believe it when she said she had a fifteen-year-old boy—she seemed so unspoiled, in a way."

"But you don't mean to tell me you didn't know who she was?"

"How the hell should I have, then? I never read poetry. She said she wrote, but so do a thousand women."

"But you must have seen her name in bookstores—in newspaper reviews—good heavens, Whitney, she was one of the best-known women writers in the country!"

"Look, Elizabeth," said Whitney patiently. "I didn't know it the first time I met her. I didn't catch on till I came back from Africa." He took a long drink and sighed. "I guess I didn't catch on very much even then—"

"To what?" asked Elizabeth gently.

"To the kind of woman she really was. Or rather, women. Olivia wasn't one person . . ."

I couldn't blame Whitney for his bewilderment. The woman he met when he came back from Africa and the woman he married were indeed different in many ways.

I didn't think of Whitney much while he was in Africa, although he wrote several times and I wrote back. I continued the kind of life I had led ever since I had given up Brian as a lost cause; lost to Mary, lost to the war, which he was now serving in England. For three years I held on, hoping, for he had asked me to wait. Then hopelessness seized me and with it a form of self-destruction which is due as much to a loss of faith in self as in others. I drank a great deal and I knew a great many men. I say "knew," because "lived with" is not accurate and "slept with" is too limited. I suppose I could say "loved" because in most cases some facet of love was present; but ever since Brian, I had been chary of the word and scrupulous about its use.

On his trips to New York after his return from Africa, Whitney would spend most of his evenings at my apartment, deep in an armchair, highball in hand, listening to me read to Philip and Auriol, watching me cook his dinner. Later, in the quiet house, in the darkened bedroom, Whitney would know the other side.

What he knew least about was my writing. I spoke little of it, afraid of frightening him, afraid of seeming like the "intellectual" woman. I avoided serious discussions with him, partly because I didn't want to tire him, partly because I had a deep instinct that we might clash on a number of things. And then, I was tired of talk. I interposed Whitney's great body between myself and doubt, between myself and the recurring ghost of Brian.

There were times when the bulwark was inadequate; times

when I cried to myself: What am I doing? What am I doing with anyone but Brian? What am I doing with a man who thinks so differently on so many things? For Whitney was a cynic about the world. He spoke with contempt of foreigners, with hate and mistrust of the administration. Resistance fighters he usually referred to as "Commies," men of vision as "do-gooders" and "star-gazers," the President, of course, as "that man." He spoke of all these things without savagery and with a barrage of factual documentation which I was never able adequately to counter, no matter how strong my opposition. He was not Jesuitical, like Max. He was merely secure.

"Livvy," he would say, after my remonstrances, "I wish the world were the way you think it is, but it just isn't. If you'd been where I've been—" And yet, I told myself, here is a man who has worked with the resistance, who has given important aid to foreigners, who has fought for "that man," who has been the living embodiment of American courage. Talk is unimportant, I told myself; it is the human being, the acting human being that matters.

And what did Whitney find in me, who actually was not his kind of person at all?

I had known several men in the period after leaving Max and before knowing Brian—the men of the letters and others less articulate—though I deny that the word promiscuous could fairly be applied to me because of this knowledge. According to Roget's *Thesaurus*, promiscuity can mean indiscrimination, want of distinction, uncertainty; the adjective can also mean hybrid, mongrel, miscellaneous.

I liked the race of men. I liked all the adjuncts of their presence: their voices, their clothes, the way their legs are put on, the way they move, the shape of their shoes, the bones of their ankles underneath their socks. Not all of them, to be sure; the immature, the dishonest, the ignorant, left me cold. But with those I knew intimately I was constantly surprised and touched by their innate tenderness, their generosity, and their profound romanticism. Possibly these qualities, inherent in most men, are evoked only by their equivalents in women.

Liking men, then, I felt it natural to serve them and to give to them, especially if they liked and wanted me. Some of them were weak, some clumsy, some perverse; and there were times when I looked down on a sleeping man and felt immeasurably lost. But intimacy often brought a compassion, a mutual perception that absolved one of all feeling of evil and waste. And later, when the man, emerging disheveled from his brief deep sleep, would stir and reach for my hand, I felt whole and at peace. If this was promiscuity, then Roget's should add another definition.

But Roget did have a definition which made the word apply to me during the two years before my marriage with Whitney. Aimless, undirected, without purpose—this indeed meant promiscuous. Without Brian there was no wonder; and without wonder, succeeding intimacies become a pattern and a formula. I began to hear myself saying the same thing to different men in the space of a month. I used "darling" too often to too many people. I found myself using toward one man inflections of voice, little gestures that another had found charming. I told about my life too often, making it braver than it was, watching the light of attraction growing in their eyes. Even my tenderness became a pattern of certain acts, certain words. The rumpled beds, the fierce and then helpless bodies of men, the weary dressing—all these multiplied themselves as if in a hall of mirrors. And then I really began to feel a tart— a high-class tart, an intellectual, sensitive tart, but still a tart.

It was this, with enormous irony, that so attracted Whitney. With all his virility, with all his competence, Whitney was an innocent man. Profoundly attached to his mother and very idealistic about women in general, Whitney divided them sharply in two classes: the ladies, whom one married; and the "girls," whom one slept with. The idea that the two could be combined never entered his mind. The further idea that a third quality could be added to this already preposterous combination—intelligence—was unthinkable. It was only after his return from Africa that he believed, against all his convictions, that it was possible. To him, I was that combination.

Whitney was returned to the United States and given a desk job in Washington in 1943 because of a wound in his knee which stiffened his leg considerably. I saw him a few days after he had landed: bronzed, handsome, and decorated, limping only slightly. Suddenly, he seemed like some sort of salvation; the oaken spar to cling to, saving me from the engulfing ocean of doubt, fatigue, and horror of the war. I made myself fall in love with him. It is something which women are able to do. The deception was deliberate, but it was directed at myself as much as at him. I made myself into his image of me; the brave little woman, the good mother, the hard worker—and the experienced lover.

If he had asked himself ever how I came to be so experienced, he never questioned me. Nor did I tell him how my life these years had been spent. We never spoke of men other than my former husband, Max; or of women other than his mother and his wife. He was either so secure that he felt superior to whatever past I had had; or so insecure that he could not bear to open the door to it.

For my part, everything that could be spoken of had been thrashed out between Brian and me. There was nothing we did not know about each other, for we felt that only on complete knowledge could complete love be safely based. Contrary to current philosophic opinion, we believed in affinity. You could live with any number of people for varying periods of time, you could live with them quite happily and in intimacy; but the complete fusion, the joining of two halves to make one whole, happened only once, if at all. I was sure that it was futile to try to build up with Whitney what I had had with Brian. But it did not seem futile to build a good life with him, and for the children.

Actually it was Auriol and Philip who tipped the scales, particularly Auriol who adored him. Whitney was wonderful with them; the perfect father type—strong, dependable and kind, a good provider; and I felt that they both needed a man in the house. The responsibility for them and for their growing needs had been a heavy weight on my shoulders and I was ready to share it.

Shortly after his return from Africa, Whitney asked me to marry him. He had just been transferred to New York and we were spending the evening at the Persian Room. After dining and dancing and drinking and looking at his fine broad shoulders across the table from me, at the big hand laid over mine and then up again to the steady gray eyes and the almost Augustin brow, I said I would. The warmth that flooded us both at that moment, the sense of mutual need, seemed to give some sort of benediction to this act.

"It wasn't until after we were married," Whitney was saying to Elizabeth, "that I realized her radical side—"

"You mean her marriage to that Jew?" asked Elizabeth.

"No—I knew all about that. I mean her feeling about things in general. I knew she was full of cockeyed illusions about the world, but I put that down to poetry. I didn't think she really felt that way."

"You didn't know much about her, did you, Whitney?" said Elizabeth in her soft, lyric voice. Her honey-colored hair was now in a low chignon at the base of her neck; and with the dark-blue dress she wore, high-necked and extravagantly simple, she was the picture of what the fashion magazines call "restrained elegance." Brian had taught me a great deal about dress, but whatever style I had was haphazard and I could not help but admire Elizabeth's consistent art.

"Well, the point is," said Whitney, "it didn't go with the rest of her. She was a damn good mother—although I think she spoiled Phil too much—and worked like blazes most of the time. Not one of these Bohemian types at all. Why, hell, Liz, we would have been happier than most people—if only she'd thought straight."

Elizabeth looked at the diamond-encrusted watch on her wrist. "I think we had better eat pretty soon if we want to make the concert," she said. "Can I refresh your drink—dear?"

Whitney stood up, but he didn't seem to have heard her question because he said, "Liz—don't get me wrong about all this. I mean, about Olivia. She was sort of like a child, in some ways. She lived in a kind of world of her own—you know, full of illusions."

"And what were you supposed to be," asked Elizabeth very softly, "just an illusion?"

Whitney sighed deeply. "I don't know, Liz—I don't know. I used to think she really loved me—but now . . ." He looked up at Elizabeth, squared his shoulders as if to shake off his oppression and confusion and said, "Come on, Liz. Let's go!" She smiled, put her hand lightly and only for an instant on his shoulder, and turned toward her bedroom to fetch her coat. Whitney looked after her, his eye traveling from the golden bun down to the small well-girdled hips down to the spike heels of her dark-blue kid pumps.

The orchestra was already seated and tuning up as the late arrivals streamed into their seats in Carnegie Hall. I wondered why I was there until I saw Brian, alone, finding a seat on the sixth row aisle and settling in it, stowing his coat and hat under the seat and looking about him. A moment later, Whitney and Elizabeth walked into a first-tier box and sat down. But I was as restless as the fluttering hands of the audience turning over program pages, pulling out of coats, removing hats, waving, smoothing its hair. Neither Brian nor Whitney nor Elizabeth were thinking of me enough to demand my presence, and even Philip, whom I finally spotted in the top gallery with Micaela next to him, was distracted by the crowd. I was suspended helplessly in the middle of Carnegie Hall waiting for the concert to begin and for someone to establish my presence.

Finally the house-lights lowered, the men stopped tuning, and the conductor, a stocky man with bushy white hair, walked out on the stage and up to his podium. I should have known it would be Eric Steiner.

He raised his baton, held it suspended for a moment as the men brought their instruments into place, and came down on the first beat of the Bach *Passacaglia and Fugue in C Minor.* After the first profound and austere measure, Brian pulled me toward him but I could not wholly respond, for I found myself inside the music itself. It is hard to define this: one of the great elements of music is this capacity to envelop the listener entirely, to transport him to an extra-terrestrial plane of feeling which has no counterpart in human experience.

I began to feel, as the *Passacaglia* rolled on, that here was the first tangible bridge between my state and the living; and the motion in which I was suspended and which palpitated in the air of the hall itself had now achieved a pure and definable pattern, becoming part and parcel of the audible harmony. It was more than sound waves invading the molecular structure of space; it was literally the penetration of mind into matter and the ordering of matter by mind. This was Bach's mind— or if you prefer it, spirit—and Bach had been dead almost two hundred years. Were men like him the great interpreters, moving freely and forever between the living and the dead and fusing them? For surely there was more in Carnegie Hall than this visible audience. There was a host like myself, sharing resurrection in each phrase.

Because this music transcended personal love I did not share it with Brian; instead he was himself transported momentarily into the realm where I now existed, becoming himself a part of organic harmony. It was a kind of death, and one could see it on the faces of those who, like myself, were actually inside the music. Steiner, conducting, had it in his face; Kraus, the first cellist, had it in his. So did the second flute and the French horn. They were closed to the outer world, toward which they turned a mask that appeared to be—as death masks often do— listening to the inward ear. It was a form of transfiguration, in which the impurities of the human soul were washed away and which approached, as far as I could see, the state of divinity from which we had receded steadily for so many thousands of years.

But the Bach *Passacaglia* did not have the same effect on all the members of the audience, by any means. I looked at Elizabeth sitting beautiful and erect in the front of the box, her chin tilted up, her eyes closed. Elizabeth had been on the Board of Trustees of the Symphony and had been to a concert a week as long as she could remember. Like many of her kind she spoke with great authority on music, commending this, criticizing that, but more often sighing with rapture at the end of a piece, particularly if it was played by a soloist of great technical brilliance. But of the structure and quality of music she knew nothing; and of performance, only the relative speed of playing. "I do think Steiner took that very fast," she would say. Or—"Halavic's tempo in the second movement was superb, wasn't it?"

I used to wonder what Elizabeth thought of during music. On this occasion, at least, I knew: Elizabeth was mapping her campaign with Whitney, down to the last word and the last gesture. The music was giving her a sensation of irresistible power; and as she sat there with her eyes closed in pretended rapture, she was sure that Whitney was examining, with growing excitement, the purity of her profile.

Actually, he was far away. Whitney was worrying about a financial transaction that was coming up in the morning and trying to decide how he would handle it. Now and then an upsurge in the volume of the music would scatter these thoughts and fill him instead with a sense of sadness and unease which he could not define. Whitney always used to say that he liked music but that he didn't know anything about it. What he liked was music with a definite rhythm, often repeated, and an easy melody: martial music, "story" music, dance music. These he would enjoy, tapping his foot in time or humming along a little out of key. But the more abstract the music became the more he lost himself either in undefinable sensations, like the one in him now, or in personal speculations that had no connection with the music. The only definable sensation then was boredom; and with it a desire to be almost anywhere but in a concert hall.

Looking about, I could hardly blame him. A musical audience is at best uninspiring, at worst definitely drab. In the bleak half-light the people look colorless and negative. Respectability hangs like a pall over the orchestra and the boxes; a sort of sterile sobriety ill-fitted to the passionate geometry of music. The hall is full of tired men and women, many of them like Miss Furman and her friend Niles, embracing music, drinking it, giving themselves to it in an orgy of self-immolation. The boxes are full of the socially or financially prominent who, like Elizabeth, use music as a vehicle to culture.

But there were many in the concert hall for whom this music was above all an affirmation of faith. Brian was one of these; so was Philip; and so was his girl, Micaela. To each of them, although in different ways, the *Passacaglia* was one answer to the hardest question in the world: What are we here for? To

Brian it was incontrovertible testimony to the greatness, the
goodness in man. In the purity, compassion, and grandeur of
these intervals and chords, all the obstructing pettinesses were
washed away, leaving him clean, at peace, and humble. This
music was a catharsis, like great tragedy; and the humility with
which it left one was the same kind of humility felt on looking
up at the night sky; a sense of wonder, not at the smallness of
man but at the grandeur of the universe.

Brian said: While I listen to this I am afraid of nothing;
neither loneliness nor failure nor evil. Olivia, you are not near
me, you are in me, as the sound of this music is in me and I
in it. And because of that, I am—for this moment at least—
whole.

I could see in his face that this was so. The lines of his cheek
were softened, the mouth relaxed, almost smiling.

Philip and Micaela were holding hands as they listened,
and both leaned forward in their seats as if by doing so they
could lessen the distance between them and the source of the
sound. Wild and wonderful thoughts were taking wing in the
boy's mind and he had already projected himself into a future
in which he alone, Philip Aronson, was saving humanity through
his own sacrifice. As the *Passacaglia* rolled on Philip was warning
the peoples of the world about their coming destruction through
greed and blindness, and they were stoning him and jeering.
He seemed to skip a number of stages in this heroic story, for
the next tableau had him bound to a stake on top of a hill while
great masses of people went on jeering. I found it interesting
that a boy born in 1927 could find no more modern method of
torture than the stake, considering the great advances in tech-
nology. But the stake it was, and fire was already flickering in
the pupils of Philip's eyes, now distended in anguish.

The flames apparently held off long enough for him to compose a testament to the world of such nobility and tenderness
that his eyes filled with water. Then, possibly because of

a slight pressure of her hand, Micaela entered the picture of his last moments and "they" were killing her too, but exactly how was too hazy in his mind to be communicable to mine.

Micaela, on her part, was off on quite another tangent as she listened with her large brown eyes fixed on Steiner. She was going through a sort of litany of service: I will take care of Phil, I will go with him where he goes, anywhere in the world, I will serve him, I will understand him, I will tend him if he is ill, I will feed him when he is hungry, I will scrub floors for him if need be. This is the first time I have felt that way about any boy, this is the most wonderful thing that has ever happened to me, I am so glad that I could cry. If we are together this frightening world cannot harm us.

She turned to look at Philip and said to herself, with great love for him: How much he looks like the pictures of his mother. As if he had heard it he turned to look at her, thinking: Strange—just now she reminds me of Mother. . . .

I could see from Brian's program that the next piece was Mozart's *Symphony in E Flat Major.* While Steiner was waiting for the audience to settle he turned to look at a woman hurrying to her seat in the second row. There must have been something about her that reminded Steiner of me, for suddenly I was there beside him, close to his heavy worn face and the grizzled hair brushed back from his large ears. But it was only for a fraction of a second: when Steiner lifted his baton there was no thought in his mind but the music. With his own tension he held the orchestra to him in the slow and serene introduction, somehow prophetic of Mozart's final maturity.

I had met Steiner first in 1934 or so when he conducted a contemporary composition based on something I had written. It was a sort of free-style poem called "Ride on the El"; a penetration of the windows lining the elevated into the lives behind them. The young composer Matthew Ordway put it to music; he made it an effective tone poem in the modern idiom, with the narration sung by a baritone voice and the intermittent roar of the El translated into an orchestral texture that bound together and sometimes underlay the lyrical episodes.

I had heard of Steiner's amatory prowess long before I had met him. People—usually unattractive women or the husbands of attractive ones—would call him "a disgusting old man," a "garter-snapper," or an "old lecher"; and would murmur in the same breath, "Poor Mrs. Steiner—I wonder how she stands it—" The truth of the matter was that Mrs. Steiner had stood it with great advantage to herself for over twenty years, achieving a position which her very limited capacities would never have managed without him. Like many wives of distinguished men, she had long since ceased to grow with him, intellectually or emotionally. Physically she must have failed his gargantuan appetite very early in their marriage, and this was the only thing for which Steiner reproached himself: "I asked too much of her," he would say. "I was a greedy monster."

He still was greedy, in spite of his sixty years and the enormous energy he poured into his conducting. But he gave as much as he took. In spirit, in vitality, in imagination, he was younger than most men of thirty. That his hair was gray, his face deeply lined, and his skin coarsened with age was immaterial as far as I was concerned. They were merely the price of knowledge and labor. And when I looked at his hard dry hands or felt their touch, I did not think "These are old hands" but "These are the hands that can pull music out of air."

He was not an easy man to know well, for his moods were violent and his demands great. Although he liked what he called "free women," he could tolerate no competing ego. To love him meant to submit to him. This was good training; for too much independence in a woman, I had learned, disturbs, and can destroy the fundamental human equation. Steiner was the master, and his need for me—which lasted nearly a year—was a command.

I learned a great deal from Steiner. What he got from me I could not, even now, tell. A number of people had a word for it, but I doubt if they were entirely right. Steiner knew women far more beautiful and desirable than myself; if all he had needed was physical diversion he could have done a better job with them. Certainly he was no more in love with me than I with him, although we were very close. Now, as I looked at him in the highly creative moment of conducting, I thought the fact that we were both reaching for the same things had something to do with our feeling for each other. We were both, in a sense, dedicated. We both had separate lives in work which were inviolate and sustaining. And yet we both needed, not in spite of this capacity for withdrawal but because of it, continual intimate human contact. Without it we were only half alive. Human passion, human closeness was the source of our energy, re-charging the batteries of the imagination.

The intermission followed, and most of the audience rose to stretch and meet and smoke in the corridors and on the stairs and in the lounge. I saw Whitney and Elizabeth and their box-companions rise and leave. I saw Brian moving slowly up the aisle with the crowd. I saw Philip and Micaela leave their seats. But I was with Steiner as he went into the greenroom.

As always he was dripping wet after an hour's conducting. Sweat poured down his forehead, his neck, his back to such an extent that he had to change his clothes from the skin out during the intermission, and then again after the concert before he went out to go home.

Tonight he saw no one while he changed. He looked very tired and much older than while he was conducting. His cheeks sagged, his eyes were dull, and his hands fumbled with his clothes.

After he had changed, he sank down on the couch, his heavy, oversized head hung forward, his eyes half-closed, his hands limp on his knees. The continuous applause after the Mozart symphony seemed not to have stimulated him tonight, and I imagined he was dissatisfied with his part of the performance. I say imagined because I was not close enough to him now to know. He had summoned me to him, but his fatigue had blurred the image and I seemed to be fluctuating in and out of his consciousness. I believe he needed me, at that moment; not necessarily for myself alone but as a symbol of the vitality and intensity which was ebbing slowly out of him and for which he now felt an overwhelming nostalgia. For Steiner was now seventy-two years old. And when, a few minutes later, a young girl knocked and entered (she looked like a music student) and faced him with submissive adoration, and he said "Hello, Betty" and drew her down on his lap and fondled her neck under its bushy tail of hair, he was repeating an old mechanical pattern. Steiner had begun to fool himself. The "old lecher," the "disgusting old man," had become a reality.

Philip and the girl were making their way down the stairs through the crowd.

"We will never get back in time," said Micaela.

"Oh, yes we will," said Philip. "Anyway I always like to look at the upper classes."

The girl smiled. "But you are the upper classes, Phil!"

"Pure accident, Mike. Actually I feel like a one-man underground at home."

Laughing, Micaela said, "Oh, Philip, you're so silly. I'm sure your stepfather is much nicer than you say."

"I didn't say he wasn't nice," said Phil. "It's just that when I'm with him I feel subversive. The backbone of the country always has that effect on me."

They had reached the ground floor and were edging their way with difficulty toward the lounge when Philip said, "Speak of the Devil—"

Whitney had seen him and raised his hand in greeting. He spoke to Elizabeth and she looked at Philip too and smiled.

"Is that your stepfather?" asked Micaela. "He's very handsome."

"Yes. I guess we'll have to go over." They pushed toward the older couple.

"Who is that with him?" asked the girl.

"That's Mrs. Warren—friend of the family." Elizabeth at the same time asked Whitney, "Who's the girl with Philip?"

"Haven't any idea," said Whitney.

"Rather exotic type."

They finally met. "This is Miss Vidal—my stepfather," said Philip, introducing Micaela. "Mrs. Warren—"

Elizabeth held out her hand to the girl and they shook. "Wasn't that Mozart exquisite? Steiner is so dynamic," she said; then to Philip, "I didn't know you were a concertgoer, Philip."

"I'm not," said Philip. "I just like certain things."

Elizabeth turned to Micaela. "I suppose you're the musical influence, then?"

"Oh, no," said Micaela. "I think it was his mother . . ." she trailed off, embarrassed. Elizabeth cut in quickly, turning to Philip. "Back to college soon, I suppose, Philip?"

"Yes. Next Monday, I guess."

"'Bout exhausted the town, haven't you Phil?" said his stepfather.

Philip smiled. "In a way," he said.

The bell announcing the second half of the concert had begun to ring, and Whitney, starting to move toward the door to the orchestra, said to Philip, "See you later," and bowed his head slightly to Micaela. Elizabeth smiled a brilliant farewell, then murmured to Whitney, "I wonder where he picked her up."

"Oh, he moves in strange circles. I've tried to get him to go to dances and things but he won't do it."

"Would you like me to throw him a party, Whitney? I know some awfully nice girls around his age."

Whitney looked at her gratefully. "I wish you would, Liz. I—I can't seem to handle him alone."

While they found their way back to their box, Philip and Micaela were climbing up to their gallery perch. When they settled into their seats, the girl turned to Philip and said, with a half-smile on her mobile face, "I don't think they approved of me, Phil."

"Mother would have," he said.

"I wish she were here," said Micaela.

"Sometimes I almost feel she is," said Philip.

"Do you believe in ghosts?" asked the girl.

"No, I don't think there's any shape," he said slowly, "just a kind of—hell, I don't know."

"A kind of presence?"

"Yes, like the smell of fear. Only there's no fear about this."

Steiner had come out on the stage. Philip took hold of Micaela's hand and they looked at each other for a brief moment before the music began.

When Brian came back to his seat after the intermission, the chair next to him—which had been empty during the first part of the concert—was filled. There was a woman in it, unknown to me but apparently familiar to Brian, for he said. "Good evening, Lilian."

Startled, she turned to look up at him. "Oh, Mr. Littleton!"

"Too bad you missed the first part," said Brian settling in his seat. "It was pretty fine."

"Oh, I'm furious, Mr. Littleton, but I got all tied up at home. Momma's sick, and I had to wash up after dinner and then there wasn't any bus for half an hour and, oh, just everything went wrong!" She seemed genuinely disturbed. As I looked at her more closely I began to realize who she was. She was the receptionist at Brian's office, and I used to tease Brian about having such a cover-girl in his outfit. She was, actually, spectacular; long, shining dyed-blond hair, a masklike perfect face, and the kind of mouth that seems designed for one purpose only. I remembered her walk: the belt around her narrow waist moved up and down diagonally like the walking-beam on old paddle-wheelers.

"It was awfully sweet of you to give me the ticket," said the girl. "I was just thrilled when you asked me."

"Well, I heard you liked music," said Brian, "and Mr. Howe couldn't go at the last minute."

He stole a quick look at her; Brian was adept at looking when he knew a woman would not intercept his gaze. As he did so, a remark which he had often made to me flashed through his mind: "I don't believe in mixing business and personal life." And, more specifically, after I twitted him on his personable secretaries, "I've never taken out any girl in the office and never will. It doesn't work." Then he rationalized, as if explaining to me now: But I haven't taken this girl out. I merely gave her a ticket.

But still I must have haunted him, for he continued to behave with almost icy correctness toward her, keeping his eyes from her profile and from the long white hands with their long red nails lying in her lap. But whether he meant it or not, her nearness was beginning to assail him and with it the perfume she was wearing, because Brian's nostrils were distending slightly, and I could see the color of his neck deepening.

Ravel's *Bolero* was the last piece on the program, but I left before the last dissonant climax. For the devilish mounting tempo and volume, the hypnotic oriental repetitions, the rising hot whine of the brass, was driving me from the minds of those in whom I had resided.

The blood was rising in Philip and Micaela, the pressure of their hands, interlocked, tightened, their breathing had accelerated, and they gave themselves over to the potency of sound and desire.

In a box below them, the *Bolero* was having its effect on Whitney and Elizabeth. In Elizabeth the tide of power was rising and she felt the hour of her triumph near. The music to her was not an incitement to the blood but a statement of her infallibility. As for Whitney, it conjured up the brothels of Cairo during the war and he became hot, uncomfortable, and ashamed without knowing why.

Brian was seized by a kind of wildness as the music mounted. With deliberate recklessness, he turned to look at the girl next to him, focusing on her mouth. She felt it and looked back. In the heat of that interchange I vanished from the hall.

I came into the apartment with Auriol that same evening. The clock on the foyer table said ten-thirty, and I was surprised, knowing my daughter's hectic social life, that she should be home so early—and alone. She looked angry and disturbed, and from the way she threw her hat and coat on a chair in her bedroom, I imagined she must have had a quarrel of some sort. She wandered around the apartment, opened the door to Whitney's room and looked in, then went to the living room and turned on the radio. She listened for a moment to some dance-music, turned it off, and went into my study. The contents of the trunk which she and Philip had sorted were still on the floor, the trunk open. She hesitated a minute, then bent down to the pile of letters and started to look through them. A frown of incomprehension clouded her forehead, and she started to look through the other piles. Not finding what she wanted, she sat down on the floor trying to find the solution to its disappearance. Her frown deepened as she thought.

While she was sitting there a key turned in the lock of the front door. Auriol heard the click, rose quickly to her feet, and was standing in the doorway of my study when Whitney came past and saw her there.

"Hello, Sis," he said. "It's a pleasure to find you home so early."

"Hello, Dad," said Auriol. She was looking straight at him in a strange way. Whitney glanced past her into the study and at the piles on the floor.

"Been working?" he asked, trying to sound casual.

"No," said the girl. "I came to get a book." She turned out the light in the study and went into the living room while Whitney hung up his coat and hat in the hall closet.

As he came out of it and into the living room, Auriol cleared her throat and said haltingly, "Have you—have you looked over the things?"

Whitney was at the bar table pouring himself a highball with his back to her. "No," he said. "I haven't had a chance to get at them yet."

When he turned around he found Auriol still looking at him, and this time their eyes met. Each one knew that the other was lying. The love letters that Auriol had read and Whitney had destroyed hung there in the silence between them—mute evidence; to one, of his wife's promiscuity; to the other, of her mother's vulnerability. To speak of them was to open Pandora's box; and neither of them dared.

"Good night," said Auriol, finally turning to go.

"Hey—what about a good-night kiss?" said Whitney. The girl turned, slowly went toward him, and lifted her cheek to his. He bent and kissed her, putting his hands on her shoulders. "I think my girl needs a change," he said. "What about a couple of weeks at Aunt Eleanor's?"

"Let's talk about it in the morning," said the girl, turning again. "I'm bushed, Daddy."

"I'll write her," Whitney said. "A little sun and air will be just the thing for you." But Auriol was already out of the room, so he put out the light in the living room and went into his bedroom, drink in hand. What that kid needs, he thought to himself, is the influence of a good woman. Then he caught himself short as he found himself wondering whether Auriol had inherited my bad blood. Nonsense, he thought, she's a sound girl with a head on her shoulders. No illusions there to worry about. Then as the drink began to warm him he remembered the look on Elizabeth's face as he left her at her door only a few minutes ago. She looked so pure and calm and beautiful, he thought. "Whitney," she had said, "if you ever need me for anything . . ." and then she had turned and gone inside the door. Elizabeth was pure goodness, pure generosity; a true friend. It was no treachery to the memory of me to see her as often as he did. The loneliness would get him if he didn't. Then suddenly a wave of bitterness washed over Whitney as the images of our early months together rose before him. My God, he said, and to think I believed her. To think I believed her all that time!

Auriol, lying on her bed with her clothes on, staring up at the ceiling, was asking herself over and over again: What is true love?

It must have been only a few hours later when I found myself in a dark room. I did not need any light, however, to tell me that it was Brian's bedroom; or that he was not alone on his bed. The surprise was not that this should be so, but that I should be there to see it.

The woman was, of course, the girl who had been next to him at the concert—the receptionist called Lilian. Enough light came through the crack of the bathroom door to show her dress sprawled over the armchair, her stockings and shoes on the floor.

Brian was turned away from her, and she was bending over him trying to pull his head around to her. He pushed her away, gently but firmly.

"Please—" he said.

"What's the matter, darling? I was only loving you."

"Well, don't."

She continued to look down at him as she sat up in the bed, white and perfectly made. "Gee," she sighed reminiscently. "I never knew you were like that. I always thought you were high-hat—you know—frigid!"

"The truth of it is, I am," Brian sat up too, smoothing back his hair. Then he spoke to me: Are you seeing me now, Olivia? And how do you like me?

Lilian laughed, gayly. "If that's frigid, give me the North Pole!" She put her hands on either side of his head and kissed him. This time he put her hands down roughly, and got out of bed.

"I'll take you home now. It's pretty late." He switched on the light and went to the chair where his clothes were.

Lilian blinked at the light, then bounded out of bed and stood close to him. "Aw, darling, what's the hurry?"

Brian, ignoring her nearness, started to dress.

"Look, you don't have to take me home. Why don't I stay here tonight?"

Brian turned to look at her. "I want you to get something straight. I like to sleep alone. You're beautiful and I had a good time with you, but that's that. I want to sleep alone."

She was silent for a moment, then, "You're not going to stop loving me, are you?"

"I never started loving you," said Brian. "I took you because I wanted to get something out of my system. I did—for about fifteen minutes."

"You just talk," she said. "You can't fool me."

He barked at her: "Get dressed—quickly." (Olivia—how do you like this? Nice picture of a bastard, isn't it?)

Slowly the girl began drawing on her stockings. "You don't have to act that way, do you? Whose idea was this, anyway?"

"I had the strong impression that the idea was mutual," said Brian buttoning his shirt. "Did you feel coerced?"

"You and your goddamn vocabulary," muttered Lilian. She pulled the round garters up above her knee, stepped into her platform sandals, then reached for her dress and slipped it over her head. Apparently that was all she wore.

Brian faced her squarely and said, "If you don't mind, I'd like to make quite sure that we understand each other. Did you or did you not want to come back with me tonight?"

Sulkily, Lilian said, "Who said I didn't?"

"All right. Did I at any time mention the word love?"

"I don't know what you're driving at. You're always talking—"

"I just want to ask you one thing more," said Brian, pulling on his pants. "Did you or did you not enjoy yourself?"

The girl had gone into the bathroom and was combing her long brassy hair. "What the hell do you think I was doing?" she snapped.

"All right, then. We both enjoyed ourselves. How about leaving it at that?"

The girl turned around to stare at Brian. "Well, of all the goddamned nerve," she said slowly.

"Will it make you feel any better," said Brian, "if I call myself a low, mean bastard? Or would you rather do it?"

The girl's eyes softened a little. "I didn't mean that," she said. "I just don't understand you. A little while ago—"

"I know," said Brian. "A little while ago I made love to you. I did so for inexcusable reasons, and I want to apologize for them."

"What reasons?"

"I used you to keep myself from feeling."

"I don't get you. That's double-talk."

"Not really," said Brian. "It's the truth. You were just a means—not an end."

"So what," said the girl. "What does all this add up to? You're giving me the air?"

Brian put his hands on her shoulders. "Call it that if you like. You can get any man you want at any time. Just count me off as a dead loss. Or pretend that nothing ever happened. Nothing really did, you know."

Lilian laughed harshly. "That's a good one. That's the best yet!"

Brian went to his closet and got his coat and put it on. Then he picked up the girl's coat and held it for her to get into.

"I don't want you to take me home," she said.

"I'd like to," said Brian.

"Well, you can't," snapped the girl. "I'm not goin' home anyway."

"Then I'll take you to where you're going."

She turned and snarled at him. "Don't be a sap," she said. "I've got a late date!"

Brian went to the door and opened it for her. "I'll put you in a taxi then," he said, and closed the door after them. They did not talk for the five minutes they spent waiting for a taxi. When it finally drew up, Brian handed the driver a dollar, then turned back to the girl. "Better luck next time," he said; and the cab drew off.

He turned back to his brownstone and walked slowly up the three flights to his apartment and let himself in. Wearily he took off the clothes he had only just put on and was about to get into bed when he looked at the tossed sheets and blanket and the tumbled pillows (one was on the floor) and made the whole bed over again. Then he went into the bathroom and took a shower. Coming back, he opened one of the windows

and crawled into bed. He reached for a book on his bed-table—it
happened to be the *Pensées* of Pascal—opened it at random and
started to read. But after only a few seconds he closed the book
and put out the light and we talked together.

You saw all that, didn't you? he asked.

Not all, I said.

No—there were moments when I really managed not to
think of you. That's what I wanted, you know; to put you out
of my mind, just for a while.

What brought me back, Brian?

Something she did—right afterward.

Something that reminded you of me?

No, something that you would never have done—or said.
Something that made me realize where I was—and who I was
with. Olivia, why don't you answer—why don't you say something? How is it to see someone you love in bed with another
person? Are you full of revulsion—are you angry? Are you hurt,
Olivia? Or are you beyond all these things? You are still so
alive to me that I feel you must still be vulnerable.

It's only what I imagined before, Brian.

Brian lay in the dark, confronting this last phrase. Then
finally he said: You knew, then?

I said I "imagined." You were away from me for long times,
Brian. How could I expect you not to sleep with others?

You never spoke of that, Olivia.

No. Why should I have? So long as you were the same with
me—when we were together.

And you? Brian smiled bitterly to himself. No—you had
Whitney, of course.

Of course. After you went away.

After a pause, Brian said: Do you remember how I used to talk
about whorehouses—how much better they were than this
sort of thing I've done tonight?

I remember.

A whorehouse is entirely impersonal. But what I did tonight has involved me personally with someone I never want to see again—and whom I can't insult by paying.

Why not?

Why not? Because she's in this border-world we've set up between prostitution and "affairs." She's a professional with an amateur standing, which makes her a "lady." Then, of course, there are ladies with professional standing. They all want something for their efforts, but so long as it isn't a ten-dollar bill their record's clean.

You asked for it, I said.

Certainly I asked for it! I wanted flesh and excitement. I wanted to wipe out this perpetual ache—

Well, you did—for a while.

For a little while, Olivia. It's worse now. Much worse. Because I need someone next to me all night—quietly, now, without passion—and you're not here.

The sounds of taxi horns came from the street outside and the beam of a headlight veered across the ceiling of the room. I could hear the faint tick of Brian's alarm clock on his bed-table, accentuating now the muffled silence.

Olivia—

Yes?

Olivia—when we talk like this, are you really answering me, or is it just a voice inside my head—my own voice?

What do you think, Brian?

God, I don't know. They say there's no such thing as communication with the dead. Certainly there's no proof.

No proof . . .

Perhaps you and I are so close that we have become part of each other. In that case, darling, you're not really dead.

Not really dead . . .

Why are you echoing my voice? Or are you agreeing?

Sleep was overtaking Brian. He turned on his side, with one knee up and the other leg straight, one hand under the pillow and the other arm stretched in front of him; as he always lay when he was ready for sleep.

Olivia—I've never asked you whether you were happy. That's the stock question everyone puts to the dead. Are you happy, Olivia—dearest? Wherever you are?

There was nothing I could say. Instead I lay down beside him and the outstretched arm moved slightly to give me space.

The fourth month . . . Having avoided the place during my life, I was rather surprised to find myself in Florida after my death.

The scene was an open patio rimmed with awnings, under one of which a luncheon party was in session. There must have been about twenty seated at the long narrow table and it took me a while before Auriol came into focus as one of them. Somewhat later I recognized Whitney's sister, Eleanor; and realized that this must be her place on an island where Auriol was visiting, as she had once before, a year ago.

Actually, most of the faces turned out to be vaguely familiar: they were the same faces that used to be on transatlantic liners before the war, at Nice, at Cannes, or at Antibes; and who were confined to the south shore of Long Island during the war. Except for Auriol, another young girl, and two young men, the guests were well over middle age. Sunburn and make-up and the constant ministrations of a masseuse gave some of the women the appearance of youth; they were slim and well-groomed and wore their clothes well. These consisted of "simple" little silk dresses or slack-suits which were used as understatements for the magnificent modern jewels they wore. But the bracelets dangled on hard bony wrists, the thin legs had the corded quality of age, their necks were dry, and their faces wore the restless harassed look of women who are constantly battling for the surface qualities of youth. Their voices were too loud, their laughs too sudden, their gestures too contrived.

If age hardens women, it seems to soften men. At least, it
softens the rich American men. They, too, were dark with sun
and oil, their hair (if they had it) either well-greased or bleached
yellow-gray. But their faces were flabby under the tan, and
nearly all of them had soft shoulders and loose flesh around their
hips. Most of them wore Tahitian shirts or shorts; a habit I
had always found touching. There is a definite pathos in the
attempt of the over-civilized to become primitive; the figurative
hibiscus stuck behind the ear of an ageing banker.

At this luncheon I noticed Ralph Corrigan. Ten years before
he had been "America's most promising playwright." He had
written a passionate play about southern sharecroppers which
gave evidence of an important talent. It was his fifth play, but
the first that had succeeded and the first time that Ralph had
more than fifty dollars in the bank. When M-G-M brought him
out to the Coast to work on a picture, he was full of apologies
to his friends. "I don't want to go out to that factory," he said,
"but what can you do? All I want to do is make some dough
fast and then come back here and write serious stuff. All I need
is some dough in the bank and then I'll be free to write what I
want. I'll be back in six months," he said, the night before he
left.

He never came back, except for brief visits. Nor did he ever
write "serious stuff" or a good play. He turned out slick brittle
dialogue for slick brittle movies at one thousand dollars a week,
bought himself a house with a swimming pool, had good Filipino
servants and a series of starlet mistresses. Nobody in his right
mind could blame him.

He himself kept apologizing for a year. "Christ, this is a mad-
house," he would say. "It's driving me nuts. You can't do anything really good in pictures. Too many cooks. Too many strings.
All they think of out here is box-office. Jesus, I can't wait to get
back to New York and see some white people."

But he did wait. And to Brian, his publisher, he sent a significant letter after two years in Hollywood. "After all," it went, "the important thing is to reach as many people as possible. What's the use of talking to an audience of a thousand when you can talk to eighty million?"

"Funny," mused Brian as he read the letter to me. "He doesn't say what the talk is about." Then, "Maybe he's forgotten that making a thousand people think is possibly more satisfying than making eighty million stop thinking."

I looked at other guests and recognized the painter who had done Elizabeth's portrait. Alan Reddiker was sitting next to Auriol and it would be only a matter of moments, I felt sure, before he asked to do hers. Unlike Corrigan, who kept apologizing for writing tripe, Reddiker dismissed "pure" art as of no consequence in the modern world. "The only good painting is commercial painting," he once said after winning a prize in a soft-drink competition; "all the rest is merely incompetence." This made him popular with businessmen, who liked to say, "No long-hair stuff about Reddiker"; and with their wives, who could have him around the house without fear, thanks to his leanings, of involvement.

I did not recognize the other guests, but as Eleanor Whittredge, Whitney's sister, had married an oil tycoon I imagined there must have been a liberal sprinking of associates in utility and manufacturing fields. The older men looked flushed under their tan, and I noticed a number of shaking hands. Eleanor herself was a fine-looking woman of fifty or so; not unlike Whitney in her straight shoulders and the regularity of her features, for which her white hair, blued and crisply curled about her head, made a handsome frame.

As I watched all this I was increasingly bewildered as to the reason for my presence. The conversation had so far not mentioned me, Auriol was not thinking of me, and although I knew both Corrigan and Reddiker, they were very unlikely to have me in their thoughts. As for Eleanor, she had always disliked me intensely.

The only thing about me that Eleanor did approve was Auriol. "A lovely child," she would say to me; to others, "Thank heaven Whitney got hold of her in time. She's got to begin meeting the right people, you know."

So here was Auriol among the right people. Certainly she looked at ease and happy; and more beautiful than ever in a strapless bronze-colored dress with a white camellia pinned in her long russet hair. She was not sunburned like the rest, and her skin in contrast seemed almost phosphorescent.

"I think there should be a law against it," Eleanor was saying.

"Against what?" asked Reddiker.

"Against changing their names like that—you know, that appalling man who tried to join the club."

"Oh, you mean Shaw—nee Shapiro," said Reddiker.

"Wouldn't you change Shapiro if you had it?" Corrigan asked the company in general.

"That's a rather academic question," said an older man, laughing. "But the point is, they shouldn't be allowed to take perfectly good family names. I don't blame the Cabots for raising hell at those immigrants who took over their name."

Eleanor sighed wearily. "Well, what can you do? Those people own the earth now. The way they breed—" She trailed off.

Another woman said, "One Jew isn't so bad, it's always that they bring along their families. Why, if you let one in—"

Auriol was looking down at her plate. Guilt and shame were crowding her mind and she felt me now as an accusing specter saying: Don't let them go on like that, Auriol, don't sit there and say nothing. But Auriol remained silent.

Reddiker was off on a new angle. "One of the chief troubles is physical," he said. "I've painted them and I know. They're a warped and misshapen race; even their skin is unappetizing!"

Auriol, I said, why don't you tell them that your father is a handsome man? Auriol said nothing, her hands clenched underneath the table. She had stopped eating, her plate still heaped with food.

"Now look at Miss Corning here," Reddiker went on. "Look at the articulation of her nose, look at the texture of her skin— you'd never find that on a Jew, it's a product purely of northern civilizations."

A slow flush crept up Auriol's face, but she only laughed self-consciously and lowered her eyes. Eleanor took the situation in hand.

"I hear Brian Littleton's staying at Belinda's," she said. So this, I thought, explained these last images I had had of him, striding along a beach. They were brief and hazy, and although at the time I recognized the tropical quality of the sea and shore I could not exactly place where he was. Nor, oddly enough, did we talk together. There seemed to be a definite obstruction, whether in him or in his environment, that weakened our communication.

Auriol lifted her head at the mention of his name.

"Smart publisher," said an older man. "Last book of his is a national best-seller."

"I've met him," said one of the women. "He's frightfully attractive, but Belinda says she hardly ever sees him. He's always wandering off on the beach somewhere."

"Strong silent men are so tiresome," said Alan Reddiker. "It's really the ultimate expression of the ego to want to be alone."

"Who says he's alone?" laughed another woman. "The beach is hardly deserted!"

"It is where he goes," said the first. "Belinda says he has a passion for Potter's Point—"

"Well, he can keep it," said Reddiker. "It's utter desolation, as far as I'm concerned."

The conversation changed course. Auriol's plate was taken

away, still full, and dessert brought in. She pecked at it but
seemed to have regained her composure otherwise, talking and
laughing with the young man next to her. The entire scene
blotted out for me as suddenly as it had come into focus, but
less surprisingly. Every element of it was against the evocation
of spirit: the size and tone of the group; the bright midday air;
the food and the heat; the absorption in immediacy; all these
were hardly conducive to my kind of state. It was only shame in
Auriol, borrowed from the shadow of myself, which brought me
here, if only for a moment. Shame and the plan that was slowly
taking shape in her mind when she heard of Brian.

It must have been later that afternoon that I saw her again,
this time alone. She was bicycling along one of the smooth
shaded roads that led—as all roads must on an island—to the
sea. She wore white shorts and a long-sleeved white shirt and a
big sun-hat, now hung by a cord from her neck and down her
back. Her hair was tied back with a dark green ribbon and I
could see that her neck was moist under the dark red shining tail.

As she pedaled along under the low vault of pines, palms, and
tamarisks that intercepted the sun except for a light dappling,
the corners of her mouth turned down and her eyes darkened
with worry and confusion.

She was angry and ashamed, angry at her father for being a
Jew, angry at the people for talking that way about Jews, angry
at herself for being quiescent, and above all angry at me for
being the cause of her shame. The talks we had had in her childhood kept coming back to her, against her will: the will to be
happy and popular and free of shame.

"People will says things about Jews," I had told her and
Philip in the days before I married Whitney and both children
bore Max's name. "Stupid things, vicious things, false things.
Don't let them get under your skin. Half the time they're only
repeating the catchwords of prejudice and don't really mean
them. Even if they do mean them, even if they do think of you

as a race apart, never allow yourself that particular luxury. You're not a race apart: you're Americans—"

"You mean," said Philip, "we've got to just sit there and take it?"

"No. But your job is to show them—not by words, but by your own restraint and dignity—what utter fools they are."

It was easy to say, I knew. And yet I wanted above all to avoid making an issue of their Jewish blood, even if others did. "It's not a matter of either pride or shame," I told Auriol once. "It's not only inaccurate but pointless to rise up and beat your breast and say, "I am a Jew!" And it's morally dishonest to deny that you are, in part. Again it's that extremely difficult road you have to tread: the middle one. And don't let extremists on either side push you off it."

Actually, the children suffered few distressing incidents of a racial sort. Auriol's beauty was partly responsible for her immunity: and whatever unpopularity Philip may have created was due to a voluntary withdrawal from the "crowd" on his part. Once or twice Auriol insisted, weeping, that she had not been asked to a certain party because of her name. Once or twice Philip had a scrap on account of some slur. But the schools they went to and the people they met at home were on the whole singularly free of bias. It was not until the advent of Whitney that the fact of their blood became an issue. And it was only kindness in Whitney—or rather, his concept of kindness—that made it so.

Pedaling along, the blood rose to Auriol's head as she remembered the joy with which she took his offered name, the joy with which she abandoned her own, the joy with which she changed schools and entered the golden portals of Gentility. Gone were her former friends: the Greenberg girl, the Halasz sisters, Toni Mancino. Her bosom companions now had the good, clean names: the Hoyts, the Sedgewicks, the Carters, the Masons. Auriol Corning belonged to them.

I saw what was happening but made no comment except one. "What's become of Sidonie?" I asked her one day. "You never see her any more." Auriol turned her face away and said, "Oh— nothing." "Ashamed?" I said. There was no answer; until now, in Auriol's mind, three years later.

Well, what was I supposed to do today at lunch, cried Auriol angrily to herself—and to me. Make a scene? Embarrass everybody?

Shaking her tail of hair like a young filly, she tried to shake the whole business from her mind, forcing it into pleasanter channels. A sign reading "Potter's Point—2 miles" spurred her into thoughts of Brian, the solitary man on the beach, her mother's publisher. What was impelling her to him? Curiosity? Some unacknowledged desire to find a link with me? Defiance of the crowd?

Auriol passed several side-roads until she came to a sign that led off left. Turning, she cycled down a narrow lane bedded with russet needles.

After a few hundred yards the path came to an end. Auriol propped her bicycle against one of the last of the trees and stood looking at the broad space of sand between her and the brilliant aquamarine sea, empty of ship along the whole horizon.

But this was no ordinary beach. It was a sparse and silver forest of dead trees, stuck in sand. They had the driftwood shapes of animal and human beings; gray satin-surfaced arms and muscles and legs, and twisting, contorted torsos. One had the blunt, blind head of a sloth, another a bird head with a twisted neck, another a stag head, antlered and rearing. Motionless, they seemed to possess an inward movement of their own, caught in space and time.

The trees near the edge of the sea stood in iridescent pools. In the wide spaces between one and another, bleached shells and smooth white pebbles and small gray sticks made a pattern of loneliness. As Auriol looked at all this, her eyes widened with wonder and delight, as if she had found a hidden though expected treasure. The interesting thing about the whole place was that although the trees were dead, the forest was alive. I think Auriol perceived this, although she would have said "haunted."

Auriol walked down near the water's edge and sat down on a driftwood log, the same ash color, the same satin texture, as the trees. She did not see what I saw, several miles away, walking in her direction, Nor did she now expect it, having told herself that her half-admitted quest was vain and foolish.

Brian was walking on the hard wet sand with a fast and almost harried step. Now I could see him with brilliant clarity. He was in shorts, shirtless and barefoot. His hard legs and his chest and face were copper-colored; Brian, being sandy-haired and with a freckled pigment, burned more than he tanned. Although slight and wiry, he had the kind of chest that sculptors like, in which rib-cage and diaphragm formed a pattern in low relief. I had always marveled at his fitness, for he never had the time—in winter certainly—to exercise or to be massaged. But he was a fairly light eater and held himself together with a springlike tension that could alternate, as it does in animals, with complete relaxation.

Where have you been all this time? he said. Then answered himself: I know, I've been thinking of every damn thing on earth but you. This is about the first moment since I've been here that you've come.

I walked along beside him, silently. Each time his foot stepped on the wet iridescent sand, the sand would dry up around his step as the water gathered in the footprint, making a blotted area. Keeping always about ten yards ahead a covey of sandpipers ran along the water's edge propelled by their fussy mechanical legs.

I suppose you want to know what in hell I'm doing here, said Brian. Well, it's business, partially. And it's that craving I sometimes get for the soft life. You know, we've talked about it: the servants, the thick towels, the camellias in bowls, the liquor, the food, and that wonderful absence of guilt.

Is it really as much fun as it used to be? I asked.

Brian thought a moment. Actually—no, he said. Fear runs through them like wind in a wheat field. All except the most stupid know they are having their last days of ease. The only trouble is that they blame this on everything but themselves.

That's what you call the absence of guilt, then.

Yes. I'm not saying that they're all like that: there are good and bad rich just as much as there are good and bad poor. But money, even with the best of them, becomes a moat between them and reality. It insulates them.

Against what? I asked.

Against doubt. Against compassion. Against that kind of humility that can be felt only when there is no real shelter.

You sound like a monk, Brian!

I feel like a monk—down here!

And yet you wouldn't be here if you didn't like it—in some way.

I came here, said Brian, because I was sure you wouldn't be here too. (But I discounted this.) His eyes scanned the beach, the empty turquoise horizon, the bland incredible sky, empty of cloud. I didn't believe, he said, that you could survive in bright sunlight.

The light has nothing to do with it. It is yourself.

He walked on and I walked at his side. We had once walked on northern beaches together, with the damp wind blowing around our heads and with it the smell of shifting fathoms. Now and then we would stoop to pick up a pebble or a shell, always showing it to the other with a childish pride of discovery, as if this were the best pebble or the best shell, as if we had each found something unique and valuable. Now Brian did not stoop; instead his eyes, narrowed against the light, were fixed on the forest of dead trees, and among them a small seated figure looking seaward.

Damn, said Brian, who's sitting in my forest? Our forest, he said to me, half-smiling; I wonder why I never brought you here before. It's your kind of place, Olivia.

When he finally approached the first of the trees he went up to touch it, stroking the bleached satin surface—broad and muscular—as one strokes the neck of a horse. Then he gazed about at the others, noticing the animal shapes, the imprisoned twistings, the sense of life in death. When he came within sixty feet of Auriol he stopped. Auriol turned to look at him, then quickly away, embarrassed. This must be him, she thought; but if I turn to stare again it would look like, well, like a pick-up. The best thing was to pay no attention, conveying the idea that she wanted to be alone and undisturbed.

But that first look pierced Brian's memory. My God, Olivia— isn't that your child? And if it is, what a fantastic thing.

Auriol was finding it hard to keep her face averted. She had had enough solitude by now; curiosity was succeeding caution. The distress and rebellion that had played their parts in leading her to this deserted beach had now been dissipated by its enchantment, and she was ready for the excitement which now pervaded her. She turned again to look at Brian, and smiled in answer to the slight nod of his head and his own smile as he approached her.

God, Olivia, but she's beautiful. Frighteningly beautiful!

Auriol's face, now shaded against the sun by her broad straw hat, had, through reflection and shadow, the iridescence of the shallow pools of water near the sea's edge. Her eyes had deepened to the green of the water and her mouth, slightly open with surprise, added a childish softness to its usual sensuality.

"How do you do," said Brian, as Auriol rose to greet him. "Aren't you Miss Corning?"

"Why, yes," she said. "Hello. You're—aren't you Mister—"

"Brian Littleton. I'm your mother's publisher."

"Yes—yes," said Auriol. "I was sure that was it. You came to the house once or twice—a long time ago."

"Centuries ago," said Brian. "Before the war."

"I guess I was very young then," said Auriol.

"I guess you were," said Brian. "In fact I remember you first in a sort of cotton nightgown just before you went to bed."

"Oh goodness," cried Auriol in mock dismay, "how awful! With those awful pigtails—Mother made me wear them and I *loathed* it!"

"I don't remember them as being especially repulsive," said Brian. "But then I like pigtails on the young."

Auriol laughed, looking at him now with heightened interest. For a pretty old man, she thought, he's not bad.

"I must say," Brian went on, "it's rather extraordinary finding someone you know sitting in a patch of dead trees ten miles from nowhere. Is this a usual practice?"

"Oh, no," said the girl. "I just—well, I just wanted to get away from some people."

"So did I."

They looked at each other and laughed. Brian was searching her face for traces of me. She's got your forehead, he said to me, and your nose. And she's got your voice. I find all this uncanny—and upsetting.

"Have you been here long?" asked Auriol in her best social manner.

"Only three days," said Brian. "And I'm off on Monday. What about you?"

"Oh, I'm staying with my aunt. She has a sort of house-party. I'm going to be here another week, I guess."

"Vacation?" asked Brian. "Or are you through with higher education?"

"Oh, I finished school last year," said the girl. "I'm not going to college."

"What are you going to do?"

Auriol hesitated a moment; then, in a small and rather lost voice said, "I just don't know."

I must talk about Olivia, said Brian. I must bring Olivia into this somehow. Funny how it is imperative to hear others speak about the person you love.

"What about writing," said Brian. "Ever wanted to try it?"

Auriol turned to look at him, her eyes wide with dismay, almost as if Brian had accused her of something.

"Oh no!" she cried. "I don't want to write—" Then, feeling that she may have sounded disloyal to my memory in the violence of her repudiation, added, "I mean, I don't think I could."

"I suppose one's enough in the family, anyway," said Brian.

"Well, it isn't just that," said Auriol, "but I think writing's awfully lonely. I mean you just stay in a room all day, and I couldn't do that. Anyway," she added, "there's no money in it."

"No," said Brian, "not in the sort of writing your mother did."

They were silent for a moment, and then Auriol said, "She didn't care about a lot of things."

"Like what, for instance?"

"Oh—clothes and jewels and things. And parties. She didn't really care."

"Is that what you have to have?" asked Brian.

The girl turned to look at him, and said with complete gravity, "I couldn't live without them." Then, "I guess that sounds terrible, and Mother always hated the way I felt, but that's the way I am. You see, she didn't seem to need those things. She had a sort of secret life—" Auriol's eyes were now turned seaward, looking at nothing.

"In what way—secret?" My God, Olivia, what does the child know? What is she thinking?

"I mean she'd sort of go away in herself. Sometimes I was

sure she wasn't hearing anything anybody was saying. She was listening, but she wasn't listening to them."

"I guess," said Auriol, after a little pause, "I guess that's where the poetry comes from."

"The secret life?" asked Brian.

Auriol looked at him, then lowered her eyes, embarrassed. "I guess it's silly telling you where poetry comes from."

"Because I publish it? No—that's as good an explanation as any. Poetry does come from a secret life—only it has to have a public expression. The trouble with most poetry written now is that it remains secret to all but the people who write it."

"I just can't understand it," said Auriol. "I thought maybe I was dumb!"

"No. The poet's dumb, in the actual sense. He doesn't know how to speak. That is the extraordinary thing about your mother's poetry. It was never banal, never common, never obvious, and yet everybody can understand it. She speaks to the heart, not to the heads of a few frustrated intellectuals who form their own symbolic community against clarity. Your mother had the humility to be simple."

Auriol was silent for a moment. They both looked at the tranquil horizon, and at a tiny smudge near the center of it.

"A ship," said Auriol.

"Yes. Probably a fruit ship bound north."

"Mr. Littleton—"

"Yes?"

"You knew my mother well, didn't you?"

Brian looked at her profile to see whether her face betrayed any ulterior meaning. Shall I tell her, Olivia? Shall I tell her now?

"Yes," he said. "I did."

"Did she ever talk about me?"

"Sometimes . . ." Olivia, can't you see she's not ready yet?

Can't I lie? "Naturally," said Brian, "Most of our talk had to do with work—"

"What did she say?"

"She was worried about you. She thought you were after the wrong things."

"Oh, my God," said Auriol, turning pleading eyes to Brian. "She would. You see, she didn't understand me. She was always trying to make me do things I didn't want to do."

"Isn't that the function of parents?" said Brian, smiling.

"Well, she wasn't that way with Philip. Philip was always perfect."

"Couldn't it have been," said Brian, "that she expected a lot of you?"

Auriol raised her eyebrows in a triangle of distress. "Gosh, I don't know. But things change after people die. I don't feel that way so much now. I keep wishing—"

"You keep wishing?" said Brian.

"I keep wishing I could talk to her. I could explain things better now."

The two said nothing for a while. Brian was the first to break the silence, which was full of thought.

"If you should ever want any help about getting jobs or things, let me know, I might be able to help. Although," he went on, "maybe you don't want to work at anything."

Auriol turned quickly toward him. "Oh, yes, I do. I've got to do something. I can't just sit around—"

"I should have thought the stage might have tempted you," said Brian, struck anew by Auriol's almost sensational beauty.

Auriol's face lit up and she smiled at him. "How did you guess?"

"It wasn't hard!"

"As a matter of fact, I'm dying to try the stage. But I don't think Whitney would ever let me."

"That sounds rather Victorian. Does he think an actress is a lady of joy?"

Laughing, Auriol said, "Oh, I don't think it's that. It's just the publicity. His family's sort of—well—sort of stuffy."

"Well, maybe he'll relent. If he does, maybe I can get you started with the right people. Or at least give you some tips as to how to learn the trade."

"That's terribly nice of you, Mr. Littleton." She looked at him warmly and Brian blushed for himself and to me. My God, Olivia, I sound just like one of those old men who dangle careers before young girls they want to make.

Auriol shoved up the full sleeve of her white shirt to look at her watch. "Heavens," she cried. "I've got to beat it." She stood up, and Brian rose with her.

"It's been lots of fun meeting this way!" She held out her hand.

Taking it, Brian said, "For me, too. Maybe we'll meet in more conventional circumstances some time again! Are you walking back, by the way?"

"No, I've got my bike back there."

"Well, I'll slog along on the sand."

"Good-by," said Auriol, lifting her hand as she turned back to look at him.

"Good-by!" said Brian. He watched her climb up the shallow dune, walk toward the trees, and pull the handlebars of her bicycle free from the trunk of the tree. Then she waved once more to him and disappeared. Brian turned back and walked slowly down past the dead silver trees to the wet sand near the water's edge and stood there for a while.

Olivia, he said. You know, don't you, you know the terrible thoughts that went through my head with that girl. You know everything; the full infamy of the male. I desired that girl. Not only because she was desirable but because she was part of you and in a queer way has part of your fire. I thought (but only for

the smallest instant, and I knew the thought to be evil and obscene): If I could have her I could live again. But don't worry,
Olivia, I would never do that to your child. It would be the
worst kind of incest.

You say nothing, do you, Olivia? But then, what is there to
say? But you have two things to be happy about, if you are
capable of happiness. Auriol's all right. She may have bad
times ahead, but she's all right. The second thing is that no one
knows of our love. Not even your children. We were good about
that.

Brian started slowly to walk back along the water's edge.
The light was softening now, the sea darker, and a slight warm
breeze had lifted.

Don't go away, said Brian, I feel you are going away. Is it
because of the girl?

No. But you must get used to being without me, Brian.

It isn't because you're hurt, is it Olivia? It isn't because you're
jealous?

What is the use of dying if feeling persists?

That's what I want to know, said Brian. Is there no feeling
at all in you as you look at us, living?

Yes. But it is not jealousy, or anger, or disappointment, or
grief.

What is it then?

It is something I never thought I could feel completely,
Brian.

And you can't tell me?

That is the only thing I can't tell you, Brian. I can only say
that everyone living feels it—at least once in his life.

Then it *is* feeling!

I don't know any other word, Brian. Even now.

Auriol, on her bicycle, was headed for home. I saw her only
for a brief instant, as she said to herself: I am sure that man was

her lover. But why didn't she keep his letters? They must have been wonderful. . . .

As I left her, she was saying: I am going to be a famous actress, with the world at my feet. . . .

For what must have been several weeks I did not see Auriol again. I could only infer that she was having a good time, full of boys and parties; for a young girl in gaiety is not apt to think of her mother. Auriol remembered me only in times of need or confusion; or when she was with someone closer to me than she was.

I was with Brian often during that southern week, but only on the beaches when he was alone; and then calmly, as though we had reached some peaceful equation along with the sun, the benevolent winds, the sea and the sand underfoot.

On the trip up to New York by train (Brian preferred it to air) he immersed himself in a briefcase-full of manuscripts; a fact of which I was made aware only when he exploded with irritation at a specific short story.

Damn it, Olivia, here's another one of those bright and sick young men obsessed with decay! He's got it all in: degenerate family; drunken father; incestuous mother; crippled son; insane sister, all described with infinite lugubrious or obscene detail. Sort of thing you read in the smart intellectual magazines, which seem to put a premium on pathology. The authors, of course, call it "life"—though it's no more life than Pollyanna or Elsie Dinsmore. But corruption and decay are fashionable now, and goodness unpopular. If you make everybody a heel and a jerk you're sophisticated. If you imply of any of your characters: "this is a good man," you are dishing out corn. I suppose it's the fault of popular mediums like radio and movies. In their scrupulous avoidance of the elementary facts and truths of life, they drive the imaginative into extremes of dissection. Because

they make a fetish of "normality"—the regular guy, the pretty
girl and so forth—these young rebels make a fetish of abnor-
mality. But perhaps it's no more abnormal than the insides of
the body, Brian continued. We know there are entrails in it
but we don't spread them out on a table, for the simple reason
that they're not pretty.

Doctors might think they are, I said.

All right then, spread them out for doctors. But writers like
this (and Brian tossed the manuscript down to the foot of his
berth) take delight in exposing their entrails to the public at
large, when only a trained psychiatrist should see them.

He picked up another manuscript. The title was *Children
of the Sun—An Anthology of American Indian Song.* Brian
groaned inaudibly and said, Now why in hell did Howe want
me to read this? He knows what I think of anthologies, and
anyway American Indians bore me as a race.

He turned a few pages listlessly, hardly reading them. Then
suddenly he sat up and began to read carefully one particular
poem.

Olivia! he cried.

Yes?

Olivia—look at this. Please look at this!

Over his shoulder I read what he saw on the page.

"The spirit of life is hidden, but the children of the sun can
be seen. Every man is a spirit, visible in the sunlight. Our lives
are not hidden. We close our eyes in darkness to rise in sunlight. My grandfather has gone away. He has hidden his face
like the sun in winter. But when the sun shines, I shall see the
face of my brother. When evening comes, I too shall be
hidden . . ."

Olivia, cried Brian, is that it? Is that near it?

His eyes were straining into the night as though he could
pierce the walls of his compartment, could pierce the intangible

layers between us by sheer effort of will and of listening.

That's near it, I said. Like the children's game, you're getting warm.

But how could they know? he cried. How could they possibly know?

The Blackfoot Indians? Maybe because nothing artificial came between them and their instinct, I said.

But aren't primitive instincts mainly concerned with food and shelter—with procreation and self-preservation?

Those are animal instincts.

You mean human beings have added instincts—like a spiritual instinct—toward truth?

What a question from you! I chided.

If that's true, Olivia, only those who know nothing or those who know everything have developed that instinct for truth. It's either the Blackfoot Indian or Shakespeare, then.

Not necessarily. The instinct can come to anyone who waits for it—alone and in silence.

Like Christ, said Brian.

Like Christ, I said. Like everyone who has faith in what he cannot see.

And which he assumes to be greater than himself.

Yes.

Brian, the manuscript on his lap, closed his eyes.

My love has gone away, he said. She has hidden her face like the sun in winter. But when the sun shines, I shall see the face of my love. . . . What sun, Olivia, what sun will show your face?

But I could not answer. Instead I was whirled away from Brian and the speeding night train to Philip, in Cambridge, who had called me there.

Philip was in a small beer joint, complete with juke-box and wooden table compartments, in one of which he and two

other boys were sitting. They seemed older than he; and the
first thing I heard was one of them saying to him, "Don't
be a sucker!"

"I can't see what's being a sucker about not wanting to get
blown up!" said Philip heatedly.

"Just how do you figure you can stop it?" asked the third boy.

"I didn't say I could," said Philip. "But somebody's got to
know what's going on in the rest of the world."

"Look, kid," said the first one patiently. "With one notable
exception, the rest of the world's kaput—phutt—finished. I
know because I've seen it."

"I know, I know," said Phil. "Those lousy frogs, those dirty
wops, those goddam limeys. I've heard all that before. The
only people you guys seem to end up liking are the Germans—"

"Well, at least they're white," said the boy. "And they use
plumbing."

"That's a fine basis for civilization," snorted Philip.

"It's about the only one, if you've been overseas," said the
second. The veterans looked at each other and laughed, comfortable in the fraternity of their experience. Philip felt young
and innocent, and hated it. He took a long swig of beer.

"What beats me," said the second veteran, "is why you
want to work for the government when you can get ten times
as much dough in private business."

"I happen to think there won't *be* any private business if
somebody doesn't try to dope things out."

"What makes you think the government's doping things
out?" said the first veteran. "Governments are no damn good—
look how they keep balling things up. Jesus, what a bunch of
dumb bastards!"

"A lot of them are," said Philip. "But Christ, you've got to
believe in something."

"I believe in twenty grand a year!" said the second boy, raising
his beer glass.

"I believe in sex!" said the other.

"Sex is here to stay!" said the first.

"Speaking of which," said the second veteran, scanning the opposite booths, "take a load of that broad over there." The two proceeded with agreeable speculations as to the size, weight, and shape of her obvious endowments. The talk excited Philip and he found himself wishing that he were alone with Micaela and then—followed by a spasm of self-reproach—that she were built like that. Philip still confused the external attributes of sex with passion, since they aroused it in him. He had yet to discover that a woman can look like a walking orgy and be cold; or that a woman can look pure and be passionate. I was quite sure, first, that he did not know Micaela intimately; and second, that she would be a revelation when he did.

In the interval between my withdrawal from the beer-joint and my reunion with Philip later in his room, I wondered why I had attended this scene with the two veterans, impersonal as it was. It dawned on me then that the conversation they had was almost an echo—an oversimplified and vulgarized echo, to be sure—of one that Whitney and I had had, overheard by Philip. Philip now was taking my part; the veterans, Whitney's.

The prototype argument happened soon after the end of the war. Whitney had been reading an article in the paper about black market manipulations with relief supplies in Europe and he threw down the paper with exasperation.

"What in God's name is the use," he fumed, "of helping these people when they haven't the faintest concept of decency or honesty!"

"What people?" I asked.

"Oh, all of them," he said. "The Italians, the French, the Balkans—they're all the same. A corrupt, lawless rabble. Give them an inch and they'll take everything."

"I wouldn't say we were particularly law-abiding," I said. "And we haven't got starvation as an excuse."

"Starvation, nuts," said Whitney. "I just talked to a fellow who'd been in Italy last week, and he said he had steak every day and all the sugar and butter he could handle."

"Did he say how much it cost?"

"Oh, sure, it's expensive. It's expensive here, too. The point is that plenty of people can afford it."

I knew the people he meant: the charmed fraction of every country in western Europe who have managed so far to survive war and revolution with their houses, their objects, and their corruption intact. But the cupidity of the rich is always more attractive than the desperation of the poor, if only because it achieves its ends without the ugliness of violence; and all I said to Whitney was, "Do you deny the existence of a decent element in every country except us?"

"No, of course I don't. But it's too small to count. We've got to stop being suckers and giving our shirt away where it isn't even appreciated."

"We seem to have plenty of shirts left."

"God, Livvy, you're impossible!" Whitney said this smiling. He was so secure in his thoughts that he took my heckling as the stubborn opposition of a child and treated it with good-humored indulgence.

There was nothing extraordinary about this conversation. It must have gone on in thousands of different homes in America, and it was going on now in beer-joints.

But it affected Philip profoundly, and troubled him. I had taught him to believe rather than disbelieve, to trust rather than distrust, to act in the affirmative rather than in the negative, since life itself was an affirmation. What were the great steps in history but affirmations? The Magna Charta, the Rights of Man, the Declaration of Independence? Were they not based on trust in the dignity and virtue of man?

But now, with betrayal and corruption spreading across the
world like a cankerous lichen, it was easier to say "Believe in
the baseness of man," for by the same token you proclaimed
yourself base and therefore not accountable to your conscience.
The marshaling of facts seemed always to be a marshaling of
evil. And the small single acts of virtue, so often unrecorded,
seemed in the aggregate to have no more strength than the
fragrance of grass in a factory town.

Thoughts like these were assailing Philip as he walked home
in the chilly dampness to his room. I wondered why the
words of two boys hardly older than himself should have concerned him so, and then—almost as if in answer to my question, he talked to me.

Mother, said Philip, those boys have been through something.
They've been through the war. They ought to know. They've
been there. I know: they're tough and they've never read
anything but comics and they wear lousy ties, but they've been
through something and they ought to know. They ought to
know more than all the rest of us who like books and pictures
and wine and Viennese waltzes. Maybe they're the only people
who *do* know. Maybe all the rest of us just don't exist. Maybe
we're all dreamers, like you. That's why I hang around with
them, to learn what life is really like, without illusion.

Philip walked on, his hands in the pockets of his flapping
trench-coat, his head bowed and his black forelock jogging over
his forehead with each step. How could I tell him that a man
could sleep with fifty women and still know nothing about
love? How could I tell him that a man could fight a war and
learn nothing of life or death? Or that a stupid man would
emerge from catastrophe still stupid? In a sense I was telling
him, for he suddenly thought of a phrase I used to din into him
as a boy: "You get exactly what you give, Phil—no more, no
less. That goes for love, work, everything. You can't get something for nothing."

Maybe that's one of the troubles, mused Phil. Those guys I was with tonight—they want something for nothing. They want twenty grand a year without working for it. They want an angle, a gimmick, a short cut, to everything. They want to lay a girl and then forget about her. They want to marry without losing freedom. But the damn thing is, they know what they want, even if they want it for free. While I flounder around waiting for some final truth to dawn.

In his room, Phil snapped on the light, tossed his coat on the bed, and sat down next to the round table by the window where his books and papers were spread. Among them was a well-known liberal magazine, thin, of rough white paper. He opened it to an article, "This Way Out," by Max Aronson.

Philip must have read it before, because he glanced through it, skipping paragraphs, a frown on his face. Before he slapped the magazine closed and shoved it across the table, I had time enough to see that the article was a blast against current government policy and mentioned the phrase "common man" at least five times. I could not help thinking, again, how easy was the formula for professional liberalism. All you had to do was to sit at a desk, disagree with the government, and talk about the man in the street. For facts you could substitute indignation, for information a self-righteous dogmatism just as inflexible as its reactionary equivalent. Max and his more temperate colleagues were very often right, as a critic is very often right, having the advantage of the spectator over the protagonist. Given positions of power, how long could they cleave to the purity of their convictions? Nine times out of ten this purity was derived from half-knowledge. The less you knew the easier it was to act. With increasing knowledge, black and white merged into gray and the sharp outlines projected by emotion blurred into amorphous shapes until time and perspective drew them again into a different focus.

But what stuck in Philip's craw in this moment was "the

common man." Who is the common man, for God's sake? he
demanded. If it's those boys I was with, they never read this
sheet and they care less. If it's me, I'm no more common than
they are. A man's only common so long as you put a uniform
on him and call him a soldier; or put him in overalls and call
him a worker. Out of uniform and out of overalls he is an
individual—uncommon as hell.

I was delighted at this private debate going on in Philip.
The sooner he could discard the clichés of Right and Left, the
better off he would be—so far, that was, as intellectual honesty
was concerned. To both extremes the middle way seems the
coward's choice. I wanted to tell Philip that in actuality the
middle of the road was perilous territory, only for the brave. In
an age of violence, deliberation is unpopular. To use it, Philip
would need all the courage and wisdom at his command.

The boy rose, yawned, stretched, and scratched his head with
both his hands. Then, abstractedly, he started to undress. His
neck, broad at the base but long and forward-sprung, still had
the loose and uncertain look of adolescence, accentuated by the
peak of black hair that grew between the two spinal tendons.
But his shoulders were widening, his long legs were becoming
muscular, and I could see the man forming beneath my eyes.

In a pair of rumpled and not very clean pajamas, Philip sat
on the edge of his bed, chin in hand, staring at nothing.

Mother, he said finally, you must know by now, wherever
you are. What the hell is it all about?

Hearing no answer, Philip got into bed, put out his light,
and gave himself over to thoughts of Micaela. I left him, dream-
ing, with his eyes open, of their perfect life together on some
remote and marvelous island, free of doubt.

That same night Whitney was tossing and turning in his
bed. Again I could not see him at first very clearly, but I felt

that the visual "static" between us was caused by another element: the thought and need of his mother, like me no longer living, like me given life by the memory of the living.

Mrs. Corning had died a few years before I met Whitney and what I knew of her came from his comments and descriptions. She was apparently a great lady in the Hudson Valley tradition. The great gloomy house overlooking the river north of Poughkeepsie had been sold, but Whitney had an album full of pictures of the place so that it was easy to visualize the background against which his childhood had taken place. The house was furnished almost entirely in the taste of the early nineteen-hundreds: an atrocious mixture, I thought, of heavy black oak furniture, oriental knickknacks, and dark damasks. Yet the place had a kind of settled grandeur, however ugly, that must have given its inhabitants as well as its visitors a feeling of unassailable security. Mrs. Corning expressed that security in human form. She was a tall handsome woman (I could see how much Whitney and Eleanor looked like her) but with the carriage of the Dowager Queen Mary and the kind of period figure in which the massive undivided bosom sloped gradually down to a constricted waist, forming a shelf for pearls and assuming an impersonality quite alien to the nature of breasts. In all her photographs, young or old, Mrs. Corning had the thin mouth and the level gaze of the impeccable matron; it was hard to imagine either kindled. Her nose was ruler-straight and delicate; her chin square and imperious.

There were a great many snapshots of Mrs. Corning on horseback: hunting, jumping, in horse shows, or just mounted in the courtyard of her stables. She was really at her best on a horse, for it was a position of command; and Mrs. Corning belonged to a vanishing race of people who are enhanced by the outward trappings of superiority if only because they handle them so well.

According to Whitney, his mother was acutely aware of her responsibilities, which, it seems, were conveniently confined to her family and her class.

Whitney must have been the apple of her eye, for his devotion to her was constantly in evidence. No matter what he talked about, Whitney would relate Mrs. Corning to the subject. "Mother always thought"—"Mother used to say"—"Mother felt"— Mother was the wisest, the finest, the dearest, the most infallible person on earth. Nothing, no one, could ever quite come up to her.

I had never come across this American phenomenon of man-and-mother love before, and only began to realize what it meant as the months of our marriage grew into years. What it meant was, actually, an incapacity for passion. Whitney had all the equipment, but none of the psychology, of virility. The pride and intensity which gives a man power over women had long since been drained by maternal demand and boyish dependence. Whitney could make love but he could never give himself to it. He could be aroused, easily: a love song, a few drinks, a romantic movie, would make him tender and sentimental, and afterward his need for love seemed real enough. But the act itself was more a means than an end, and I always felt that he was glad when it was over. He would go back to his bed and fall asleep immediately, like a child after a bottle, satisfied and at peace. There was, to be sure, no law against satisfaction; but the speed with which it was achieved left no time for those prologues and epilogues without which women are only partially possessed.

In a way I loved this in Whitney; it was part of the simplicity and almost innocence of his nature which had attracted me in the first place. Even if I had not loved this, I felt for the first time in my life that my own desires were of minimal importance. Having deceived myself, and deceived Whitney, into a wholly disparate union, the least I could do in atonement was to make Whitney as happy as I was able. He had given me trust, affection, and security. It was up to me to make myself as much as possible into his image of a wife.

To do this, the first step was to eradicate, brutally if necessary, the memory of Brian. This was not only difficult; it proved virtually impossible. The second was to be faithful to him; which I was. The third was to avoid, in writing or in action, anything that might bring embarrassment to him. This was not easy for anyone endowed with a persistent curiosity for the truth.

Finally, kind as he was to Auriol and Philip, Whitney, I felt, should have children of his own. He had told me that his first wife could not bear him any; and although he never spoke to me about it I could see the wistfulness in his eyes when he looked at my two. Not long after we were married, I said to him, "Darling—don't you think we ought to have a baby?" To say this gave me a deep excitement: there is nothing more wonderful, really, than to want a child; and the expression of this want, in man and woman equally, is a moment of transport. Whitney said nothing, but as he embraced me I could feel that his cheeks were wet; and that night was one of the happiest of our three years together. But while in European men the thought or fact of pregnancy in the woman they love is if anything a sexual stimulant, in Whitney—as I imagined it must be in many Americans like him—it inspired a tenderness which actually inhibited passion. I had become a mother, entitled to that respect and purity of approach which the maternal inspires.

Ironically, and sadly, no child appeared. After a year I went to a doctor, but was assured that there was nothing wrong about me to prevent conception. I never told Whitney this, afraid that he would draw the inevitable inference of his own sterility (he had never attributed his lack of issue in his first marriage to himself). Instead I hinted at some fault in myself: tension, fatigue, whatever it might be; telling him that something might ultimately happen when we least expected it.

Tonight in the restless dark Whitney was bitter about this failure to bear him children. With the illogicality of bitterness, he linked it with my work, believing that whatever creative energy I possessed had been channeled into written words. He thought with a spasm of jealousy of Max, who had twice impregnated me. But then she was young, he thought; young and clean.

Evil thoughts assailed him that night as he sighed and tossed. Images of intimacy arose before him and he thrust them down in disgust, for they were images of pleasure and he did not want them to be. She was a tart, he said. I loved a tart. A man should marry a virgin. Once a woman began sleeping around, you could never trust her entirely. It was all very well to talk about the advantage of experience; it was fine for a man but it made a woman shoddy, like used clothing.

No wonder she was good in bed, with all that practice. Savagely he thought of the letters again and thinking of them searched back in his memory for times when I might have been deceiving him. That night she said she couldn't go to the Club dinner—she said she wanted to work, and I believed her. That and a number of other times: days when I was in Washington, what was she doing? Whom was she with? How could I have been such a sucker, believing her? And the afternoons, Whitney went on, the afternoons: sometimes she would come in after six, after I got home from the office—where had she been? Sleeping with Eric, with Carlo, with who-in-hell? And then sleeping with me as if she wanted it.

My God, he groaned inaudibly, how can I think that way about the dead, how can I think that way about Olivia, after the happiness we had together. She was just a kid, Livvy; just a crazy kid who didn't know what she was doing. Then he laughed shortly: crazy kid of thirty-seven, thirty-eight! There I go, hooked again by those enormous eyes, by that laugh of hers, by the way we were in bed. There was always something stirring when she was here, an excitement in the house. Now it is dead, in spite of Auriol. Cold and dead.

He tried to conjure up Elizabeth, in her beauty, her purity, and her fastidiousness, but the face would not form, it was intercepted constantly by this tortured shifting image of myself in all the shapes he had known: gay, angry, pensive, tired, gentle, abstracted. And then the final image, drained and dying, the face on the pillow.

Whitney switched on the light, sick of his thoughts, sick of his own confusion. The room was so still that you could hear the stillness humming. He looked about the familiar room and then at the space on the other side of the night-table where the second bed had been. (A week after the funeral it had been moved into Auriol's room and made into a couch.) Now Whitney's bed stood alone; and where my dressing table had been stood a guncase full of old rifles and pistols, handsomely shown. Only the two reproductions of Ingres drawings and three small gouaches by a painter friend remained as traces of my habitation—those and my own presence, which Whitney now felt, sharply and with pain.

"Christ, how I hate living alone!" he said aloud. He pulled out the drawer of the night-table and took two luminal tablets out of a small bottle and washed them down with water. Then he turned out the light and settled himself to wait for the merciful oblivion which would come. Waiting, he forced his memory into happier channels: the days and months of the war, when he knew what he was doing, and what it was all about. Then darkness came: the darkness of sleep and the shadow of his mother bending over him and blotting me out.

The seventh month... Another night, another time. Through the palpitating density of my atmosphere the outlines of a house began to form: a white clapboard house set in a grove of tall elms and surrounded with lawns. There was a sign on the porch which said "Room and Breakfast." Moonlight touched the early leaves, the short new grass with earth still showing, the closed-budded lilac bush by the porch steps; and the cool thin air proclaimed the late New England spring.

Then, as in a movie dissolve (and I thought how often and how unwittingly the arts stumbled on truth) I penetrated through the gabled roof into an attic room. On an old-fashioned double bed lay my son, face downward. Next to him was Micaela, raised on one elbow looking down at him with compassion. Her long black hair, unbraided, fell down on her delicate shoulders and on the white cotton gown she was wearing.

"Please—please darling," begged the girl. "Don't. You mustn't, darling, you mustn't."

Between convulsive sobs, dry and difficult as they are when a man cries and doubly painful because of their difficulty, Philip said, "God, what you must think of me—what you must think of me—"

"I don't think of you, I love you. Don't you understand? What happened wasn't important at all. Please, Phil, believe me!"

Phil said nothing for a while. He tried to control his sobbing,

144

but his shoulders still jerked and shuddered. Micaela stroked them slowly, regularly. A little later he calmed down and turned his face sideways on the pillow, away from her. His hair was damp and disordered, his thin cheeks wet with tears.

"The first time with you—and this had to happen." He shook his head from side to side in abject misery. "I wanted it to be just right. I've dreamed of it for months and months, Mike. And now— Oh, God, Mike, I'm a failure, I'm no good, you must hate me, any woman would!"

"You're so silly, Phil. So very silly. Don't you know it doesn't make any difference?" She smoothed his hair back from his forehead and said, very gently, "Why, darling—we just don't know each other yet!"

Philip jerked his head away from her hand. "Stop trying to comfort me. It's no use. I've let you down terribly, and you know it. . . ."

"Philip—listen to me. Listen. You made me happy. You made me happier than I ever have been."

Slowly Philip shifted himself around to look at her. "I made you happy? Christ, Mike, any truck driver could have made you happier. At least, he could have made the grade—" He turned away again, facing the wall.

"Philip—I think I know what was the matter," said the girl. "I think we love each other too much. I think we were frightened—"

Philip said nothing. The moon touched the foot of the bed and one of Micaela's small bare feet.

"I read that somewhere once, darling. I read that when people want something too much they—they can't—" her voice trailed off.

Philip spoke in a muffled voice, "There was nothing the matter with you—"

"There is nothing the matter with you, darling."

"Do you believe that? Or are you just being kind?"

"I know it."

"How do you know it? After what happened?"

"I know it," said the girl, "because you're wonderful."

Philip snorted. "Wonderful—the great lover!"

Angrily Micaela said, "If you say that again I shall leave you, Phil!"

"I'm surprised you haven't left me already—"

"And let you go?" The girl slid off the bed, walked around and knelt on the side which Philip was facing. She was smiling now and there was a mischievous teasing look in her shining brown eyes. "Before breakfast?"

Philip looked at her and suddenly his face lighted and the corners of his mouth began to lift. With one sudden movement he leaned forward, put his arms around her under her shoulders and dragged her off the floor and onto the bed next to him.

"Come close to me," he said. "As close as you can." She put her arms around his neck and he gathered her so tightly to him that she gasped for breath. "Closer," he said. "Mike—are you very hungry?" he whispered into her mouth.

"Yes," she said, and put her lips on his.

I left them there to their re-discovery. I had come because the scene was so much like the night when Brian and I had been together for the first time. I had come to tell this to Philip, to tell him what this meant, to give him comfort and hope. Micaela had done it for me, out of the promptings of love; which, as the poets have often said, is stronger than death.

While I had known him, Whitney had never been active in any political group, in spite of his solid conservatism. As a figure of some financial importance in the city, he was chairman or member of several civic and philanthropic committees, and there was small question that his sympathies lay with unrestricted private enterprise and all it implied. He had the average American's pathological hatred of communism; and I was constantly worried lest my own distrust and dislike of Communist doctrine make me share this pathology. Whitney also was deeply antagonistic to any form of government planning. Socialism to Whitney meant "taking away." He never bothered to examine what it gave, or to how many.

Yet he himself was a conspicuously generous man, giving freely to the most vital causes in the country, from cancer research to education, from community chests to planned parenthood. Whitney had a strong sense of civic responsibility; to call him or his kind "enemies of progress and of the common man" was sheer nonsense. In the three years I lived with Whitney I had seen him perform more acts of spontaneous kindness to individuals—black, white, native, foreign—(not merely in the way of financial aid but by efforts of friendship) than Max, with all his love for humanity, made time for in a decade. What made Whitney reactionary, then, was not lack of heart or lack of conscience but the enormous fear to which the wealthy are prey: fear of change, since change to them is synonymous with loss; and fear of "They," who would initiate this change. Here was the root of that hate which, pursued to its end, could turn Whitney and men like him into destructive or at best, obstructive, forces. So far, from all I could see, Whitney's record was far more constructive than his words.

I was surprised then, this particular evening, to find him in his car on the way to a dinner-meeting which I subsequently found to be sponsored by the leading nationalist group in the country.

Elizabeth and Auriol were in the car with him. A young man with close fair hair and features which magazine serials describe as "clean-cut" occupied the folding seat next to Auriol. I imagined he was Curtis James, Elizabeth's nephew, whom I had seen once or twice at the subscription dances Auriol went to.

Whitney seemed nervous and preoccupied, glancing at his watch and showing irritation at traffic lights.

"Don't fret, Whitney," said Elizabeth. "We have hours yet."

"We have exactly ten minutes," said Whitney. "I have to be at that damned table by seven-fifteen."

Auriol was thinking: Mother always hated these big dinners—I don't think she would have liked this one tonight. She had fixed her hair in a thick low chignon held by a tortoise-shell brooch and looked older than her seventeen years. The boy could not keep his eyes off her profile, off the incredible curve of her chin and her long round neck. Elizabeth herself stole glances at the girl, jealously searching for traces of me, for qualities that were superior to her own. After deciding that Auriol's was a cheap kind of beauty ("obvious," she told herself) she turned her attention to Whitney and I did not see any of them until the dinner was well under way and Whitney in the middle of his speech.

Superficially, the crowded ballroom where the dinner was held looked like any one of the hundred occasions that had preceded it. From bitter experience in the days when I believed such dinners (if the cause seemed good) should be attended, I knew all the details by heart. There again were the green trailing plant decorations of the boxes; the American flag hung behind the speakers' table; the hundred round tables ringed by people in evening dress; the harassed and flustered waiters squeezing their tray-loaded way between the tables; the twenty men or women at the table of honor, self-conscious and public-conscious; the microphone and all the glasses of water.

Elizabeth was presiding over a table of ten right below the speakers' table. The only others I recognized besides Auriol and the James boy were Eleanor and her husband and Alan Reddiker, still tanned from his southern sojourn. They had turned their chairs to face the dais, and the table was cleared except for coffee cups and ash trays and a standing dish of small cakes.

"There are certain groups in this country," Whitney was saying, "who are bored with the Constitution, just as some of our so-called intellectuals are bored with the basic American virtues." (Ha! I thought, this is where I come in.) "They find it smart to jeer at patriotism and at loyalty—although it is very doubtful if they know, in spite of their superior education, exactly what loyalty means."

Applause greeted this remark, and Eleanor nodded at Elizabeth with common pride and agreement.

"These same people, some of whom unfortunately occupy positions of public trust or prominence, are far more interested in saving other nations from the wages of their stupidities than in saving their own country from its enemies!"

I wondered who wrote this. It was certainly not Whitney's way of speaking, although it was Whitney's way of thinking. I looked more closely at the crowd of faces in the ballroom all fixed—as they would be later in the flash-bulb photograph of the banquet—toward the speaker. They were mostly middle-aged. The men in their dinner coats had bland faces with hard mouths, skin slightly pink from sunlamp or massage, white hair or little hair; and many of them had stomachs which spread below their vests and rested on their knees. Their hands seemed capable of only two functions: signing checks or holding golf-clubs. Certainly the appearance of their wives seemed to belie other functions: they looked as if they had not been touched for the last twenty years. Because of this obvious lack, they lavished attention on their hair and face and dress, not to attract their husbands (that was too late) but to stand up to each other. I kept having to remind myself that they had once lain with men and in childbirth; that they had lost sons in battle; or that they might even be dying, now, slowly from disease. Some were certainly kind and charitable. All had standards of cleanliness and deportment which made them more attractive in mass than a gathering of less successful human beings.

But in their faces I could find no sign of that one emotion without which no face can be beautiful: grief. I do not mean the tortured mask of tragedy, but I do mean that acquaintance with sorrow which makes the old wise and valuable, and which is the source of compassion. Whatever suffering they may have had—these people here tonight—remained a local pain, like a broken leg or a headache; it was not transmuted into the texture of the soul, then to be translated into the lines of the face and the radiance of the eye. They had no serenity, for true serenity comes after knowledge of pain. They had only the stillness of spiritual inertia. They were half alive.

"I think it is time we stopped deceiving ourselves," said Whitney, "that the world is one big happy family sitting around a Christmas tree—paid for by us. Like every family, the world is full of brats and delinquent cousins and dishonest relatives who must be taught or put away in safekeeping or punished. One world may be a nice idea for poets—who, I might add, have always left the realities of life to people like us—but it is hardly a practical basis for doing business. And whether the poets and the radicals and the longhairs like it or not, this country means—business!"

In the surge of applause that greeted this, I thought: this is Whitney's revenge. He is speaking to me, against me, against everything I have believed, against everything I have tried to convey to others. This is Whitney's revenge, and that is why I am forced to be present.

Auriol knew this too. She was inwardly disturbed and uncomfortable; torn between pride in her stepfather's success tonight and a nagging fear that there was something ugly in his words and ugly in the measure of the applause.

Young Curtis James leaned toward her and said, "Good going! I didn't know your father did this stuff. . . ."

Auriol only smiled back at him, not knowing what to say.

"It's time," Whitney went on, "that we distinguished between true American democracy and the kind of spineless tolerance that passes for democracy now. When you discover a cancer in a living body, you cut it out. If you don't, it spreads to every cell and kills the organism. I don't have to tell you what that cancer is in the organism of America. It has been spreading unchecked for many years, growing within but fed from without. Some of our bright citizens have said, 'Nonsense. Pure imagination. There is nothing wrong that a little fresh air and sunshine won't cure.' Other bright citizens—the quack doctors for the ills of the world—have said, 'Sure it's there, but leave it alone and it'll work itself out.' I ask you, ladies and gentlemen, have you ever heard of a cancer that has worked itself out?"

Whitney paused; he held his audience in absolute silence. "There are only two things that can stop a cancer, ladies and gentlemen. One is the knife. Cut it out. Cut out the malignant cells so that the healthy ones can regain their sovereignty. Cut it out with the one weapon we have: law. There is only one other way, I am afraid. A way that none of us want to use. A way that others must not use. A way that we may have to use. That way is atomic energy." Whitney paused again, conscious of the gravity of his words and the atmosphere they invoked. "So far law has not been signally successful: it seems to have degenerated into a squabble between a number of foreign gentlemen who have settled—rather conspicuously—in our midst. . . ." There was scattered laughter, and Elizabeth this time smiled at Eleanor.

"That is why I say—and I say it with complete knowledge of all its implications—that if law cannot cut out this cancer in the tissue of America—if law cannot control the powerful and sinister agency of this cancer—the atom must."

As Whitney sat down in the prolonged burst of applause, I looked again at the people who were clapping. But I saw no terror. What I saw instead was the look—at once self-righteous, stern, and exalted—that a Puritan crowd must have worn at the execution of a witch.

"Auriol dear," said Elizabeth, bending across the table. "You might at least give your father a hand!" Auriol started as if suddenly awakened, raised her hands from her lap and gave a few slow claps. But in the depths of her green eyes I saw the fear for which I had been looking.

What must have been a few days later Auriol was in her room reading a letter from Philip.

"From what I read in the papers," it said, "that meeting you went to must have been something. Mother must be turning over in her grave. God knows my stomach turned over at some of the things Whitney said. What gets me is how a guy can be so nice and decent in the home and calmly advocate mass extermination in public. My God, all he was doing was screaming for another war.

"I'm getting so that I don't blame Father—or maybe I should say, my father—for the way he feels. It's people like Whitney who make roaring Commies out of other people. I used to think maybe it was vice versa, but now I'm not so sure. But if only Whitney and his ilk had the sense to meet Max and his ilk half-way, they'd take the wind out of their sails. That's why I keep yapping about some form of modified socialism; it's the only thing that communism can't react strongly against or even offer better breaks. But setting up a purely capitalistic society with a free-profit system is just asking for communism.

"I don't know why in hell I should be writing all this to you, because, (a) you're too young to understand it, and, (b) you seem to thrive in the society of economic royalists.

"But an older brother is supposed to assume the functions of a mentor, so I feel it incumbent upon me to preserve you from the abysmal ignorance in which you are inclined to wallow.

"Yours fraternally, and somewhat contemptuously,

"Phil"

"Smart aleck," snorted Auriol. Then she saw a P.S. scrawled vertically along the side of the letter. "I'm coming down next Saturday to hear what Poppa has to say at Madison Square. There's some sort of Peace Rally going on. I'd take you if you weren't too delicate for a proletarian gathering."

Philip went alone that Saturday night, as I found out later. My first introduction to this meeting was a phenomenon I had experienced before.

The molecular void had become agitated in the way I now recognized as evil. The points about me wheeled and jerked and darted among one another like waterbugs; and I myself was part of the erratic vibration. The reason for this dislocation of matter was soon evident, for I found myself in Madison Square Garden along with twenty thousand people on a hot spring night. I knew it was hot because of the sweaty faces of the people, because of the men in open rumpled shirts and the women in their sleeveless cotton dresses and bare legs.

The group of men on the platform, one standing and speaking, and the American flags generously stacked and hung, made it clear that this was a political rally. Max was one of six men on the platform.

I came and stood beside Philip just as the speaker was sitting down and Max rose and stepped forward. Philip was gazing intently at his father while the chairman of the meeting —a well-known radio commentator who had been fired from his station the previous year—was introducing him.

"It gives me great pleasure to introduce to you one of our most fearless fighters for democracy, one of our most eloquent and uncompromising American liberals, Max Aronson—"

There was considerable applause. Philip looked about him to see who was clapping, but most of the response seemed to come from the ringside seats. He noticed the same common denominator, humanly speaking, that I had: ugliness.

Tonight's crowd was particularly ugly, not only in the physical sense but in the quality—and this assailed me violently—of its emanation. They were there for the kill. They were there to knock down something because they themselves felt knocked down. Twenty thousand chips sat on twenty thousand shoulders: a legion of standard-bearers of inferiority. They were there because they wanted someone to pay for their ugliness, their lack of grace, their lack of stature.

This was not a poor crowd, in the economic sense. The men were no proof of this, since even a twenty-thousand-dollar-a-year American can look like a bag of soiled laundry in hot weather. But most of the women, however gross, however vulgar in the deepest sense of the word, wore good clothes and showed the attentions of hairdressers and manicurists. Their sense of inferiority came, then, not from having no money but from having no attraction. The patent fact that they attracted one another was not enough. They felt themselves shut out of a golden world to which they secretly aspired but which they openly condemned. The philosophy of proletarianism made commonness not only obligatory but desirable. The onus of excellence was removed, and with it inferiority.

Max was stoking the fires of their chronic discontent. "Must we stand by, then, while the very principles for which we fought and died are being sold for thirty pieces of silver?" he was crying. There was a roar from the crowd and loud clapping. "Must we stand by while the bankers mortgage the life of the common man and while politicians and office-seekers gamble with the American dream?"

With a few small changes this might have been used at almost any rally.

"Must we stand by," repeated Max, "while we exchange one imperialism for another, while we substitute chains of platinum for chains of gold on the legs of the captive peoples of the world?"

This went over big, and the row in which Philip sat contributed its share of clapping and whistling.

I was again struck at how old-fashioned all this sounded, and how far below Max's real intelligence. Surely Max could not be unaware of what had happened to the British Empire; or of what was happening in Russia? Think up another word, boys. How about Superialism, or Cashination, or Fiscality? How about a little basic reading?

But Max was as happily angry as his audience. "Some of us have been laboring under the misapprehension," he continued with that pause of gentle reasonableness which all good orators alternate with their climaxes, "that this was a government for the people, by the people, and of the people. Perhaps it would be wise to examine for a moment just who the people are. Are they the people who, by some extraordinary chance, now dictate our policies in Washington and Wall Street—or are they—" and Max's voice rose again, mounting toward a crescendo—"or are they—by an equally extraordinary chance—us?" As his arm swept around the vast hall the crowd burst into roars of approval.

Philip looked increasingly uncomfortable. He was less disturbed, I knew, by the actual words Max had spoken than by the reactions of the audience. We had seen newsreels of Nazi meetings together often and talked about them afterwards with fear and horror. The sound of the Nazi crowd was not much different. It was channeled, to be sure, into "Sieg Heils" and "Heil Hitlers," and they used their own flags for decorations, but the blood lust was the same, the hysteria was the same, the prejudices were the same. While Max talked of substituting one imperialism for another, the crowd in reality was thinking of substituting one governing power for another: themselves for those now seated.

There were other speakers. A well-known union leader got up

to denounce contemporary labor-legislation. A Negro spoke of the injustices committed against Negro troops in the war and Negro veterans now, with ample substantiation and in a gentle voice. The radio commentator spoke of the forces in America who were sabotaging any hope of peace by sabotaging world government. A woman magazine editor who had just come back from Russia spoke of the wonderful life artists led there and how much happier the people were than our own, since they lived for an ideal. A foreign correspondent, known for the heat of his dispatches, raged against the British in Palestine, the Chinese government, the Greek industrialists, and several other groups whom he considered purely vicious. A man who was expelled from the State Department denounced the State Department as a fascist organization solely concerned with keeping the oppressors of humanity in power. A dance troupe did some Spanish dances, and a Negro quartet sang a song about freedom.

Philip left at midnight while it was still going on. He was in a turmoil of confusion. Much that had been said struck him as right and just; much as distorted and pandering to the basest instincts of revenge and inferiority. Again, it was not so much what was said as how the audience reacted to it. Control and moderation (and some of the speakers had both) were greeted with coldness and indifference. Excess and violence—the instruments of ignorance—fired their blood.

Is that the brave new proletarian world, Mother? asked Philip. Are these ugly, graceless, harsh, intemperate people really my brothers? Must I choose between them and the stuffed, myopic ladies and gentlemen of Whitney's persuasion? Must I choose between the over-civilized Right and the under-civilized Left? Must I choose, when both of them fill me with disgust at the human race? Thus Philip, as he walked home in the stifling night, where the sides of buildings and the streets beneath threw back into his face the stale old heat of the day.

Auriol was in bed reading when Philip passed her room to go to his own and saw her door ajar. Even he, like most brothers unimpressed by their sister's charms, was startled by her beauty as she lay propped up against two pillows, her long dark red hair cascading over them, her face innocent of make-up.

"Hello," she said as he stuck his head through the door. "Have fun?"

Philip walked in and shrugged. "Poppa's missed his vocation," he said.

"How come?"

"He should have been an actor. Boy, how he can pull out those stops!"

Auriol sat up, interested, her book on her lap. "I wish I'd seen him—"

Philip shook his head. "You wouldn't have liked it. It wasn't up your alley."

"I gather it was up yours, though."

"Not all of it," said Philip. "Not by a long shot."

"Funny," mused Auriol, "how Whitney and Max are both sort of . . . in the ring . . ."

"In opposite corners. Your two fathers, Red, are mortal enemies!"

Auriol was staring into space, beyond Philip, beyond the wall of her room. "Mother certainly made a jump between the two."

"Until tonight," said Philip, "I wondered what in hell had driven her to Whitney. Now I know. Although," he went on, more to himself than to Auriol, "I bet that didn't satisfy her either."

"She had everything, didn't she?" said Auriol with a hint of her old defiance.

"People like that never have everything. . . ." The boy and girl were silent for a while. *If ever I were with my children, it was now, in this room.* Philip, aware of this, broke the moment

by saying, "Well—guess I'll turn in—" and left Auriol's room
for his own.

Auriol herself lay thinking of his remark: "People like that
never have everything," and began to relate it to herself. But
before long another thought occupied her mind: Philip's comment that his father should have been an actor. Maybe that is
why I want to act, she said. Maybe there's genius in my veins.

She leaped out of bed and sat in front of her dressing-table
mirror. I left her as she was expressing Agony, her mouth drawn
down, her brows drawn up, her hands clutching the sides of her
head. It seemed to me she had talent.

From his office Brian lifted the receiver of his telephone and
dialed my number, or, rather, the number of Whitney's apartment.

"Could I speak to Miss Corning, please? . . . Mr. Littleton.
. . . No, Littleton . . ."

After a considerable pause, Auriol's voice said "Hello?" In
the advantageous position of seeing both ends of the line at
once, it was clear to me that Auriol had been awakened from a
deep sleep. Her hair was over her eyes and she had bare feet
and no wrapper.

"Is this Auriol Corning?" asked Brian.

"Yes—hello—I mean—"

"I hope I didn't wake you—"

"Oh, no," said Auriol stifling a yawn, "not at all. I was just
eating breakfast—"

"Well, I called because I need your help."

"My help?"

"Yes. I wondered if you could come by my office some-
time soon. You see, I'm planning to publish a complete edition
of your mother's work, with a sort of biographical foreword—
and I may need some help on the details—"

"Oh," said Auriol. "Yes, of course—"

"I also wondered whether you or your brother had any additional manuscripts that might be included—you know, unpublished work that she may not have shown me."

"Why, yes," said Auriol. She was still struggling up through the muffled layers of her childlike sleep, and by now Brian was aware of it.

"Look, I don't want to bother you now, but just give me an idea when you'd like to come in, and I'll explain it more fully then."

"Why, any time," said Auriol. "I could—I could today—"

"Fine. How about three?"

"Yes, that would be fine—"

"Good," said Brian. "I'll try not to keep you too long—" and hung up.

Auriol padded back to her bed and in five minutes was asleep again. As her bedside clock said eleven I imagined she must have been out till dawn the night before and could not help wondering with whom. One of the irritating things about my present state was that I missed great gaps in the lives of the people close to me. I was present only at those moments when they brought me back by force of thought or feeling. And as the impact of my death wore slowly away, as it must, the intervals between those moments of presence seemed to be getting longer and longer. In a way I welcomed this as a sign of ultimate release from the purgatory of dependence on the living. In another way human curiosity—so intense in my life— seemed to have extended itself even into death. Especially with my children, it seemed strange that I should not know every moment of their growth as I knew it when they were little. But then, did I? Can any mother know the secret hours of her young? There were times when I would look into Philip's eyes and speak to him and know that he was not there at all. There were times when Auriol, playing in the same room with me, would be enclosed in that private impenetrable world which children inhabit for their own protection. I wondered now whether this world of theirs was not indeed an extension of their state before birth; just as my death was an extension of my life, and I still shadowed by it. For if life were not the only condition of the human being, and I now knew that it was not, there must be a condition preceding life, preceding the embryo, preceding the foetus, preceding the sperm. And it was this condition, this knowledge, that still persisted in the eyes of children, giving them a kind of inviolability.

"I brought all we had," said Auriol, "but I'm afraid it isn't very much." They were in Brian's office, and she had laid a large envelope on his desk. He opened it and pulled out the contents, pipe in mouth.

"Philip got a lot of unfinished stuff—sort of different versions of the same poem," she went on. "He said please not to lose them."

"Don't worry, I'll be very careful." Brian was studying various pages with interest.

"And there's a radio play. It never got broadcast."

"I remember your mother speaking about it," said Brian, "but I never read it."

"Philip thinks it's very hot," said Auriol.

"Some of this might be very interesting to publish—as indications of her work methods. If you'll leave it all with me I'll go over it and weed out the best. In any case, I promise you'll get all the originals back."

"Thanks."

Auriol studied his face as he bent over the typewritten sheets, following with her eyes as I used to with my fingers the line down the broad high forehead, the slightly crooked nose, the long upper lip and the strong square chin, slightly cleft.

He raised his head, looked at her directly, and said, "What I need you for is to fill in some gaps in the story of her life.

You see, I was in England all during the war; and anyway, a publisher's contact with an author is rather intermittent . . ." Why did I have to add that, Olivia? Why do I have to pile it on when the girl already has an instinctive knowledge that I'm lying?

Auriol said nothing, so Brian proceeded. "Did your mother leave any papers that might give point to the autobiographical section—copies of interchanges about her work, letters—"

The girl felt herself blushing as she answered slowly, "There were—there were some letters—"

"Can you remember offhand the contents of any of them?"

"They were—they were personal. From different people." The tone of Auriol's voice made Brian look up from the manuscripts on his desk.

"Love letters?" said Brian.

"Yes," said Auriol, and lowered her eyes.

After a pause, Brian said, "Are they yours? I mean, did she leave them to you?"

"No—I—I think they got mixed in by mistake."

"Where are they now? Have you got them?"

"No," said Auriol. "I think—I think my stepfather tore them up."

"Auriol," said Brian, "do you mind if I call you Auriol?"

"No—of course not."

"Did these letters upset you a lot?"

Still looking down, Auriol said, "Sort of."

"Did it change the concept you had of your mother?"

"I don't know," said Auriol, "I guess I just didn't think—"

"You didn't think that she had men in her life—outside of your father and stepfather?"

"It's awfully hard to explain."

"I think I know. I was almost twenty before I realized my father was a man, and my mother a woman. All of one's childhood they are just—parents."

"I should have known," said Auriol. "I mean, if you read her poetry—"

"It doesn't always follow. Great poetry of love has been written by virgins—or, at least, by deeply frustrated women."

Auriol was silent again, looking at her lap.

"Forgive me for going into this," said Brian. "It isn't just idle curiosity. I don't want you to get mixed up by it."

"Mixed up?"

"Yes. I don't know what these letters were like, but I do know what your mother was like; and I don't want you to get a distorted image of her."

"I don't know what you mean," said Auriol.

"I mean this," said Brian. "Do you feel that because your mother was a much loved woman—because she knew a number of men—that her memory is cheapened?"

"I—I did a little. At first." Her voice was barely audible.

"And now?"

"It's changed, somehow."

"What changed it?"

Auriol raised her head and looked straight into Brian's eyes. "You," she said.

Olivia, cried Brian, let her know, let her know!

"You loved her too, didn't you?" said Auriol. And then she began to cry like a child, her chin and mouth compressed and trembling, her eyes swimming in tears, and her hands clenched in her lap. Brian left his chair and went over to her and knelt beside her, taking both her fists in his hands. "Auriol, please. Please!"

"I'm sorry," she gulped between sobs, "I didn't mean—to do this. I'm sorry."

"Forgive me," said Brian. "I didn't mean to tear you up like this."

"It isn't that," gasped the girl. "You didn't do it. It's just me. I don't know what to do. I don't know what to do about love!" She almost wailed this, and if Brian had not been so moved by her he would have smiled, it was so desperately young.

Brian released her hands and thrust his own handkerchief into them. Auriol wiped the tears away, but fresh ones came as she sat there, shaking and talking. "I—I just get passes all the time and I get all excited and I don't ever know whether it's love or not, and they always want me and I don't always want to and I don't know what to do!"

"Auriol—please. Dear child, please!" said Brian, with the helplessness of men in the presence of tears.

"Mother always knew!" the girl burst out, "Mother always knew—that's why I hate her sometimes, she never was mixed up like this, she always knew what to do!"

"Listen to me a minute, Auriol. Listen to me!"

"She did, she did, she did!" cried Auriol.

"Auriol," said Brian, almost sharply, so that the girl stopped sobbing in spite of herself. "Auriol, will you please listen to me!" She raised her tear-streaked face to his, now snuffling a little, shuddering a little.

"Listen to me, Auriol. Your mother didn't know until she was thirty-seven years old! I didn't know until I was forty. And you sit there crying because at seventeen you don't know what love is!"

Olivia, I want to take her in my arms, but I don't dare.

Auriol sniffled a little but said nothing.

"Blow your nose!" said Brian. The girl complied and then said ruefully, "I'm sorry about your handkerchief."

"I can survive that."

"You must—you must think I'm a terrible fool. I didn't mean —I didn't want—"

"We never do," said Brian. "These things just happen. Especially when something's been stored up for a long time inside." Brian rose and went back to his desk while Auriol took her

compact out of her bag and surveyed her face in the mirror.
"Oh, dear," she said, "I look simply horrible!"

"I don't think the damage is permanent."

Auriol powdered her face and put on lipstick. "How about
the dramatic career?" said Brian. "Any prospects?"

"I want to do it," said Auriol. "I can't stand sitting around
doing nothing."

"And waiting for love?"

Auriol smiled. "You shouldn't tease. It's not fair."

"I wasn't teasing. I highly recommend work as one way out
of confusion. Your mother was proof of that. The reason she
had so much to give to men was because she could draw on a
world apart from them. The trouble with most women is that
they have only one world—and unless that's a very good one,
it can suffocate. Knowing your mother satisfied all the polygamous instincts in man: she was at least five different women—"

"Maybe," said Auriol, "that's why I want to act—"

"To satisfy the polygamous instincts of man?"

The girl laughed.

"Seriously, Auriol, if you'll lunch with me one day next week
we'll explore the whole field of training in the theater. I haven't
time now, but I think you ought to get started and enroll in
some school for next fall."

"Couldn't I try to get a job in some play?"

"Just like that?"

"Lots of girls do."

"Lots of girls are showgirls or get screen tests and go to Hollywood and get five thousand dollars a week for having the right
measurements. Is that what you're after?"

"I wouldn't mind being a movie star."

"Would you mind being a bad actress?"

"Well—"

"Answer me, Yes or No!" insisted Brian.

"Yes—I would mind."

"Well, then you'd better go at it the hard way. Nobody is worth a good goddamn who doesn't." He rose, and so did Auriol, and they stood facing each other.

"Will you call me on Monday? It will have to be next week because I'm flying to England on the fifteenth and won't be back until August."

"I'll call you," said Auriol. She held out her hand and raised her face to his. "I'm awfully ashamed of myself, Mr. Littleton. You asked me here to help and all I've done is bawl on your shoulder."

"You have helped," said Brian taking her hand, "and my shoulder is waterproof." He led her to the door of his office and relinquished her hand. Auriol turned to face him, leaning against the door.

"Do you want to know why I cried like that—really?" Brian said nothing, suddenly overcome by her beauty, not trusting himself to speak.

"I cried because I'm in love with you. And because I know," said Auriol, giving herself entirely to him with the light that shone from her eyes, "that it's hopeless!"

Brian's arms began to lift slowly, but I pulled them back. In one instant Auriol was out of the room and the door shut after her. Brian's hand went to the knob of the door but I held it back. His eyes were closed, the color drained from his face.

It is only because she is yours, Olivia, that I wanted to take her in my arms.

Only, Brian? Only?

He took a deep breath, walked back to his desk, and sat down. He set his elbows on the manuscripts, and put his face down in his hands.

Brian, you know that it's no good, don't you? You know it?

Olivia, he groaned, why must you know everything!

You know that it is hopeless?

Olivia, don't go, don't go!

You wanted to hold her, Brian.

I wanted to hold her because she is your child.

And because you are growing old?

His fingers tightened on his face, and I could feel the contraction of his heart.

You're cruel, Olivia. . . . You're accusing me of what I haven't done.

But of what you have thought.

The thought does not exist any more, and will not.

But it exists in Auriol, Brian.

Auriol is a bewildered child.

She is my child.

What shall I do? Never see her again—even to help her?

You must see her—and help her.

But it will make her suffer.

You too, Brian.

No—I'm all right—so long as you are with me.

That's up to you.

Miss Evans, Brian's secretary, stuck her head into the office and said, "Mr. Waldron is waiting outside . . ." Brian jerked his head up. "Yes—yes, of course. Tell him to come in." As she withdrew Miss Evans said, "Miss Corning looks quite a lot like Rita Hayworth, don't you think?"

Brian nodded abstractedly. I left him as his visitor came in.

I did not know then whether Brian saw Auriol before he left or not. If he did, I was not there. That could mean either complete impersonality in the meeting or the presence of an outsider; or it could mean a new direct relationship between them both which would have precluded my presence. But I did not think that was the case. For I trusted them both.

The big plane was over the Atlantic at night when I next rejoined Brian for any length of time.

The interior of the cabin was dark, the chairs were tilted back and nearly all the passengers, tucked in blankets, seemed to be asleep, their heads askew on their pillows. One reading light was on, casting a thin small beam on the page of some insomniac's book; and the stewardess was walking up the aisle and into the pilot's cabin, closing the door behind her.

Brian was awake although his eyes were closed. He was seeing, as he always did, the black lonely reaches of water underneath; aware, as he always was, of the steady drone that kept the plane from this water, that pulled it through the long black hours of the night toward ultimate land. He was never without a sense of wonder that this should be: the battle against gravity seemed so fallible. Once he thought he heard a slight change in the pitch of one of the propellers and he opened his eyes to look out at the engines, pressing his face close to the window. A small red glow, baleful against the blackness, issued from under the cowling, giving just enough light to show that the wing was wet. Beyond that, nothing but space. Below that, nothing but water. That both were peopled he knew; but the illusion of illimitable loneliness in that outer darkness remained. He closed his eyes again and shifted his position, putting his pillow in the angle between the window and seat-arm and trying to stretch his long legs under the chair in front of him. If only I could sleep, he said. Those damn capsules aren't working. . . . If only every eastward flight I take didn't conjure up these flights away from you, Olivia. . . .

Two flights away from me, Brian. And the second was to be the last.

The second was the last.

The first time Brian went to England away from me was in 1937, two months after we had first met. He was to be away for over four months, and our parting was painful and sweet and full of reassurances; although I still wondered how much Mary would hold of him, and although Brian wondered what our new and sudden love would do to his relationship with her.

His letters during that first separation seemed to belie our fears. "Mary and I," he wrote in one of them, "have slipped back with surprising ease in the old ways of comradeship. She appears to demand nothing from me except a sort of fraternal solidity, is as independent as ever, and very flippant about my life in America, which she insists on describing to others as very colorful. Never anything specific and always with high good nature, but apparently friends have been telling her what a hell of a gay dog I am in New York—the perennial extra-man. I am glad it's as general as that. In one way I keep wanting to shout to everybody 'I am in love with O.B.!' But on the other hand, invulnerable as she seems, I can't bear to have Mary hurt. She is like a child under all that brilliance, and I can't help feeling that she needs me in a strange sort of way, even though she accepts our separations with complete equanimity. But I can't say that I am in a very happy state. There is something basically and profoundly wrong about living under the same roof with one woman while you give your entire soul to another. I hate myself for being so good an actor . . . and I find myself wishing, too often, that Mary were not such a superior human being. . . ."

My work and the children kept me busy during that first separation; and I found for the first time that there was only one alternative to the presence of Brian and that was solitude. I preferred to be alone so that I could be with him, three thousand miles away. This might have been self-protection—fear of myself in the presence of other men—but I don't think so. Faithfulness is not necessarily non-deception; it is a positive affirmation of choice. I wanted to deny myself minor pleasures in order to be ready, without blemish, for the major joy.

The winter after Brian's return was reward enough for this denial. I had never before known the deep satisfaction of working impersonally with the individual one loved. I was busy all that time on a long poem that tackled the nature of nostalgia; a form and a subject which would have frightened away any publisher but Brian. Because he thought I was capable of handling this poetic form, which can be more turgid, inept, and tedious than any other, and because he shared my obsession with this common human pang for things lost or things never had, he was largely responsible for its completion. For there were moments when I despaired of conveying the full beauty of nostalgia without lapsing into bathos or the fashionable obscurity of those who do not know exactly what they mean. It was Brian who prevented both. He was a watchdog, ferocious about the sloppy line, the superfluous phrase, the ambiguous image. "What do you mean by this?" he would insist. "Why drag that in, when you've said it three lines above?" "Why use an archaism when a good Anglo-Saxon word will do?"

Sometimes his criticisms would enrage me. My immediate reaction would be to defend the passage criticized as being not only beyond fault but probably beyond his loutish comprehension. Brian always smiled when I was angry. "Okay," he would say, "leave it in. Nobody'll know the difference anyway." Hours later, I would usually alter the passage.

Our professional contact was always kept scrupulously impersonal. Although there might be in our meeting glances remembrance of the night past and prelude to the night ahead, we neither touched each other nor used endearments toward each other. Brian, moreover, was not a demonstrative man. He disliked the casual intimacies practiced by men who are usually incapable of serious ones; men who pat and stroke and kiss their women in public and in so doing (I had always suspected) progressively slacken that tension which feeds on restraint. That might have been why so few knew of our love although so many knew of our professional friendship.

It might seem strange in the light of our complete happiness together that we did not speak sooner about its future resolution. But it was not until the spring of 1939, after two years of increasing intimacy, that we talked of marriage.

Brian was lying on his bed smoking, I with my head on his shoulder, when he said, "Olivia—we can't go on like this."

"I know—"

"We have got to live together. Really together. Always." I took his hand, saying nothing.

"Olivia—would you marry me?"

My heart turned over and I wanted to cry. No matter how much one has loved or been loved, those words which are the total offering of the human being are hallowed. I could not speak, instead I turned toward him and put my arms around him. We lay that way for what seemed a very long time until I found my voice.

"I want a child by you, Brian."

We clung to each other then, so fiercely that we might have been drowning. Brian shuddered and we did not even kiss. Finally he said, "I've tried not to face up to this. You know why—"

"I know. I never would have spoken."

"If Mary had shown any sign—"

"I tell you she still loves you."

"No," said Brian. "It's not love. I don't know what it is. I sometimes feel like her father—or her brother—" We said nothing for a while. Brian loosened his hold and sat up higher, reaching for his pipe on the bed-table.

"When I go back this time," he said, "I will have to tell her. It can't go on like this."

"It could, maybe. But I don't know what it would do to us in the long run."

Brian shook his head. "It's impossible. No relationship can stay static. It either grows or diminishes—or breaks. You know as well as I do that what we have will grow—and there's only one way to let it."

"Do you think Mary has any idea—"

"She must have by now," said Brian. "She can't believe that

I can go on indefinitely like this—a sort of intermittent intellectual escort."

It hurt me to say this but I had to. "Brian, shouldn't you try once again to bring her here—with you?"

"I suggested it again last summer. She smiled and shook her head and said, 'Thanks, Brian, but it wouldn't work. This is the right way for both of us.' You see," he said with irony, "I made her think I was a happy man."

"With her?"

"With the way things were."

"But surely she must have some life of her own all that time you're away?"

"I wish to God she had," said Brian. "But so far as I can see she is in love with no one. Or rather, she's only in love with her work."

"But that's only half of it."

Brian rose and went over to the bar-table in the living room. "Drink, darling?"

"Yes, please."

He poured two highballs and brought them back to the bedroom. We were both suddenly very depressed, not only by our personal problem, which was common to the point of banality, but by that sense of impending disaster which the events of the outside world had made a part of our sleeping and waking consciousness. It was this sense that made Brian say, "A lot of things will have to be cleared up this summer—"

"Of which ours is the least," I said.

"No," said Brian looking at me gravely, "not the least. Part of the whole thing. In the face of chaos we've got to hold fast to our own truth."

"I think I could face anything if you were with me," I said.

"I can't conceive," he said, "of not being with you."

And so, in June of 1939 Brian flew to England. "If things work out all right," he said, "I ought to be back in August."

He noticed a look on my face and suddenly drew me to him, for the first time before people, right at the gate at LaGuardia where the passengers waited to board the plane. "It's got to work," he said, and then turned and left and walked out through the passage without a backward look. I went up on the terrace to watch the plane go off. The Clipper sat there like a huge squat silver hen roosting on water. It took a while before the passengers stepped on, and I caught one brief glimpse of Brian as he boarded it. Finally, four engines roaring and four propellers invisibly slicing the air, the plane moved forward; and I watched its ponderous take-off across the bay and up into the pale transparent sky. Then I went downstairs and took a taxi home. I felt as if I had undergone a major operation, without anaesthetic. Only in such separations can one know the incompleteness of the single human being. Only at this separation did I know that Brian was, in actuality, a part of me.

He sent a cable from Newfoundland and another from Southampton when he landed. After that, two weeks went by without a word; two weeks punctuated by newspaper headlines that froze the heart with foreboding. I had moved down with Philip and Auriol to a small rented cottage on the south shore of Long Island and was occupied, on the surface at least, with housekeeping details, preparations for Philip's summer at camp, and a certain amount of proofreading. Only at night did my longing for Brian become acute; and then I would take out his cables, like any schoolgirl in love, and read their brief messages. The last one read: "I have never left you."

The first letter finally arrived, but it was disquieting in its ambiguity. Brian was seldom ambiguous, never to me. He said he was extremely busy, that the situation looked even uglier from England than from here, and that circumstances had so far conspired against any airing of our own situation. "Mary is in a very tense and exalted state and is almost visibly girding herself for the showdown. Since all her passions seem confined to world matters (her column, incidentally, is considered one of the best in England) she does not mean our showdown. And the moment hasn't yet arrived when I can talk to her about that." Later he added: "The only times when I don't think of you are when I read the papers. Then I think of us all—we humans, I mean—and of the frightful rope we're splicing for our necks. I feel also an increasing rage against the Master Race and their monstrous souls. Words won't stop them, and I find myself wishing I were ten years younger and handy with a gun. You and I have been angry since nineteen thirty-three, but even here—a few hundred miles from annihilating doom—there are people in clubs who flick their fingers at it. No wonder the U.S.—thousands of miles away—is angry only at an umpire's mistake. What is the matter with us, anyway? Too much breakfast-food?"

A few days later another letter said, "Mary has gone to spend the night at Chequers to interview the P. M., so I have twenty-four hours to be exclusively with you. I showed Alec [that was Brian's representative in London] the rough proof of *Rowan's Loss* and he is extremely excited about it. I can't help agreeing (after you pruned out those *Redbook* moments). I am very proud of you, quite aside from my chronic infatuation. I never thought a woman could be both noble and absurd, but you are."

Two more weeks passed with still no news of himself and Mary or, for that matter, of us. He had been gone a month now and I muffled my apprehensions by telling myself that his return was one month nearer, whatever the decision. I tried not to count on our marriage, but I found it impossible to blot out images of breakfast together in the country, of Brian's key in the lock, and increasingly of the child that would be ours. The thought made me sick with desire.

In the first week of July, on a day so sultry that breathing was an effort, a letter arrived with news. Auriol had gone to the

beach with friends and I was sitting on the screen-porch, half
clothed and trying to write, when the postman brought it.

"It happened so simply," wrote Brian, "that I still can't believe it. This morning, out of the blue, Mary said, 'You're in
love with somebody, aren't you?' I said nothing and she went
on: 'You want to leave me, don't you?' She seemed perfectly
calm and said this looking directly at me and in an even voice.
I told her, finally. Much as I had rehearsed it and much as I
needed to say it, it hurt like hell. I must have sounded like a
floundering adolescent. I ended up by calling myself any lousy
name I could think of. She stopped me in the middle of these
protestations and said, 'You needn't go on like that, Brian. This
is no kind of life for you, anyway. I've known that for a long
time. I just thought there was no one else you liked more.' A
little later, she said, 'I suppose it's up to me to get the divorce,
isn't it?' By this time, speech was so hard that I could hardly
get anything out, so I just nodded my head. If she had given
the slightest indication of emotion I think I would have made
a mess of things by taking her hands or getting on my knees or
something. But she was entirely cold. Right after that she looked
at her watch, said 'I've got to be going,' and walked out.

"Dearest, dearest, dearest—you will know what I mean if I
say that there is as much misery as release in all this. I know
the first will wear off, but right now I feel abject, rotten—oh,
everything. You must have felt that when you left Max. No
matter what has been lacking between two people, no matter
how much may have gone wrong, the final parting is terrible.
It is a kind of drowning, in which all good, shared moments
pass in a piteous parade. You can actually feel the tearing of
that intricate binding membrane of common memory; and it
hurts, badly. Divorce may sometimes be the agency of happiness; but in itself it is a hideous thing." The letter ended:
"One thing you must be sure of: I have never for one instant

doubted that this was right—or that I must live with you. You are as essential to me as my breath."

The letter left me profoundly anxious; not only because I shared his distress but because of the manner in which the break had happened. It was too quick, too simple; there was something wrong with the picture. Superficially Brian was now free and we could be married in due course. But the letter, airmail tissue though it was, weighed as heavily in my hand as the air weighed on my flesh. No breath stirred its pages as no breath stirred the maple leaves outside. The lawn was now a poisonous, lurid green in the sickening light. The moment had the gathered silence of a panther ready to spring; motionless but charged. This calm was merely an overture to disaster.

The storm broke an hour after that letter, violent and torrential. But the doom I awaited came seven days after it; and even before I opened the letter I said: Now it's here. Brian wrote almost incoherently but, as in all the letters of that summer, I remember every word. "Something fearful has happened —I don't know how to convey it. That night after we had that talk, the police-station called and told me Mary had collapsed in the street. They picked her up and found out who she was. I can't go into all the horror after that. The point is that she's had a complete nervous breakdown. She's in a nursing home now. She can't talk and she doesn't seem to hear. Doctors and psychiatrists say it's some sort of traumatic shock—nothing physically wrong that they know of. She just lies there with her eyes open. But when I try to go out of the room she gets very agitated, so I hardly dare leave. Christ, to see her that way— she of all people.

"I can't write any more. I don't know what to write. Hold on, for God's sake, Olivia. . . ."

The next few letters told the rest of the story. Mary came out of her shock state with only a slight slowness of speech but

with a profound depression that made her inert. She slept a
great deal, and when awake took no interest in anything. Little
by little she grew more normal, went out with a nurse for walks
and began to read again. But she was not fit for work and the
psychiatrists told Brian there was no way of telling when she
would be.

"Dr. Meyer," wrote Brian, "knows the whole background
of the case but hasn't told me yet what conclusions he has
drawn except that Mary has battened down on something ever
since the kid died and that my talk of a split has blown it up.
He appears to attach no blame to me directly, but he does think
that Mary's general behavior warranted observation some time
past. There was quite a lot of talk about a 'father-attachment'
which was transferred to me and about suppressed Lesbianism—
something which I had never allowed myself to think. My own
conclusions are that I have been criminally stupid. All I can
say for myself—as I have said it to you so many times—is that
I honestly believed our marriage to have become an off-and-on
companionship which had lost all sense of urgency or need.
We did not legally separate—before I knew you—simply because neither of us particularly wanted more freedom than we
already had. Anyway, you have always known how much I have
admired her and been fond of her. It was she, I thought, who
had deliberately killed the sentimental element of our marriage.
Now, haunted by inadequacy and helplessness in the face of
her collapse, I force myself to think back to moments where a
word or gesture from me might have released her. . . ."

The summer wore on, perversely calm and beautiful while
the fuse of human destruction burned slowly up its length. I
tried very hard to work but found I could not; the times lay
so heavily on my mind and soul. Instead I wrote to Brian,
trying to sustain him.

Toward the end of July, he wrote that Mary was getting
perceptibly better and more like her old self, although she was

still unable to work and fell easily into fatigue and depression. "If she continues like this," he said, "I may be able to get back late in August—at least for a while. The atmosphere is extremely tense here, but most of the people still can't believe that Hitler will act. The British have been called devious and tricky, but from where I sit they seem almost simple-minded in their refusal to be alarmed. I suppose their lack of imagination is what saves them. That and a generous amount of guts."

In August came a short letter. "Today I broached the idea of my returning for a short visit to the U. S. to the psychiatrist. He was silent a moment and then said, 'Littleton, if you leave her in her present condition she may kill herself.' I asked him how long he thought she would be in that danger. 'I can't possibly say,' he said. 'It might be weeks, it might be months.' I told him about you, about my business, about the urgency of getting back before the outbreak of war. He shrugged his shoulders slowly and said, 'You're in a bad spot, I know. And if you want to take the chance of leaving Mary, it's up to you. No one can positively prophesy her reaction. All I can do is repeat that in her present state she is capable of doing away with herself—if you leave.' What can I say? What can I do but wait? Oh, my dearest, we've got to hold on—somehow, someway. There is nothing else for us to do."

A few days later, toward the end of August (the day Philip came home from camp, thin and brown) Brian wrote, "Today I asked Mary whether she would not come back with me to New York. It seemed the only alternative, although I did not dare to think of what would happen once we were all there together. She looked at me in amazement and said, 'Leave England—now?' Then, in a toneless voice that always frightened me, she said, 'You go. You've got to get back, you belong in America. You go—' I said, 'Nonsense, we're in this thing together.'

"Actually, I meant what I said to Mary. The Russo-German

pact has, of course, stunned everybody. I can't help feeling
that to leave England now is a form of desertion. You would
feel that way too if you were here. The mobilization here is
more than a country preparing for war. It is a mobilization
against evil. An evil that may engulf us all, even that great
remote sleeping country of ours."

I heard nothing more until two weeks after the outbreak of
war, in September of 1939. Then Brian wrote: "I have joined
up. I can't see it any other way. The thought of you will sustain
me, for that is the most precious thing I have. But until this
is over our own lives are irrelevant. Or rather, we won't be able
to live them. That will come afterward. Olivia—dearest, dearest
Olivia—is it asking too much to ask you to wait for me?" At
the end of the letter, he wrote, "Olivia—for Christ's sake hold
on. . . ."

I held on. We wrote each other fairly regularly during the
first year of the war. Then, after the fall of France, over three
months went by without word. Finally I got a brief note saying,
"I've been traveling about a bit." The last paragraph was about
Mary. "The war has really been her salvation, and she's doing
magnificently by it. They wanted her to do broadcasting and
lecturing and that sort of stuff, but she flatly refused and went
into a munitions factory instead. She is working on the night-
shift at the moment. Her Joan of Arc spirit is back and you can
almost see the shining armor."

At that time I was writing and lecturing and broadcasting
about the war and our imperative obligations toward it. Except
for a poem about Dunkerque which appeared in the magazine
section of the *New York Times*, I wrote no verse. This was no
time for verse. It was soon to be no time for words.

After I had taken the War Department job, a few months
after Pearl Harbor, I met an English Intelligence Officer who
had seen Brian in London. "Doing a splendid job," he said.
Then he added that he had seen Brian and Mary in a restaurant

one evening. "She's a smasher," said the Major. "They looked positively bride-and-groomish."

Now that I was dead—five years later, in 1947—Brian interrogated me while his plane flew over the Atlantic night and he could not sleep.

You wrote a strange letter after that.

I felt you and Mary had found yourselves.

I never told you that.

No, you didn't. But I thought you were being kind. And for a year I heard nothing from you.

You knew why. You knew what I was doing.

I guessed, yes. But I thought somehow, some word—if you had wanted to—

You guessed, you thought—

I loved you, always—

But you married Whitney.

That was after four years without you—a half-year without word.

And two years of promiscuity?

I've told you about that. Without you I felt my life had no value—and certainly not my virtue.

Brian stirred, stretched again, moving his pillow to the other side of his seat.

And you, Brian? Were you one-minded all that time?

No. There were times when you became a remote dream, when you lost reality. You are nearer to me now than you were then.

I withdrew from you purposely. There seemed to be no hope.

There were only two other dates of importance: my marriage to Whitney in 1943; and the letter I got from Brian one week after the wedding. It was the first in six months.

"Beloved," it read. "Mary herself has suggested that we divorce as soon as the war is ended. God knows when that will be, but at least it's a definite thing. She is completely fit now in every way, so I have no fears about her at all any more. Hold on. It's been a long, long time, and it may be still longer, but there's a light at the end of the tunnel. . . ."

I tore the letter up into small pieces and threw them away. But they stuck in my throat forever, like the lump that is the prelude to tears that never come.

There was no need to answer it. My letter telling Brian of the marriage had been mailed.

One week more, said Brian. If you had waited one week more—

Two years more. Two years added to four.

Before I could come to you, yes. But I thought our love was independent of time.

It was. It is. But not independent of human need. I was lonely.

You not only married another man. You excluded me. You never wrote to me after that.

How could I? To torture you and myself? To make the life I had chosen with Whitney impossible?

You must have known it wouldn't work.

I knew in that first week.

But you kept on with it—

Until I died.

Are you forgetting our last meeting, Olivia?

I've tried to.

I can forget no single moment of it.

It was in September 1945 that Brian first came back to this country after the war. I had gone to see his partner Howe about some business matter and it was he who told me of Brian's imminent arrival. "It will be wonderful to have him back again, won't it?" said Mr. Howe. "Although I wonder if he'll be able to settle down in the old routine after all he's done."

Brian called me up one morning, a few minutes after Whitney had left for the office. "Olivia," he said, "I must see you. If you don't want to make it anywhere else, come to the office."

"I think it's crazy," I said.

"I don't care what you think. It's impossible to avoid."

"I suppose it is."

"When will you come?"

"This afternoon, if you want."

"Come at four."

"All right."

As I came into his office, Brian rose from his desk but did not move toward me. I in turn stood half-way in the room.

"Hello, Olivia," he said.

"Hello, Brian." Six years had not changed him much. He looked lined and tired, but indefinably stronger, as if he had been tempered.

"Cigarette?" He held a pack toward me.

"No thanks."

"You look well—and prosperous."

"Thank you."

"More like a magazine cover than a poet."

I smiled. "Should I be insulted?" He indicated the chair opposite his and I sat down.

"No. You do dress better."

"One learns, in time—"

"This is a bloody silly conversation, Olivia."

"You *do* sound English!"

"It's still bloody silly!"

I had been trying not to look directly into his eyes, but finally I did. Nothing had changed. We said nothing for quite a while. Then he cleared his throat and spoke.

"What are we going to do?"

"We?"

"All right then, you."

"I don't know. Or rather I do. I'm committed—for life."

"I don't believe you."

"But it's true—"

"Do you love Whitney?"

"Please, Brian!"

"Do you love him?"

"That isn't the question."

"It's my question."

"Brian, I will not leave him. I can't."

He paused for a moment. "Made your bed and lain on it, is that it?"

"It isn't that sordid."

"Then what is it?"

"It's affection . . . and a code of behavior. I've never had one before."

"And you really think you can stick to it?" Brian rose and started pacing back and forth behind my chair.

"I've got to." I began to tremble a little and Brian came around in front of me, half leaning on his desk.

"What does that make me—the clandestine lover?"

"It needn't make you anything." My head was lowered as I said this, in a barely audible voice.

"Look at me!" Brian barked, "and say that again!"

I said nothing but I looked at him.

"Do you honestly think," he said, "that we can live on the same continent and live apart?"

"We've been away from each other a long time, Brian. It has almost become a habit."

"Do you think it's a good one?"

I had risen and was standing facing him, but again with my head lowered. Brian raised my chin up. In another moment we were in each other's arms, rocking in a tight painful embrace, wordless and miserable. Tears streamed down my cheeks and onto the lapels of his jacket. We did not kiss, we just held each other in the common knowledge, suddenly perceived, that we would not hold each other again.

Six years had been too long. Too much had happened in the world, too much had happened in our hearts. That we still loved each other neither of us questioned. But that we could go on where we left off both of us now doubted, profoundly. The alteration of the world had left us altered. It was not only age that made us tacitly renounce each other; age and distance or obligations or codes of behavior. It was something far deeper in both of us: a knowledge, sharpened by the awful years of war, that our personal happiness was of little importance. The fact of our love may indeed have been important, as we had given each other the best of ourselves; but its consummation now, at the expense of others, was not to be demanded. Perhaps age had much to do with it, since it brings at the same time a weariness of spirit toward human relationships and an enlargement of spirit toward humankind. It is a progression painfully formed by experience, from the part to the whole.

We broke away, finally. I dried my cheeks with my handkerchief while Brian looked on. I don't remember clearly just what we said after that, before I left. There was some talk about a reprint of an early book and about rights in an anthology. Brian mentioned that he would cut short his American stay. And then I asked him to come to the house some afternoon; "To see the children," I said.

In the few months following we saw each other as little as possible: each meeting had become torture. He did, however, come once to the flat, while Philip was down from Cambridge. Whitney was there, jovial and innocent; and he and Brian talked of war while Philip questioned, avidly. Auriol did not come home until after Brian had left, although I had asked her expressly to be there. But there were several other guests, and the occasion was casual enough.

"That publisher of yours," said Whitney after we were alone. "He's a pretty sound fellow. Not like some of your looney friends."

I smiled and said nothing. Whitney was a little tight that night, and became affectionate and sentimental. There was a quality of despair in my love-making that he mistook for ardor. "You little bitch," he whispered in my ear. "You little bitch—"

As it happened, he was absolutely right.

You wrote your best poetry, you know, that winter of '45— said Brian on the plane at night, seven months after my death.

It's a strong argument for misery.

I took mine out in another way. I can't remember all their names.

Don't try!

What I don't understand, Olivia, is the strength of this thing between us, after all the time and happenings that kept us apart. Do you realize how little we saw of each other even in the year before you died?

That's one of the reasons, Brian—

You mean that if you had divorced Whitney and we had lived together before you died, this tie would have been dissipated?

No. But we have kept it in a pure state by renouncing it.

You sound like a Christian martyr.

That's not it. I mean that we cast our bread on the waters.

Brian pondered a while in the vibrating semi-darkness. The stewardess came out of the door that led to the pilot's cabin and walked down the aisle, looking to right and left to see if she was needed. At the seat across the aisle from Brian, she stopped to pick up a blanket that had slipped from an elderly woman's knees and tucked it around her sleeping form. Then she passed down the aisle toward the rear section where she stayed. Brian watched her, thinking how wonderful was the ministrant woman, especially if she were pretty and young.

In Hollywood, said Brian, our story wouldn't have ended this way.

In Hollywood, I said, people over twenty-five are incapable of love.

In Hollywood, said Brian, love always finds a way.

It was getting cold in the plane. Brian turned off the little ventilator above the window and pulled his blanket higher over his shoulders. The plane droned eastward toward the morning; and already in his mind's eye Brian saw the wet green fields of Ireland emerging through the mists of weather and night. Half-drowsy he said, When will you leave me entirely, Olivia?

I don't know.

I suppose it will happen?

Will happen. . . .

Not yet, Olivia! Not yet!

Not yet. . . .

Finally, Brian slept.

I saw very little of him on the rest of that trip. But one day I rejoined him in a Soho restaurant lunching with a woman. She seemed middle-aged and inclined to stoutness, and her fair hair—short and rather untidy—was streaked with gray. It was not until I looked at her eyes—dark, brilliant blue—and at the finely modeled nose and mouth that I recognized who it was.

"I was shocked," Mary was saying, "to read of her death."

"It was very sudden."

"Brian," Mary said with distress and compassion, "I feel somehow responsible—even for that."

"Don't be absurd."

"No. I've managed to make a colossal hash of your life, and I know it."

"You didn't start the war, Mary."

"That was only part of it." They were silent a moment, and then Mary went on: "If only I had met her—long ago. I think if I had known, then, who it was—"

"What difference would it have made?"

"I don't know. Maybe I would have realized how right it was." Brian said nothing, so Mary went on. "You see—I loved her poems." They were both silent again.

"I'm all right, Mary. Anyway," he smiled at her, "I think the pursuit of happiness has been vastly overrated. It's one of our chief national weaknesses, and I'm just beginning to grow out of it."

"I wish I could say that. But ever since Colin was born—"

"How is he now?"

Mary felt around in her handbag and brought out a small leather folding frame. Unclasping it she handed it to Brian, who examined three snapshots of a plump grinning baby. "Pretty fine job," he said.

"Colin senior is quite incoherent about him. As a matter of fact, he *is* in the nature of a miracle." Brian handed the pictures back to her and when Mary saw his face she said, very low, "I know, Brian. I know there's no justice."

But Brian was speaking to me then. This, he said, is the ultimate irony. Mary a mother, happily married. And I? married to a ghost, and without issue.

"What food we have," said Mary, putting the photo-case back into her bag, "goes into him. But then it should," she said. "That's what we're living for, isn't it? That, and some state of grace." Mary reached out her hand and put it over his, lying on the table. "That's what you have, Brian . . ."

Beyond that I heard nothing of their talk, nor did I see Mary again, at any time.

Philip was graduated summa cum laude from Harvard, and I was the only member of his family present at the ceremony. Part of the time I stayed beside Micaela and shared her pride.

There was a solemnity about the graduation, about the thousand-odd young men massed there, that Micaela found as moving as I did. Whatever individual frivolity or meanness or competitiveness might have existed was momentarily dissolved in the spirit of the moment, which was, essentially, part of the ritual of manhood.

I left the girl to be with Philip as he stood with the graduates. Mother, can you see me now? Are you glad? After the ceremony I did not see him again until he and Micaela were sitting in a small restaurant having supper.

"If only your mother could have been here," said the girl.

"I know. I kept thinking that most of the time."

"Why didn't Auriol come? I thought you'd asked her?"

"I did," said Philip, "but she's got a beau who's doing the same thing at Princeton and she was all dated up. Whitney sent a telegram—you know, congratulations and all that. Even Max crashed through."

They held hands over the table and smiled at each other, for no particular reason.

"I'm glad it's over," said Phil.

"So am I."

Philip reached inside his coat and brought out a batch of papers. "I forgot to tell you. These came yesterday—" he threw them on the table before her and Micaela looked at them.

"Oh," she said, "the application!"

"Yep. The exams start in September, and I have to get this filled and sent in forty days before that."

"Heavens, what a lot of questions. This will take you days!"

"I know," said Philip. "Typical government red tape. God, Mike, I'm just getting in under the wire as far as age. At least, I'll be twenty-one by the time that application goes through."

"*If* it goes through," said Micaela.

"What do you mean, if?" asked Phil. "I've gone into the whole thing and got it all taped—qualifications and all. The exams are supposed to be hell, but if I bone up on language and economics in the summer course I don't see why I can't make it."

"I'm not worried about your marks, darling. But they don't take just everyone—" She smiled at him, but I could see that she was concerned.

"Look, Mike," he said, "when they see the names of my sponsors they'll make me an ambassador—" then, as if announcing an important speaker at a banquet and sweeping his arm toward him—"Professor Miles Maitland, English Department, Harvard University! Dr. Cyrus Metzinger, Professor of Political Science! Mr. Hiram Mason, of Corning, Mason and Company, Wall Street! Hell, it's a cinch!"

"Well," said Micaela, lifting her glass to him, "let's drink to it anyway."

"To our first post," said Philip, drinking. "Somewhere hot and beautiful—"

"I bet it will be Iceland," said the girl.

"You can warm it up," said Philip.

"I wish," said Micaela dreamily, "that it could be somewhere on the Mediterranean. What was that thing your mother wrote about it?"

"The one about the temple?"

"Yes, something about Poseidon—in Sicily—"

After a moment's silence she said, "Philip—"

"Yes?"

"Philip—do you think your mother would have liked me?"

"She'd have been nuts about you."

"There are so many things I would have wanted to ask her. What you were like as a little boy, how you looked, what you said. . . ."

"God forbid," said Philip. "I was a hellish brat!"

"I thought Auriol was the brat."

"No, she was just a bitch."

"Phil!"

"All girls are—fundamentally! But I must confess she's improving," he said, with the condescension only a brother can express fully. "Given time, she may turn into a human being!"

"Philip," said Micaela after a moment, her hand still held by his across the table. "How do you feel about Whitney marrying?"

Philip shrugged. "I don't, very much. It just moves him one step further away. She's just right for him—anyway—"

"Are you angry with him?"

"For forgetting Mother so soon? Gosh, Mike," he said shaking his long head from side to side, "I don't think he ever really knew her. If he did—he couldn't fall for a dame like Elizabeth—just like that."

"But she's nice, isn't she?"

"Oh, sure. She's nice and virtuous and beautiful and smart—but she's never dreamed of Atlantis."

Micaela smiled. "Is that a female requirement?"

"It's a human requirement, as far as I'm concerned. Mother had it. A sick kid I knew in school had it. You have it." He looked into her eyes. "There—it's there right now. You've seen other things—not just what's here, what you can touch. Jesus, how can I describe it without sounding corny? It's a kind of light—a kind of radiance . . ."

"It wouldn't have anything to do with love, would it?" said the girl.

She was right, of course; but only up to a point. I knew what Philip meant. It was a look compounded as much of wonder as of love, and fed on inward vision. The image of the tangible world was fixed on the retina of most people; only in a few did the eye give back a reflection of the invisible.

Only the few conveyed the evidence of things unseen. It was an ardor free of personal, specific passion; a love free of desire; an amazement, as if the beholder were in some chronic state of revelation. Again the mawkish cliché comes to mind: there were "stars in her eyes." Stars; or more likely the radiant energy of the world into which I now was again being drawn.

I wondered as I left the two young people there in the restaurant, lost in each other, found in each other, whether I would have been jealous had I been a living witness to their love. Even the least possessive mother was supposed to feel some pang, however transient, at the thought of another woman now closer to her son than she, now the recipient of his secret being. It was merely another separation, this time from the womb of the spirit; and there is no separation without some pain.

But all I felt as I looked at my son in love was peace, because he was in good hands. And because I was realizing more and more that any evidence of harmony in life—affection, tenderness, trust—drew its participants closer to that state of grace which seemed to be the highest human condition. It was the only shield against destruction, and against mortality.

"It will have to be handled right," said Elizabeth, "but it can be done."

She and Whitney were sitting on the terrace of her house in Oyster Bay. I had been there several times with Whitney for week-ends and knew it well. It was, again, a color-page out of *House and Garden;* in perfect taste, perfectly kept, fresh and gay. The white iron furniture had yellow cushions, the little white iron tables had glass tops, and the façade of the house behind was of whitewashed brick with a white iron-lace portico, Southern–Long Island style. An edge of lemon-yellow curtains could be seen behind the wide bay window of the living room.

Elizabeth wore a cinnamon-colored sleeveless shantung dress, her hair was swept up into an off-center bun, and Grecian sandals showed the long elegance of her feet. Whitney and she were both reclining on chaise longues with highballs in their hands. Beyond the lawn a steep wooded slope fell off toward the Sound, where a regatta of small craft, like white butterflies which had just alighted on the pale blue water, skittered along.

"The trouble is," said Whitney, "that Auriol's name has been changed only three years and there must be people who knew her as an Aronson."

"Not here," said Elizabeth smiling. "Maybe on Fourteenth Street or in Greenwich Village."

"Well, if you think you can swing it, I'm all for it," said Whitney. "It would be wonderful for Auriol to belong to the Club. Anyway, she knows most of the young people who do."

"I'm going to bring Auriol to see Charlie tomorrow."

"Charlie Treadway?"

"Yes—he's a member of the Admissions Committee."

I was wondering just why I was present at this dialogue when Whitney said, "You know, Olivia never liked changing Auriol's name."

"Why not?"

"She always acted as though there was something shady about it."

Elizabeth, looking at the Sound, said nothing.

"When I pointed out the handicaps Auriol would have with that tag on her, she said, 'The awful part of it is that you're right.'"

"What was Auriol's reaction?"

"Oh, she was all for it," said Whitney. "Even before I married Olivia, Auriol told me how she hated her name."

"I noticed that Olivia got out of using it very conveniently."

"Well, that's a writer's prerogative."

At that moment Auriol came out between the glass doors of the living room. She had on white shorts and a halter and sneakers and looked flushed with heat.

"Hi," she said, and slumped down in one of the chairs.

"Hello, Sis," said Whitney. "You look all in!"

"The last set killed me," she said.

"Where's Curtis?" asked Elizabeth.

"He took on Eddie in singles," said Auriol. "He'll be around later."

"We were just talking about you and the Club," said Whitney. "Aunt Elizabeth very kindly wants to put you up for it."

"That'd be swell," said the girl.

"There's only one thing," said Elizabeth, "and I wanted to tell you about it before I took you to see Mr. Treadway tomorrow."

"What's that?"

"Well, you know how these clubs are, dear. Just leave your father out of it, if they start asking questions."

Auriol turned to look at Elizabeth curiously, then at Whitney.

"All she means," said Whitney, "is to remember that you're a Corning. Bury your dark past!"

"Oh," said Auriol.

"I don't think there'll be the slightest question," said Elizabeth, "but there's no point complicating things."

There was a silence and then Auriol got out of her chair, said, "Think I'll get myself a coke," and went inside. I went with her.

What shall I do, Mother, she said? I want to get in that club awfully, but what should I do? Is it okay to lie for a thing like that?

It's up to you, Auriol. It's your struggle.

But you wouldn't like me to do it, would you? You'd be furious, wouldn't you?

Did that ever stop you from doing anything, Auriol?

She went to the pantry, took a bottle of Coca-Cola out of the icebox, opened it, and poured herself a drink.

I want to get in that club terribly, she said. It's no fun here without it.

I said nothing and left her shortly after.

I rejoined her again in the presence of Elizabeth and a man who I assumed was Mr. Treadway. He was a blue-eyed weather-beaten man of fifty or so with the reddish foxlike face of the country gentleman. The Club office was filled with tennis and sailing trophies, and the remaining space was taken up by ship models. It was a pleasant room, incompatible with doubt.

Treadway was holding Auriol's hand, and from her expression he had been holding it too long. "So this is the young lady we're to have with us," he was saying. "I can see that Mrs. Warren was not exaggerating!"

Auriol blushed and withdrew her hand with embarrassment.

"Well, as I told you, I've been hoping that Auriol would spend a lot of time down here with me, and of course it would be ideal for her to be able to use the Club—"

"As far as I can see," said Mr. Treadway, "it would be a pleasure for the Club to have her!"

"Normally, of course," Elizabeth went on hurriedly, "Mr. Corning would have taken out a family membership here, but being a golf-fiend I'm afraid he swears allegiance to the Fairway. It's the tennis and sailing that Auriol's after—aren't you, dear?"

Auriol nodded, with a forced smile.

"Well, I don't think there'll be the slightest trouble getting her in," said Treadway. "The Admissions Committee meets next Wednesday and the moment they know you're sponsoring her," he said to Elizabeth, "she'll go through like a breeze. We have the reputation of being very fussy, young lady," he said jocosely to Auriol, "but unfortunately we have to be. A great many rather undesirable people have moved out here lately and of course they all want to join. But as you know, if you let one Jew in, the floodgate's open." Elizabeth was about to open her mouth, but Treadway put his hand up, smiling. "Naturally, this has nothing to do with you, it's just one of the things we have to be so careful about."

"It has something to do with me," said Auriol. Her voice was small but clear. In the short pause that followed I felt suspended, hardly daring to believe that her moment of courage and clarity had come. Elizabeth looked at her apprehensively but before she could speak Treadway said to Auriol, "What was that, my dear?"

"I said it has something to do with me. I'm half-Jewish."

Laughingly Elizabeth cut in, "Don't pay any attention to the child, Charlie, she has an absolute obsession because some great-great-grandfather or other was supposed to have Jewish blood."

"Well, I honestly don't think that—"

Auriol interrupted Treadway. "It isn't any great-grandfather, it's my father and he's a Jew!"

Treadway turned in bewilderment to Elizabeth, whose mouth was now thin in anger. She shrugged and turned away from them, drawing her breath in sharply.

"But surely Mr. Corning—" Treadway began.

"He's my stepfather," said Auriol, now sullen and defiant. "I took his name. My real name's Aronson. My father's name is Max Aronson. He's a Red and a Jew."

"Mrs. Warren," said Treadway, "is this child—?"

Elizabeth wheeled around. "Auriol is Mr. Corning's legally adopted daughter," she cried. "If she insists on exaggerating the case just to be sensational—"

"You know that's not true!" said Auriol. "You know it isn't!"

"Well, I confess I'm very much confused by all this," sighed Treadway, "but even if that were the case, I'm sure your name and Mr. Corning's would hold sufficient weight. That is," he went on, "if the young lady herself is not prone to such out-bursts!"

"I'm extremely sorry about this," said Elizabeth. "Whatever she means, she's kept from me too, so naturally it's something of a shock—"

Auriol looked at her in scorn and amazement but said nothing.

"Well," said Treadway, "perhaps when we've calmed down we can go over this again. How about it, young lady?" he said to Auriol.

"I'm sorry. There's really nothing more to go over. I'm half-Jewish and you don't take Jews and that's that."

Treadway shrugged slightly, and then shook hands with Elizabeth. "Call me in a day or so," he said. "I'm sure it can be straightened out."

"You've been terribly kind," said Elizabeth, "and I don't know what to say." She looked betrayed, helpless, and charming.

They left shortly after. On the way back in Elizabeth's car the two did not speak for at least two minutes. Then Elizabeth exploded with "I simply cannot understand what got into you!"

"I guess Mother did," said Auriol.

I would have hugged her, if I could. This was the child I doubted, criticized, feared for. Child no longer, perhaps; Auriol had become a human being. And because I felt I did not deserve my fortune in her, I thanked her for what she had done. Later on there was a scene between Whitney and Auriol, but there was such a resumption of static that I could get only bits and snatches. Whitney was very angry and delivered himself of such phrases as "shameful exhibition," "completely uncalled-for," "crazy behavior." Auriol made copious use of the word "truth"; and I heard the words "hate" and "snobs" quite often. Then the air cleared for a moment as Auriol said, "Mother would have done exactly the same!"

"In the first place," Whitney said, "your mother was not

even partly Jewish. In the second place, you have deeply hurt someone who—well, who will take the place of your mother eventually."

After a pause, Auriol lowered her head and her hands fidgeted in her lap.

"You're going to marry her?" she said finally.

"Yes," said Whitney, "in the fall."

As Auriol made no comment, Whitney went on, "Aunt Elizabeth is very fond of you and Phil, Sis. She'll do everything to make you two happy."

Again Auriol was silent, her eyes lowered.

"You seem to have some chip on your shoulder. I thought you liked Aunt Elizabeth."

"She's okay," said Auriol, "but I didn't think—"

"I know, Sis, I guess you're upset by its happening so quickly—after your mother . . ."

"It's okay," she said again, tonelessly.

"Aunt Elizabeth has been very wonderful to me during all this time, Sis. And she'll be a great help to you, too."

"I don't need help."

Whitney smiled. "That's what *you* think!"

"Anyway, Phil won't like it."

"Phil is nearly a grown man, Sis. He can take care of himself—but anybody who acted as you did this afternoon certainly needs to learn a few things."

"I didn't want to lie."

"Nobody asked you to lie. All you had to do was to say nothing and let Aunt Elizabeth handle the whole thing."

"I can't see the difference."

"Well, we've been all over it and if you can't see it now you will some day. The worst thing about it is that you've deliberately cut yourself off from the kind of people who could be most useful to you. I used to think you had a head on your shoulders, Sis, but I must say I'm not so sure now."

"If those people don't want me, I don't want them."

Whitney rose and gave a sigh of exasperation. "Some day, Auriol, you'll realize that people who buck the world don't get anywhere."

"Mother bucked the world."

"Must you," Whitney exploded, "constantly bring your mother into this conversation?"

Auriol's chin was quivering by then and Whitney, possibly ashamed of his vehemence, stomped out of the room. As she sat there, motionless, I put my arm around her and she began to cry, without making a sound. Don't worry, I whispered, don't worry. You can take it. You've got to.

She must have heard, because presently she dried her tears, rose and left the room, her head held high. I don't doubt that there was a streak of the "noble martyr" in her emotions then, but that was all right too. It was an effective performance.

The ninth month . . . There was no possible gauge of time in the element in which I now resided increasingly; the only measure came from contact with the living. I did not know, therefore, how long my last interval away from them was until the next visit, which took place in my apartment and which was ushered in by a new and strange phenomenon.

I can describe it only as a series of brief, violent shocks. They differed from the more general dislocation brought about by the impact of evil in that I alone was affected. The nuclear pattern around me pursued its complicated but ordered course, while the separate molecule that I had become seemed wrenched from its orbit. It was the closest sensation to actual pain that I had yet experienced.

There was such confusion in this particular transit back to life —so much whirling substance, so much scattering of light and sound—that it took considerable time before the facts came into focus. When they did, and the outlines of my own apartment gradually clarified, I could see what the reason was. Elizabeth was moving my possessions out of the house.

Brief dialogues I had heard before should have warned me:

"I want you to feel," Whitney had said (I don't know when), "that you have a free hand in decorating the apartment. After all, it's going to be yours."

"Ours!" said Elizabeth.

"I'm all for a clean sweep," said Whitney.

198

"You're so wonderful, darling," said Elizabeth. "I was afraid—" Afraid of me? Afraid of lingering memory in Whitney?

Here she was, in any case, sending away all that remained of me. She was alone, except for the moving men. The apartment had the look of all city apartments in the heat of summer. The floors were bare, the furniture in slip-covers, the bookcases covered with sheeting. The light that came through the slats of the Venetian blinds was aqueous and stale. Although the windows were closed against the heat, dust had settled on the sills, the accumulation of weeks. Elizabeth moved carefully about the rooms as she directed the packing, so that her hands and her light silk dress would not be soiled.

They took my desk first. It was an old Victorian secretary which I had had for twenty years; not beautiful, but of good dark walnut and full of cubbyholes, drawers, and compartments. A generous piece of furniture, well-made and enduring, it wore an air of stalwart service that had always cheered me. There I had done most of my writing, there I had sat unable to write, there I had written my letters to Brian and there, in a small locked drawer, I had kept his letters until the day we parted. The desk had become a part of me. Removing it from its context was wrenching a part of my identity out of my living home.

After the desk came an old American wall-clock, shaped like the Bunker Hill Monument. Austere and elegant, it had the dignity of true craftsmanship, the inherent serenity of all things well and carefully done. It had belonged to my father's grandfather, and I loved it.

Into a packing case, along with other objects less involved, went a small bronze Cretan bull I had bought in Rome with my first big check. I had held it often in my hand, for the feeling of its back and its muzzle gave me enormous pleasure, as did the sight of its greenish-brown patina. I touched it also because three thousand years ago it had been touched, and this made a tangible link between the long past and myself. This kind of continuity was as precious as the object itself. The little bronze bull was alive not only because it was a work of art but because successive generations of hands had kept it warm.

There were other things Elizabeth put away—for what purpose, storage or sale, I could not know. A footstool covered with a tapestry bird that I had embroidered as a child; not valuable, not handsome, but an intimate, slightly comic companion of many years. The children had taken turns sitting on it while I read to them, each fighting the other for tenure of that small throne.

A Georgian toast-rack Brian had brought me once; a French side-chair; a miniature wooden chest of Holbein's time; these and a dozen more objects were taken away. My favorite pictures were taken down from the wall and packed in a box: a small Degas pastel; the Hogarth prints; an American primitive painting of peaches and grapes, which I found in a junk shop when I was married to Max; a reproduction of Lautrec's "Mlle. Avril"; an oil-painting of a deserted village by a young American romantic. All these had become threads in the texture of my living.

By the time Elizabeth had finished and the packers had gone, there was nothing left of me. Three years had not been enough to impregnate the very walls; it takes decades of living in one room or house to accomplish that, so that—empty—it can cast back the human emanations it has absorbed. Only these objects held some fraction of my living essence. With their removal I should never see my study again unless either Philip or Auriol were there; and even then, clear vision of it would become increasingly difficult and ultimately impossible.

In my lifetime, possessions as such had meant little to me. The loss or injury of something I liked would sadden me for a moment but quickly pass away. I had no desire, at any time, to accumulate or collect. On the contrary, I feared the domination of physical objects, for I had seen how craven they could

make their owners, how unfree. Human progress had so often
been checked by those who were afraid of losing what they
had. The more they had, the greater was their fear; and the
greater their fear, the more blind and deaf they became to the
voice of ordinary human need. The insulation of the rich, Brian
had called it. To fight it, after marrying Whitney, I trained
myself more toward loss than toward gain. Every day I would
say to myself: You are surrounded by comfort and beauty,
you are completely free from want. But if you should lose all
this, you will have lost little of importance. Enjoy it, but consider it ephemeral, without substance. For if you ever reach
the state where these things are essential to your happiness,
you are lost.

They were not essential to my happiness then; but I was
surprised at how important they were to my continued existence now. The desk, the Cretan bull, the clock, the footstool—
these possessed some of my living substance. Together in a room
they contained enough to conjure up my entity. Scattered,
buried, forgotten, I too was scattered, buried, forgotten.

This then, I thought, was why America had so few ghosts; a
room was so seldom given time to absorb the living. Uprooting
and change disturbed again and again that fine intangible balance between animate and inanimate. The objects themselves
were made for immediacy; their owners ignorant of the past. An
American tradition was pride in lack of tradition. Because it
was cut off by a sea, the United States was proud to think itself
cut off from the long accretion of human experience. "We are
new," was the cry. "Brand new! Nothing that happened before
us has anything to do with us!" Continuity was an unknown
word and an unrecognized concept. Age was an object of pity
or indifference in a country which idolized youth. And death?
Death was unspeakable.

We jeered at the old countries with their old attachments,
we pitied the people who clung, until they were allowed to

cling no more, to their ancient homes. And yet it was still to
be wondered whether the child brought up in new pre-fabri-
cated rooms of glass and steel, the child shifted from apartment
to apartment, did not miss the good as well as the evil of past
presences. Roots could not grow on plastic; they could be put
down only in the rich loam of human experience. And part of
that loam was physical: the clock, the chair, the wooden banis-
ter, the fading portrait. Cared for and allowed the peace of
years in which to grow in relation to one another, they evoked
an atmosphere which could be a benediction as well as a curse.
The dead were not always given their due.

So now Auriol and Philip would have to lay their own founda-
tions, without our physical help. Some day, maybe Auriol would
get the clock out of storage and put it in her home: perhaps
Philip, married to Micaela, would set the footstool in their
nursery. I hoped that Whitney would salvage at least a portion
of my things for their future use. Some day, I felt, their homes
would reflect the kind of warmth and serenity which existed in
the home of my parents and might have existed in the home of
Max's parents. A quality of taste can be inherited even if most
of the things that bred it are lost.

But it would be hard, for the link was broken; broken that
day by Elizabeth as she ordered out of her future residence all
things that might conjure up the image of their owner. Oddly
enough, in spite of the immediate pain this dislocation caused,
she had done me a service. What she had broken was one
more link in the chain of my servitude to life. I would never,
I hoped, have to return to those rooms again.

Philip interrupted his letter to Micaela long enough to read
one just received from Auriol.

"Can you *imagine* it," she wrote, "every single thing that
had anything to do with Mother she's gone and put away. I was
livid when I saw what had happened. And she has the nerve

to be sweet and lovely and ask my advice about re-decorating
the place. Why on earth didn't Mom leave those things to us
instead of to Whitney? God knows what will happen to them
now." On the next page Philip read: "Things have sort of
quieted down about the Club affair and anyway I don't need it
much because the bunch use the beach more. I've cooled off on
Curtis ever since the way he acted up about it, but I can't say
I'm exactly a wallflower otherwise. Elizabeth gave me a pretty
lethal evening dress (hush money, I guess), it's cut to here and
Mother would have a fit. . . ."

Philip threw the letter down, calling his sister a silly, frivolous,
appeasing little idiot. The part about the furniture would normally have enraged him, but such was his depression and bewilderment at the moment that he could think of nothing but his
own trouble. The letter to Micaela, lying open before him, told
the story. That morning a State Department note had informed
him that his application for Foreign Service examinations had
been regretfully turned down.

"They said," he had written, "that it had come too late and
they had been forced to cut down the number of applicants,
but I just don't believe it. Christ, Mike, they said forty days
before the exams and I sent mine two months before. There's
something else behind all this, and I'm going to run it down if
I have to see the Old Man himself. I could understand taking
the exams and then not getting passed, but this—hell, this is a
conviction without trial. . . ."

Micaela read his letter with sorrow and anger, and when they
met again they rehashed the whole thing, exhausting themselves
with surmise.

"It can't be the Jewish angle," said Philip, "because that's
unconstitutional. If anybody got wind of it you can imagine
what the press would do!"

"It must be your father," said Micaela. "There's no other
way to explain it."

"But Max is no party member—why, he told me so himself the last time I asked him!"

Micaela smiled and shook her head, "Philip, Philip, since when does that prove anything? Hundreds of them say they aren't; and anyway, didn't your father speak at that rally?"

"Sure he did, but that wasn't a purely Commie rally—there were plenty non-Commie leftists there."

"Well, for all you know, they may know things about him that you don't."

"Okay, okay, but even if he is, I'm not, and who's applying for the job anyhow?"

"They probably are afraid you're infected by him."

Philip got up and walked restlessly back and forth.

"Have you told your father?"

"Yes. He didn't seem too surprised."

"What did he say?"

"He said if I really wanted to know he could probably find out—he knows some fellows there," Philip added.

"Darling—Phil—there must be some way. Perhaps if you could see them, talk to them—"

Philip shook his head. "I wrote and asked. It's just no goddamn use. Anyway, it's too late for this year."

"It's just possible," said Micaela, "that after all your application *did* come too late and the lists were full. And anyway," she added, "you're awfully young, Phil. You can try again for next year—"

Phil wheeled on her. "Next year? What the hell has next year to do with it? Will I have a different name next year? Will I have a different father next year? Don't be a sucker, Mike. The thing's as plain as a pikestaff. They don't want Jews and they don't want radicals or sons of radicals—only they haven't got the guts to come out and say so!"

Micaela sighed and was silent for a while. Then she said, "What will you do?"

Philip shrugged and sat down near her, but with his face turned away from her. "Finish summer school, I guess. And then go out and fight."

"Fight?"

"Yes," said Philip, rising again. "I'm beginning to think Pop's got something after all. Like hell this country's a democracy. It's a nation of witch-hunting Rotarians, of blind reactionary idiots, of people who are so goddamned afraid of change that they don't even want to grow up!"

I didn't hear the rest of the tirade, for if Philip had been thinking of me he wouldn't have made it. Because I had myself been guilty of such explosive pronouncements in my youth, I deplored them in others. The overstatements induced by anger may be a relief to their speaker but they tend to have a disastrous effect on the listener. Violence begets violence, and the natural reaction to Philip's catalogue of clichés out of the *Daily Worker* would be to call him a lousy Red. From then on nothing but aggravation could be produced by further speech.

After that I saw Philip several times with his father, but very unclearly. Out of various bits of dialogue, however, and various scenes both at Max's house and at bars and other places, I could piece together what was happening to the boy. Philip was using his hurt as a fulcrum for cynicism.

His father, watching his son's resentment with pleasure, would not have called Philip's sudden conversion cynicism, for the doctrinary radical considers his ideology to be, in fact, a faith. But to the middle-of-the-roader, there is little to choose between the cynicism of the Extreme Left and the Extreme Right, because from where he sits both are predicated on contempt: on the Right, contempt for the Mass, on the Left, contempt for the Individual. Philip was feeling an urge of contempt for those individuals who constituted Authority, because they had hurt him. He was also taking on certain so-called

Jewish mannerisms—aggressiveness, over-emotionalism, over-vulnerability—which arise as much from imagined as from real persecution. Where before he chose his friends solely on the basis of qualities as individuals, he now made a point of associating with Jewish groups; abandoning his Gentile acquaintances as if the mere fact of their "gentility" condemned them.

"You make me sick," I heard Auriol say to him once that summer, "with all this Jewish stuff!"

"You're a fine one to talk," said her brother. "What about those lovely club people that threw you out on your can!"

"Oh, for heaven's sake," said Auriol, "just because a few dopes act that way is no reason for calling everybody a fascist!"

"Listen to the little philosopher."

"I mean it. Just because you can't get into the State Department and you don't even know why, you think the whole world's ganging up on you."

"I didn't say the whole world. I've merely said that the vested interests in this country are reactionary bastards."

"You sound just like your father."

"Well he makes a lot more sense than Whitney."

"I don't know what you call sense," said Auriol, "but I'll bet you a dime to a dollar that Whitney's given more to charity and done more for people than Max ever has!"

"Charity," sneered Philip. "Benevolent paternalism. So what?"

I could have boxed his ears, but as that was palpably impossible I could only stay and listen to his subsequent attack on the capitalist system. He ended it by lashing out at all moderate solutions and shaking a warning finger in his sister's face.

"You and your kind," he warned, "are on the way out. You'd better dig your head out of the sand or else you'll be caught ass up!"

"Boy, you're elegant," said Auriol. "All I can say is, I'm going to have fun on the way out. And as for what you so delicately call my ass," she added from the doorway, "I'll take care of that myself." With that she swished out of the room.

I have no idea why I was present at this rather ridiculous scene. Possibly Philip was indulging in a sort of conscious rebellion against my memory, for in the last years of my life I had been very impatient with his tendency toward wholesale indictments of things, people, or ideas. It had been my own weakness and I wanted to spare him from the consequences of this kind of intellectual arrogance, for all it bred was discord. It was, to be sure, part of the healthy violence of the young; but carried into maturity it was likely to atrophy into intolerance.

I need not have worried too much, because the next time I saw Philip closely something happened which effectively checked this course.

One very hot evening—it might have been mid-August— Philip was catching a train back to summer school, a newspaper under his arm. Micaela wasn't with him, and I could feel he was depressed and tired. Settling himself in a coach seat next to a fat woman in a limp flowered dress, Philip opened his paper and saw the following headline on the front page:

;   NOTED RED DENOUNCES PARTY

The subhead read, "Max Aronson Ready to Tell All." Shocked and fascinated, Philip read on. "Aronson, university instructor in political economy, long considered the most eloquent spokesman for extreme leftist factions in the East, delivered the following statement to the press, denying membership in the Party and denouncing Soviet policy."

The statement itself was like several that had preceded it during the last year of my life. In it Max confessed to having been misled by his idealism into working for a better human society, but that closer contact with the alleged planners of that society had convinced him of its grave dangers toward the American system. The rest of it could have been written by Whitney, "exposing" as it did the insidious Communist network in the United States and accusing several liberal organizations of harboring some of its most powerful agents.

"My God!" said Philip as he laid down the paper. The woman next to him turned sharply toward him, and Philip apologized, trying at the same time to edge away from her hot fleshy thigh. Since it expanded with space, this was a useless attempt.

My God, he said again, this time to himself and to me. What does this make him, Mother? A hero—or a heel? Where do we go from here?

Where do you go from here, Philip?

I don't know yet. Just now I feel like the sucker of the world.

Is that all you get out of it?

What do you expect me to get out of it? Doesn't it throw a whole set of values right out of the window?

Were those your values, Phil?

Hell, I don't know any more. I've got to start all over and find out. Mother—is everything built on shifting sand like that? Is nothing fixed—nothing absolute? What can a guy hold on to?

I left him to his bewilderment, wondering how long it would last and what would pull him out of it. So long as he believed nothing I would not see him, for some kind of belief was implicit in my presence. Negation as deep as that could banish me utterly.

But it could not have been very long before I saw him in his room at school, with a boy whom I recognized as his roommate this summer.

"Christ," Philip was saying disgustedly. "Not a damn thing to read."

"I can't make out why you have to read in bed. We read all day in this damn course."

"I don't mean that. I mean escape stuff."

"Take a *Reader's Digest*," said the boy, tossing it over to Philip's bed. Philip gave a short laugh. "Thanks. I'm not in the mood for that particular escape."

"Well, the only other thing I've got kicking around is the *Oxford Book of English* Verse. I don't know how you feel about poetry—"

"I feel okay about poetry. I was brought up on it."

"How come?"

"My mother was a poet. Olivia Baird."

The other boy switched his feet off the bed and onto the floor, sitting up straight and looking at Philip with a new interest.

"Well, whaddaya know!"

"Read any of her stuff?"

"Sure—mostly in magazines. Christ, I didn't know she was your mother!"

"Why should you? She never used her married name in print." Philip rose, went over and took the *Oxford Book of English* Verse from the shelf above his roommate's bed, and returned to his own bed with it.

"What was she like—as a person?"

"Kind of elusive," said Philip. "Now you see her, now you don't. She's tough to describe."

"Temperamental?"

"In a way, I guess. But she was pretty nice to everybody. People liked her. I guess you'd call it magnetism."

"It's—it's tough about her—" The boy could not seem to say "dying," and Philip said nothing. He was turning the pages of the book and scanning the poems. Then, after a while, he read:

> "When in the chronicle of wasted time
> I see descriptions of the fairest wights,
> And beauty making beautiful old rime
> In praise of Ladies dead and lovely Knights . . .

"She was nuts about the sonnets. Always reading them aloud to us. I remember all the first lines: 'O never say that I was false of heart'—'Th' expense of Spirit in a waste of shame Is lust in action . . .'" Tilting his head back against the wall and looking at the ceiling, Philip smiled. "I was only about eight when she read that first, I guess. I asked her what 'lust' was!"

"What did she say?"

"I don't remember what she said then. But I asked her again a couple of years later and she said it was 'desire without love.'"

"That about covers it."

"Will Shakespeare covers it, all right." Closing his eyes, Philip quoted with only slight pauses:

> "Th' expense of Spirit in a waste of shame
> Is lust in action; and till action, lust
> Is perjured, murderous, bloody, full of blame,
> Savage, extreme, rude, cruel, not to trust;
> Enjoy'd no sooner but despised straight;
> Past reason hunted; and, no sooner had,
> Past reason hated, as a swallow'd bait
> On purpose laid to make the taker mad:
> Mad in pursuit, and in possession so;
> Had, having, and in quest to have, extreme;
> A bliss in proof, and proved, a very woe . . ."

Philip's voice trailed off. The other boy was getting into his pajamas. "I can't go along with the Bard the whole way," he said. "I have some very pleasant memories of lust!"

Philip laughed, but the sonnet was still going through his head and he was trying to remember the last three lines.

Later, when the room was dark and the other boy asleep, Philip still had his bedlamp on, still read. His mind was filled with the cadences of the great, and as he read a profound sense of peace seemed to come over him. Finally he turned out the light and lay there.

Mother, he said, that's the only thing that counts. isn't it?

Isn't that the answer? The immortality of beauty? In words, in sounds, in shapes?

That's part of it . . .

If people really read these things or listened to Bach or looked at the Sistine Chapel they couldn't destroy one another the way they do, could they?

It isn't enough to read or listen or look. You yourself have to live creatively.

What do you mean, live creatively?

I mean live so that the pattern you make of your life is a work of art in itself. You don't have to write or paint or compose to do that.

But you have to be a Christ or an Abraham Lincoln. That's too tough on most of us, Mother!

There are degrees. The main thing is not to waste your life in irrelevancies—

Such as?

Such as the easy labels of the moment, such as the conflicting immediacies of the day. You were profoundly disturbed by these labels—Right and Left, Radical and Conservative, Liberal and Reactionary. You have teetered from one to the other in search of final truth. You have been confused by headlines, by demagoguery, by the organized conflicts of groups. You have tried to identify yourself with one or the other, and in so doing have lost yourself. You cannot stand alone in this world; on the other hand you cannot lean on such arbitrary groupings of men. You have to judge each man on his own lights. Human values are not group values. They belong to the individual.

But I thought this was the century of the common man?

That is a phrase—and a label. There may be a common faith, but there is no common man. Only an individualist would use such a term to describe his fellow men.

Philip lay there for a while thinking. Finally, he said: Mother, is it you who are speaking to me, or is it another part of myself?

Aren't you a part of me, Philip? And I of you?

Philip smiled in the dark. You're hedging, Mother! That isn't fair!

Do you expect to get the secrets of the universe ready-made?

No—but I thought you could at least give me a steer!

I have, I said. Go back to your sonnets, Phil.

Philip stretched, turned from his side to his back, and searched his memory—then recited slowly to himself:

> What is your substance, whereof are you made,
> That millions of strange shadows on you tend? . . .

That millions of strange shadows on you tend, he repeated. Together we remembered the rest of the sonnet, and several others besides, before he finally fell asleep.

Here again, as the marvelous lines inaudibly filled the air, I felt this to be—as I had felt during the music at the long-past concert—the link, the channel, the communication, between the living and the dead. This was the language in which revelation could be translated. For these writers, these musicians, these philosophers, saw beyond the fact into that intangible state to which their effort and their humility had drawn them. Genius was not the infinite capacity for taking pains; it was rather the capacity, nurtured by passionate observation, to pierce the walls of the immediate surrounding world and penetrate into the enduring substance of life. Essentially this was a labor of love, shared by all—scientist, mystic, and poet alike— who felt the inexorable drive toward truth and the need to communicate it to others.

Sleep on now, Philip, I thought as I left him again. Sleep on, but sleeping gird your loins. You have a long fight ahead of you with a great Goliath. He calls himself Realist, and he is armed with facts and figures and polls and ratings and surveys. His mouth is an amplifier, his eyes are precision lenses, his spear is tipped with cynic acid; and he is heavily insured. But he has a weakness, for he is actually blind. He believes only what he can see. And you have a strength, for the stone in your sling is made of cosmic substance—human faith. Against that his arms are impotent.

Brian, back at his New York office desk, was reading a letter. The handwriting was Spencerian and regular—extraordinary in this age—and the signature was "Emily Furman."

"Dear Mr. Littleton," it read, "I read your request in the Sunday Book Section concerning material for your autobiographical preface to Miss Olivia Baird's works, and I thought possibly you might be interested in some minor sidelights of her character. . . ."

Good God, I thought, why don't they let me alone? If my poetry's any good, let that speak for me. What difference does it make what sort of a woman I was, what I ate for breakfast, whether I slept in nightgowns?

"Miss Baird used to come into my bookshop very often to use the lending library. As a great admirer of her work it naturally interested me greatly to know what her literary taste might be. While she was working on something she invariably chose detective or mystery stories. She said she couldn't read current fiction while she was writing because it distracted her. She also once said, 'If it's good writing I get discouraged about myself, and if it's bad writing I get discouraged about the author.' Now and then she'd take out biographies. But she had an antipathy to all journalistic books—'I' books, she called them. She complained that nowadays not enough distinction was made between journalism and creative fiction."

Brian was smiling. Don't I know it, he said. It was one of your pet arguments. "Another characteristic which I remember very clearly," went Miss Furman's letter, "was her habit of dress. I could always tell when she was at work on something by the fact that she wore no hat. She wore hats only when she wasn't working. 'I can't think with a hat on,' she told me once."

Or with a girdle on, said Brian! But I guess Miss Furman wouldn't have known that.

"I hope you won't think these items too trivial. Sometimes they help to make an important figure human. Not that this was necessary with Miss Baird—she was the most human person I have ever known; and although I saw her only once a week I feel as if I had lost a very dear friend. . . ."

Nice woman, mused Brian, putting her letter in a folder marked "O.B."

This amassing of material proved to be a very busy time for me, not unlike the period immediately following my death; for Brian's published request had impelled a number of people to remember me and convey their memory to him.

There was the time, for instance, when Brian was listening to a woman in his office. She looked colorless and dowdy, with the kind of drained and formless face, with hair skinned back, that seemed the trademark of the German governess. This was not strange, for she turned out to be Fraulein Kiesewetter, who had taken care of Philip and Auriol for two years after I had left Max.

From the look on Brian's face his distaste for Fraulein Kiesewetter was intense; and from her remarks it was easy to see why. She spoke with a strong German accent in spite of twenty years' residence in the United States.

"She did not love her children," the woman was saying. "If I had not been there they would have had no mother love."

"Just what makes you think that, Miss Kiesewetter?" asked Brian.

"Everybody knew it, Mr. Littleton. All the nurses. Why, she was out every night, and always people for drinks, and then, of course, Miss Baird drank much too."

"Just what did that have to do with mother love?"

The governess opened her white-blue lashless eyes in righteous incredulity. "Why, that is no atmosphere for children. She was wanting them always around in the evening when—when— she saw all these men. She tried always to upset my routine with the children."

How well I remembered that routine! Supper five minutes late, Philip up ten minutes late, and Miss Kiesewetter would become alternatively abusive and tearful, in the German manner. Every time I took the baby Auriol in my arms, her lips would be compressed with irritation and disapproval: that was her right, not mine.

Brian, waiting, said nothing to her, but his aside to me was: How did you stand her in the house? Miss Kiesewetter obviously expected some reaction to her revelations, but receiving none decided to play her trump card.

"I know everybody thinks how sweet, how charming is this lady poetess, but I think the world should know she was not such a fine sweet lady. That is why I am here."

"That is obvious," said Brian.

The governess said "Please?" Then, in a confidential half-whisper, and bending over toward him, "I was forced to leave her house because of these things. I did not want to leave the poor little children—ach, they were like my own, you understand—but I could not stay in that house one moment longer. I may be only a nurse but I can see things."

"Miss Kiesewetter," said Brian, "I am not interested in gossip. It was kind of you to bother to come, but I am afraid you misunderstood my request—"

"Please?" said the governess again.

"I was interested chiefly in correspondence concerning Miss Baird or facts about her professional methods which might interest her public."

Miss Kiesewetter smiled—if you could call the extension of her bloodless lips a smile. "That is why I too come, Mr. Littleton. The facts—" (She pronounced them "fects.") Heedless that

Brian had risen and was shuffling the papers on his desk in an obvious desire to terminate the meeting, she went on, her voice rising, "One day I could stand this fine lady no longer. I went to her and I said, 'Miss Baird, I have been a slave for two years to your children to give them the mother love that you are not able to give, but now I wish to leave because you are a low person and I do not wish to stay in the house with you. You should be ashamed, with your drinking and kissing and goings-on, you—'" Brian cut her short by raising his hand and walking toward the door.

"I don't wish to hear any more of this," he said. "I would appreciate your leaving."

Miss Kiesewetter rose and shrugged, her lips tight. She went to the door, paused, turned back towards Brian and said with a malice of which only the servile are capable: "Naturally, you do not wish to hear. You gentlemen all like a loose woman, yes?" I saw Brian's right hand instinctively clench in a fist, as though he would have struck her, and before he had controlled himself she had slammed the door and left. He stood there shaking with anger and only a succession of telephone calls and interruptions from his secretary forced him to tamp it out. I could have made him laugh by telling him what I said to Miss Kiesewetter after her denunciation, which she reported accurately enough.

"Thank you, Fraulein," I told her, trembling. "Now I can say what *I've* been wanting to say for the past year, but haven't because of the children. You're a lying, prying, sneaking horror, Fraulein. I have enough proofs of your emotional instability to have you put under observation. Like most Prussians you are either a bully or a whining sycophant. You are quite incapable of normal instincts. I shall recommend you as a good nurse for small children; but as an impossible member of any household. Now please leave—and take your cringing, paltry virtue with you!"

I don't think Miss Kiesewetter understood half of my peroration, but she understood the gist. She was out of the house in an hour. I doubt whether any other moment of my life held such pure relief.

"Cassie," said a strange woman in a strange house, "you used to work for Miss Baird, the writer, didn't you?"

The Negro girl looked up from the sink in the small kitchen and smiled broadly. "I sure did," she said. "Three years."

I was very fond of Cassie. She was a generous soul, albeit a sloppy worker. The two seemed usually to go together. I think she would have stayed with me indefinitely if she hadn't married a shiftless fellow and got herself involved in the policy racket in Harlem.

"I see in the papers," said the lady, "that they're looking for letters she wrote—you know, for her biography."

"Letters? What kind of letters?"

"Oh, any. You know, that would give an idea what kind of a person she was."

"I got a letter. I kep' it."

"Really, Cassie?" The lady laughed, indulgently. "Well, maybe it'd be something for them. Here—" She put a section of the paper on a ledge. "Here's what it says—" She left, and Cassie picked it up, found the item, and studied it. Then she tore out the paragraph and put it into her purse.

I followed Cassie to her home in Harlem that night. It was a railroad flat, and every tumbled bed in the dismal string of rooms seemed to be occupied. There were paper flowers and religious color-prints for decoration; the rooms were cluttered and airless. She pulled a box from under a bed where a man was sleeping, clothed; set it on a table, opened it, and took a folded piece of paper out from a variety of things: sewing spools, buttons, badges, ribbons, postcards. She read it carefully, then sat down, and with a pencil laboriously wrote a note.

"Dear Sir," she wrote. "I seen by the papers you need letters by Miss Olivia Baird. I work for her three years, genral houseworker and light wash. I take care Ariol and Phil sometimes too. I am sending you a letter writ by Miss Baird to me, so maybe you could use it in your book. Please can I have it back—

"Yours truly,

"Cassie Jackson, Apt. 2, 868 West 139."

The enclosure, in my writing, went as follows:

"Cassie—I will be back at five. Philip is *not* to turn on the radio. If you take the children to the park please see that Auriol wears her old clothes. I have ordered stew for dinner. If you have time please iron my black dress. Thanks. O.B.

"P.S. One of the gentlemen who was here for dinner last night said you cooked the best yams he had ever eaten."

After Brian had read this, smiling, he called in Miss Jordan.

"Send a note with this, please," he said, handing her my note and Cassie's letter. "And enclose a check for ten dollars." Then he dictated:

"Dear Mrs. Jackson: We appreciate deeply your thoughtfulness in sending us the letter you received from Miss Baird. We have had it copied for future reference and are returning the original to you along with a small payment.

"Sincerely yours—"

After Miss Jordan had left, Brian sat musing for a moment. At that, you know, Olivia, that note to Cassie is as revealing as anything you've ever written!

There were a number of such instances in which people I scarcely knew or had not seen for years came forward with letters of reminiscences, trivial or critical, sentimental or concocted; but my vision of the world and its people was beginning to dim. Only those closest to me still retained their sharpness of outline in the moments—widely spaced—when I was present.

I next saw Philip in Brian's office.

"Thank you for letting me see these things of your mother's," said Brian. "Some of them are extremely interesting—particularly the fragments."

"Are you going to print them all?"

"No, I don't think so. But I am going to include her radio play. As a matter of fact, I'm seeing Burton at CBS tomorrow about putting it on the air. It's amazingly timely."

"I thought so too." Philip got up awkwardly and said, "Well, I guess maybe I'd better—"

Brian rose too. "By the way, what are your plans this winter?"

"Me? Well, I've got to get a job."

"What kind of a job?"

"I'm not really certain yet. Newspaper job, maybe. Some other plans I had fell through, so I—"

"What sort of thing do you want to write?"

"Oh—critical stuff, I guess. I don't think I'd be any good at original writing, but I did a lot of essays and things at school."

"Ever thought of the publishing business?"

Philip looked at him in surprise. "Why, no—not particularly. I don't know anything about it."

"I'm asking you because I may need an extra reader around here. Not much pay but at least it's a starter."

"Why—why, thanks Mr. Littleton, that's awfully nice of you. I didn't mean—"

"Look," said Brian, lifting a heavy book manuscript off his desk. "Take this home and write me a report about it. Give a brief synopsis of the plot and then let me know what you think of the writing and the approach in general." He handed the manuscript to Philip. "Try to keep it under five hundred words. And if you can," said Brian leading him to the door, "let me have it by Monday. Think you can make it?"

"Oh, sure," said Philip with elation in his voice. "I can make it."

"After that it'll be easier to get down to facts," said Brian at the door. "I don't yet know how your mind works!"

"Deviously!" said Philip, grinning. He held out his hand to Brian. "This sounds like a lucky break. Thanks!"

I was with Brian when he read Philip's subsequent report. According to the brief résumé, the book concerned the life of an adolescent boy in the slums of Detroit. The comments ran as follows:

"Mr. Litvak (the author) seems to think that a vocabulary is strong in direct proportion to its meagerness. His words are limited to one syllable and four letters. Possibly this is appropriate in a book dedicated to the exploration of obscenity. The latrine figures prominently in *Ashes in the Mouth*. Benny, the hero, is possibly the most unattractive adolescent character yet conceived. Litvak shows that his brutal environment has made Benny mean, morose, furtive and sexually distorted; but he gives no clue as to why a mean, morose, furtive, and sexually disturbed youth should warrant four hundred pages of loving attention. Martha, the older woman for whom he harbors a specific and nasty passion, is, among other attributes, a dope-addict. Benny's mother is an abortionist. The used-car dealer in love with Benny's mother is impotent.

"Throughout the book there are turgid passages in which the great assembly-lines of Detroit are described as demonic crushers of the human spirit; but as there is no spirit evident in Litvak's characters there is nothing to be crushed.

"The prevailing impression," Philip wrote in his final paragraph, "is that the author is trying to cover up some innate weakness by the constant use of verbal brutality. Like brilliant colors, shock effects in language gain most by being used sparingly. In *Ashes in the Mouth*, Mr. Litvak has painted a violent chromo which offends the senses without stimulating them."

Brian laid the report down, smiling a little. Chip off the old block, Olivia! The boy's incapable of reacting any way but strongly to anything. But he'll do. He's got the right slant—even if I have to pin his ears back from time to time for his cocksureness!

It must have been shortly after that Auriol telephoned Brian at his office.

"I just thought I'd tell you," she said. "I've enrolled in the Workshop . . ."

"Good girl," said Brian. "When does the course begin?"

"Monday. I'm terrified!"

"Don't be silly. There's nothing terrifying about learning to act."

"Oh, yes, there is. What if I'm no good?"

"Even that isn't the end."

"Oh, you're terrible! You should have said, 'Of course, you're good!'"

Brian laughed. "Tell me, Auriol, how's life in general?"

"Dizzy," said Auriol. "Rich and dizzy."

"Good. So it should be."

There was a pause at both ends of the line. Brian was merely waiting; but Auriol was waiting for something: for a word, for a sign.

"Well," she finally said, "I just thought I'd tell you."

"I'm glad you did," said Brian. "I think you'll get a lot out of the Workshop." There was another slight pause and then he added, "Invite me to the first performance, won't you? I'm a good claque!"

"That's a date," she said. "For next year . . ."

Brian ignored the hint. "Work hard," he said, "I expect fine things of you."

"Thanks—Uncle!"

Brian laughed. They said good-by to each other and hung up.

You see, Olivia? Nothing up my sleeve. There was a time when you didn't trust me with Auriol.

There was a time when you didn't trust yourself.

And Auriol? Did you hear her voice on the phone?

I heard. She wanted to see you again.

As she hung up the phone, Auriol's brow was clouded and her
mouth in the sullen down-drawn line I remembered so well in
moments of childhood recalcitrance. He treats me like a child!
she said angrily to herself. I wish he'd never known my mother,
that's why he thinks of me as her child.

She went to the mirror of her dressing-table and looked at
herself, and as she saw a certain ugliness mirrored, her mouth
softened and her brow slowly cleared. I could have him if I
wanted, she said to herself slowly. I know I could. If only he
wouldn't think of Mother. . . .

Auriol, Auriol, I said, must you have everything?

You did!

Must you keep testing your power on all you meet?

You did!

Auriol, what do you want of Brian? What do you want of a
man twenty-five years older than yourself?

What has age got to do with it?

Do you have to be told?

Auriol, sulky again, turned abruptly from her mirror as the
telephone rang in the next room. As she raced to answer it I
flew out of her mind; and so, I am reasonably sure, did the
thought of Brian. She is in love with love, I mused; a rapturous
and tormented state and one essential to the expansion of the
human spirit. But I will be glad when some of the passion is
diverted into less explosive channels; not so much for her sake,
but for the helpless human targets in its range!

My hope was partially answered when I next saw Auriol. She
was in a large bare room with wide curtainless windows at
one end, mirrors down the length of one wall, and a platform

at the far end, on which were several chairs and a table. Facing
the platform were a dozen or more young people, men and girls,
seated on cane-bottomed chairs. An older woman with very short
brown hair and an aquiline, forceful face was standing below
the platform. On the platform stood Auriol; she was pale and
her hands were trembling. In a very low voice she said: "I
am going to recite 'Deirdre,' by James Stephens." Then without a breath she started: " 'Do not let any woman read this
verse!' "

But the older woman put up her hand and stopped her,
turning toward the class.

"How many of you heard the title of the poem Miss Corning
said she would read?"

Three hands were raised. The woman turned to Auriol. "Miss
Corning, this is a diction class, not a course in lip-reading.
Would you be good enough to let us all in on the secret?"

Auriol flushed with humiliation and repeated in a loud
strained voice: "I am going to recite 'Deirdre,' by James Stephens."

"That was audible enough," said the woman, "but it sounded
more like an accusation than a statement." There was laughter
in the class and I could see that Auriol was fairly near tears. So
could the instructress.

"Come along, now, this isn't a personal issue. You've got a
job to do, Auriol. You've not only got to speak so that they
can understand every word; you've got to make them feel. You
must have chosen 'Deirdre' because it made you feel. Now go
ahead—share it."

Auriol went ahead. The first verse was still self-conscious and
a little strained; but by the fourth a new voice issued from her,
full of nostalgia and wonder:

> "More than two thousand years it is since she
> Was beautiful: she trod the waving grass;
> She saw the clouds.

> Two thousand years! The grass is still the same;
> The clouds as lovely as they were that time
> When Deirdre was alive."

Her young voice roughened as it rose and fell:

> "But there has been again no woman born
> Who was so beautiful; not one so beautiful
> Of all the women born.
>
> Let all men go apart and mourn together!
> No man can ever love her! Not a man
> Can dream to be her lover!"

The class was utterly silent, the eyes of all of them on the young girl. She herself was more beautiful than I had ever seen her; not for the perfection of her features but for the compassion which animated them, evidence that she was at last outside of herself and in some common experience.

As for me, an extraordinary thing had happened. I had shifted my position. I was now on the platform, facing the row of faces, the keen, arrested face of the woman, the window, the walls. I was part of Auriol. I was part of the voice that issued from Auriol. I was part of the cadence of the words she spoke:

> "No man can bend before her! No man say—
> What could one say to her? There are no words
> That one could say to her!
>
> Now she is but a story that is told
> Beside the fire! No man can ever be
> The friend of that poor queen!"

The last line hung in the air, piercingly sad. The room blurred, the air pulsated like the beat of blood in the veins; and the last thing I heard was the voice of the woman as she turned to the class. It was not the voice she had used before.

"I believe we all heard it that time, didn't we?"

We stepped down from the platform—Auriol and myself. And then I left.

The twelfth month... This transmutation into the actual beings of my children (for it was happening with Philip too, increasingly) made me believe that I was approaching the last stages of my enforced spectatorship. Less and less was I being compelled to stand apart as an observer of emotions and events which were somehow involved in living memory of me. More and more was my existence on earth approaching my condition in space: in the latter I was a particle of matter or energy; in the former I was becoming a particle in the spiritual tissue of my children. There was some substantiation, then, in the phrase: I will live on in my children. But the continuity was not in facial resemblance or fleshly characteristics; it resided more mysteriously in the realm of feeling and conscience. Before their birth I had nourished the children from my own body; now I was nourishing them with the residual element of my spirit. Before, they were within me; now I was within them. Not as an entity, not as a character, but merely as one small segment of their vast human inheritance. Along with me were all that had preceded them, male and female, maternal and paternal. Max too, when he died, would be a seed in their consciousness. Now, alive, he was still outside of them, his influence external; although I could see already the contribution of his blood: in Auriol, the ardent dramatic presence; in Philip, the ceaseless war between abstraction and reality. Those were inheritances; as they had inherited from me certain passions and prejudices, certain talents and weaknesses. But what I meant now, in trying to describe my new relation to them, was none of these things. It was the indescribable essence of life itself.

But something happened which checked, once again, this total absorption, yanking me back as an observer of the living. I should have suspected the cause: the publication (by Howe and Littleton) of my complete works; and, on the anniversary of my death, the broadcast of my radio play. Quite suddenly I was in the minds and thoughts of a great many people. It was a sort of mass recall which brought me so vividly and ubiquitously back to life that I seemed almost to reassume my earthly identity.

Brian had done a handsome job with the book. Its thickness surprised me: I had not remembered having written so much. As for the biographical foreword, it was restrained, accurate, and simple. The bare facts of my life took no more than a page. Contrary to popular belief and a few exceptions, the lives of creative people are not inclined to be sensational in the external sense. They are too busy either contemplating or working to indulge in colorful gestures, in audacious social episodes. A reporter, an actor, a fashionable artistic dabbler, may get drunk every night, perform outrageous deeds, embroil himself with a series of noteworthy people, and make, in short, good human copy. But the serious writer, painter, composer, the research scientist, are far more likely to lead lives of bourgeois regularity. The passions and conflict reside in their work more than in their actions, and to endure the productive strain they need some degree of form and tranquillity in their pattern of existence.

Looking over this collected work of mine, I could trace every weakness to a lack of this order in my own life. So often had I forfeited it and squandered vitality in the pursuit of personal happiness—the American goal, the sterile avoidance of grief. Casual love, drink, vanity, gregariousness—all these had at one time or other dissipated the creative current, deflected the line, dulled the edge of mind or spirit. The ivory tower has been much attacked in these last years; yet the locked door still remains an artist's major equipment.

In Brian's biographical preface, little of this turmoil in myself was apparent. He mentioned my two marriages briefly, disposed of the children in one sentence and covered all other relationships in a paragraph which contained the phrase: "Miss Baird was intensely human: she had a quality of compassion, a ready and constant response to human need which has been described by some as a 'lack of discrimination' but which is essentially the basis of her universality as an artist. She wanted above all to understand people; and, understanding, to communicate."

He touched upon my war-work, making it sound more important than it actually was; and devoted a few paragraphs to my journeys abroad and the influence they had on my thinking in general. The rest of the preface was mainly concerned with method of work, with the different "periods" or phases, with the critical evaluation of others. Brian finished with a summation of his own estimate of my value as a poet and my position in American letters. Although the expression itself was controlled, the content seemed to me extravagant. I was simply not that good.

The critics on the whole were extravagant too. The only dissenters came from the ultra-literary or ultra-leftist press. The leading esoteric literary review, noted for the brilliant unintelligibility of its essays, wrote me off as "the cut-rate Millay with a dash of *Good Housekeeping*." It conceded technical excellence ("of an orthodox and derivative sort"), but complained of overexplicitness and "unabashed sentimentality." I happened to know the author: a pale young neuter with his hair cut in a bang who spent every third month in a sanatorium for unidentified neuroses.

The leftist press stated that I was a hangover from the dead period of romanticism, and my work was wholly without social consciousness and therefore of no importance to this day and age. Readers of New York's most conservative paper, on the other hand, would have learned that "Miss Baird was sometimes overpreoccupied, for poetic good, with the struggle of human society. She is at her best in her lyrical, imaginative work."

The book appeared simultaneously in England, and the reviews were on the whole very favorable. It was not the reviews, however, that interested me. It was the actions and reactions of a certain man. I was with him first as he stood before the window of a bookstore in Victoria Street: a well-built man of forty-five or so with the kind of carriage a disciplined life always seems to produce. I could not see his face at first but I could see that his gaze was centered on a pyramidal display of books, all the same—and all mine.

The man entered the bookstore, asked for my book, paid for it, left with it under his arm. Now his face was in focus: the blue eyes, the weathered cheeks, the jutting nose—prototype of the English naval officer, in or out of uniform. It was Alan Mayberry, the writer of one of the letters seen by Auriol and Whitney, the Bermuda friend and lover of long ago.

I was with him as he walked to Victoria Station; I was with him on the train—a commuter's train, from the looks of the crowds on it, the tired men and women in mackintoshes. He leafed through the book slowly, stopping to read the shorter poems, then turning back to Brian's preface. There was no change of expression on his face but there was a slow change of expression in his mind: a change from the shabby realities about him to the twice-haloed beauties of a lost young world. He was thinking of a dark-haired girl in a white dress, of black-night water, of a girl with no white dress in his arms. He was thinking of the wordless embrace, of the short and simple rapture. Nostalgia swelled into pain, and pain into sorrow, and sorrow into a sense of loss which Alan could not define but which enveloped him entirely. I thought this kind of feeling had died, he told himself; I thought it had died.

He got out at a station called Leatherhead, walked for about ten minutes through the damp cold evening, then past a gate, up a short flagstoned walk and into a house; an ugly stucco-and-brick house typical of English suburban style of fifty years ago. There was a row of them on either side, almost identical.

He hung his raincoat on a rack behind the front door just as a woman came downstairs to meet him. Her fair hair, hardly touched with gray, was in rigid, lusterless ridges that stuck out from her head like a bad wig. Her face was bony and kind; her teeth pushing her upper lip above her lower. Her frame, narrow-shouldered and broad-hipped, was clothed in a shapeless sweater and skirt, and she wore the kind of long boatlike shoes which Englishwomen seem to favor. As she greeted Alan, her voice had a high sharp twang, overaccented, overladen with the gentility of the middle class.

"Hallo, dear," she said as she took his briefcase from him. "Had a hard day?"

"Same old stuff," said Alan, walking with her into the living room. "A lot of bloody admirals who haven't been to sea for twenty years."

"You look all in," she said. "Are you sure you feel all right?"

Alan settled into his chair and lit a pipe. "Naturally."

His wife stood and looked at the book on his lap. "What's that?" she asked.

"A book," he said. The rude finality in his tone stopped her from further questioning.

"Joan is having dinner with the Partridges, but she promised she'd be home early. I got a letter from Peter asking for more money—he says he needs a new hockey-stick."

"What's the matter with his old one?"

"Oh, you know Peter—he's always breaking things, or losing them."

Alan grunted as he drew on his pipe. "I suppose Sally wrote and asked for new riding-boots. How one is supposed to raise three children on Navy pay is something I can't fathom."

His wife sighed. "Well, don't worry about it now. I'll get your dinner ready in a mo. . . ." She went out of the room.

Alan did not open the book on his lap but one hand held it as if actual contact could sustain the spell evoked on the train. Closing his eyes, he shut out the dreary room, the niggling objects, the overfamiliarity with every square foot of this space which had once spelled comfort but now, at this time, spelled imprisonment and stagnation. He saw himself in his whites, he wandered through the harbors of his youth, he stood on the decks and watched the foaming over-curl of the bow-wave and the frothing lane of the wake. Particularly did he think of the girls—the dark, the fair, the shy, the freely given. These were the cohorts of freedom, of virility. These were the delirious echoes of a world without war, of a Navy without peer, of a young man without thought of the future.

Then, because his hand was on the book, he came back to me. He tried to imagine what his life would have been had he married me, but it took no shape. All he could think of was the days of his return from sea, with me waiting; and of the nights of leave, consistently ardent. But she would not have waited, he said to himself. She was not that kind. She would have vanished one day. Or I would have brought her to a house like this and she would have run away. She wasn't right for this.

But damn it, am *I*, he suddenly cried to himself. Was *I* meant to live like this? I was gay then, and rash and devilish. I would rise to any dare, gamble for any stakes. The world was my oyster and I awoke each morning with a premonition of excitement. There was plenty of trouble, too, plenty of departure and pain. But all that was stirring, I felt it in my guts, there was this constant heat there—damn it, Olivia has a word for it in this

book: "erection of the heart." Christ, thought Alan . . . how
can it happen here . . .

His mind traveled briefly over the war years on his destroyer,
of the violence of explosion in water, of the terrific tensions
and equally terrific releases. Was this what he had lived through
it for? Most of his closest friends were dead. Only he, Alan
Mayberry, had been permitted to survive so that he could sit
at a desk in the Admiralty and commute each evening to
Leatherhead, to Doris.

Once more he forced his mind back to the water's edge at
night, and to the feel of the sand under us, still warm from day.
God, what a wild kid you were! Wild and sweet . . . I loved
you more than you thought I did . . . and more than I thought
I had. And now you're dead. Well, so for that matter am I.

His wife reappeared, an apron over her skirt and one frizzled
corkscrew lock over her forehead.

"Come along," she said. "Kidney's on the table . . ."

He came; and I departed.

Strangely enough, except for this contact with Alan Mayberry
and the first wave of reception, the publication of the book
did very little in the way of commanding my presence among
the living. If anything, it was another freeing agent. Between
the two green cardboard covers was all I had written that mat-
tered, all I had felt, all—actually—that there was of me now
that the flesh had gone. But it had ceased to be a personal
evocation. It had reached the abstraction of all creative
things.

If you saw an Italian palace where Byron had lived, for
instance, you would conjure him up as a man, seeing his ardent
poet's eye, his free neck, hearing his uneven step on the stone
floors. But if you opened up a book of Byron's poetry, these
physical manifestations of the man would be of small account,

if any. Only the poetic mind and heart would remain. The shape, the contour, would be solely the shape and contour of the creative imagination.

I assumed then that people reading this book, these complete "works" of mine, no longer thought of me as a woman, as an individual. It was not that I had joined the ranks of immortality (although a few critics had put me there, giving me a ten-year to a century span of fame) but that a certain seal had been put upon my name, removing it from the mortal roster of personalities.

The book had also released Brian and the children to a large degree from the frequency of my presence. With Brian, the writing of the preface "fixed" me in print, drawing my image to a certain degree out of his consciousness. To name a fear goes toward dispelling it, and a dream described is less likely to haunt the dreamer. Impersonal as it was, Brian's preface was a testament of his love for me. Thus expressed, it became less of an obsession.

As for Philip and Auriol, the book made me something of a stranger. They looked upon it much as one would look at a public statue of someone intimately known. This is not really our mother, they thought, this is that other thing in her, which we never really knew. This is the other side of the locked door. These are the complete works of a modern American poet called Olivia Baird.

I did see them from time to time even then, but through a diffused and shifting light that reminded me of the gauze screen that stage designers used in *Peter Ibbetson* to convey the illusion of a dream. Their voices too were muffled and almost inaudible.

Once I saw Philip in a room where four men were playing quartet and he and Micaela were listening on the sofa. The cellist, an older man with bushy gray hair, must have been the girl's father. The music was Mozart. Here again I was in three places—or conditions—at once: in Philip, listening; in the musical cadence; and outside, observing. There was a quality of serenity in the room that matched the oscillating harmony of my present home. The two spheres seemed at these moments to have interlocked, as they had when Auriol was reciting "Deirdre," and one time later when I found her standing on some terrace at night looking across the bay hand in hand with a boy whose face I could not see but in whose silence there was reassurance. They were both torn with the beauty of the night, with the sound of waltzes coming from a house, with the revelation, commonly perceived, that they were immeasurably fortunate in a world full of pain. They turned to each other finally, not in passion but like two children protecting each other from the dark, and that is how I left them; except for that part of me that lived in Auriol and in the two stars on her white summer dress.

The cadences of Matthew Arnold, so dear to me, seemed to envelop them as they stood there:

> Ah, love, let us be true
> To one another! For the world, which seems
> To lie before us like a land of dreams,
> So various, so beautiful, so new,
> Hath really neither joy, nor love, nor light,
> Nor certitude, nor peace, nor help for pain;
> And we are here as on a darkling plain
> Swept with confused alarms of struggle and flight,
> Where ignorant armies clash by night.

The radio play, broadcast on the anniversary of the night of my death, had been going on for several minutes before I realized I had written it. This was because of the extraordinary elaborateness of modern radio technique, which has so little confidence in the spoken word that it must boost it with brassy fanfares, charge it with musical emotion, interrupt it with special effects, and bandy it back and forth between a chorus of voices all fraught with that special kind of nervous tension that is called "pace."

The play, called *People's Choice*, concerned a Senator from the Middle West who has a nightmare. The nightmare is that he has to explain to a jury every single statement made in a certain speech of his on "America for Americans." As the speech abounds in such phrases as "real American democracy," "constitutional rights," "foreign entanglements," and "fifth columns," he has rough sledding, particularly as his ignorance of history is almost as profound as his ignorance of the English language. The jury is composed of a cross-section of Americans whose verdict after no deliberation is that the Senator is incompetent, irrelevant, and immaterial. This was a simple enough frame, relying entirely on sharpness of dialogue and content.

But radio's chief production genius had not, apparently, found this sufficient, and had succeeded brilliantly in making it a cross between the "Battle Hymn of the Republic" and a Madison Square Garden pageant. Judging from the rave notices he must have been right. But I saw Brian turn it off half-way through, and Philip, who knew the script well, listen with dawning amazement at the violent potpourri that issued from his radio.

I was present also at two other reactions which had less to do with the play than with a part of my former life. I saw Carlo again, the writer of one of the letters found by Auriol, the Italian lover of fifteen years ago.

Shortly before my death I had read in a newspaper that he was to come to New York as the architect for a proposed center here of Italian handicraft, and I remember speculating as to whether we would run into each other and whether either of us would feel any of the strong physical attachment, after all this time, which had bound us together that one year in Europe. I was afraid that I would, for of all the men I had known before Brian, Carlo Vespigli had been the most attractive.

Now he was sprawled on a couch in what looked to me like a hotel room: not much changed except for the gray in his black hair and a coarsening of his Roman face. Stretched beside him, her head on his shoulder, her waist held in his arm, was a woman of thirty or so, fashionably dressed, with reddish hair and a sensual heavily made-up face. Before them on the coffee table were two tumblers of brandy.

Presently she sat up and leaned over to the other end of the couch where the radio stood and turned it on, saying, "How about background music?"

Carlo laughed indulgently and rubbed the nape of her neck with the back of his hand. "You Americans," he said. "Always turning something on . . ."

Suddenly an announcer's voice exploded over the unadjusted radio—"a commemorative program on the anniversary of her death. Olivia Baird was . . ." The woman started to turn the knob and reduce the volume.

"Wait a minute," said Carlo. "Turn that on again . . ."

"My God," said the woman, "don't tell me you want to listen to a radio play!" She turned it back to the station and the announcer continued, stopped, and was followed by a loud trumpet fanfare.

"Olivia Baird," said Carlo, "how amazing . . . !"

"What's amazing, darling?"

"I used to know her, in Rome. Long ago . . ."

"One of your five hundred conquests, darling?"

Carlo laughed. "Five hundred and one . . ." He bent forward to listen.

The woman stroked his cheek, trying to distract him. "I shouldn't think lady writers would be your type."

"Type!" snorted Carlo. "What does that mean, type . . . ?"

". . . to uphold those principles of democracy for which our forefathers . . ." thundered my Senator.

"Do you really want to listen to all that?" said the woman.

"I suppose not," said Carlo. "Turn to your music, then . . ."

"What was she like?" asked the woman after she had found a station with dance music on it, which she tuned very low.

"Olivia Baird? Why, are you jealous again?"

"I'm always jealous, and you know it!" The woman lay back in his arms and he reached his hand around under her breast.

"You needn't be," said Carlo. "She was a typical American girl—romantic and puritan."

"I bet she didn't stay puritan long."

The Italian laughed. "No—she was a willing pupil. Too willing!"

"What do you mean by that?"

"I mean she had no coquetry—no art. She was too honest—and that becomes boring!"

"God, I'd hate to know what you'll say about me some day!"

The Italian kissed her under her hair, behind the ear. "Never," he murmured, "that you are too honest."

Naturally I left them at that point. I couldn't have been further from Carlo's mind.

I fared slightly better with a sick old man who turned the radio on in bed at ten o'clock to try to forget his arm. Eric Steiner was in the bedroom of his brownstone home when the broadcast of my play brought me back to him. The twin bed on the other side of the night-table was turned down for the night and I could see through the open door to a sitting room that someone—Mrs. Steiner, probably—was sitting there.

Steiner, propped against three pillows, looked even older than on the night of the concert soon after my death; and certainly ill. From the way he sat I saw that his neuritis was giving him pain (he was prone to agonizing bouts even when I knew him); but I felt sure there was something more the matter with him than that, for his skin was loose and of bad color, and his eyes sunken under the great dome of his forehead.

I doubt if he turned to my broadcast on purpose, for Steiner had a petulant loathing of radio, never looked at the radio page, and vowed that he listened only to news, and then only during crises. Music he certainly never listened to; he made all the music he could take. Now, however, he was using it as an opiate, or as a distraction from the sharp discomfort of his body.

The moment he heard the announcement of my name, however, he shifted higher against his pillows and leaned toward the radio, turning it on louder.

Little Olivia, he said to himself, my little Olivia! Like most men who are much older than the women they love he thought of me still as a child, as a child-mistress. He listened intently to the play, smiling sardonically at much of it, shaking his big head in agreement at some of the sharper phrases.

"Eric," called a querulous voice from the next room, "must you keep that thing on so loud?"

Steiner, his face suddenly dulled again, turned down the radio, and leaned closer to it. My clever Olivia, he said, my brave and clever Olivia, who was so good to me, who asked nothing from me.

When the play ended he turned off the radio and sank back against the pillows, his eyes closed. Wherever you are, Olivia, I want to give thanks to you. I was an arrogant master in those days, and took you somehow for granted. But now you have your revenge, if you need it. You have died young, you have eternal youth, while I get older and sicker by the hour.

They are taking everything from me, Olivia. First the instrument of my love and then the instrument of my work. Let them stop me from being a man, but for God's sake let me still make music with this arm! He shifted position painfully and then roared into the next room:

"Lise! For heaven's sake where is my hot milk?"

A chair scraped in the next room, there were footsteps, and then the creak of a swing door. Steiner started to fiddle with

the knob of the radio again, turning the dial angrily through
its crazy acoustic spectrum: bands of vulgarity in speech, obscenity in jazz, puerility in thought: squawks, snatches, brassy
intervals, whispered mystery. He turned through bands of Italian, Czech, Yiddish; then more sentimental songs, more savage
jazz; then, finally, as if he had reached an oasis of crystal sanity,
to the slow movement of Bach's *Double Concerto for Two
Violins*. He sank back and closed his eyes again; and conducted
without moving his arm, without stirring. Every note, every bar,
every swell and diminution, was part of his breath and his being,
so well did he know it, so deeply did he exist in it. His pain receded and he felt again the old expansion of spirit, as if gates
had been opened on infinity. Olivia—his voice was very faint
to me—the music of the spheres. There is such a thing— Yes?
Yes?

When his wife entered with the glass of hot milk on a small
plate, Steiner was asleep, holding my hand.

I saw them all, however briefly, that night of the broadcast. To my surprise Max reappeared more vividly than at any
time since my death. He and his wife and some friends had
listened intently throughout. At the end, one of the men said,
"How come they let that through? It's one of the hottest things
radio's ever done."

"What do you think of your former spouse, Max?" said
another.

Max smiled, shaking his head. "I missed the best of her, I
guess. She did her growing up afterward."

His wife Marusia turned to him curiously. "I thought you
said she was unpolitical?"

"She was. This isn't politics, this play. It's the cockeyed
truth."

"There's a quality of rage in it that's magnificent," said the
first man. "It makes you want to go out and kill the bastards."

"It's the rage of the poet," said Max, "the rage of heaven." He rose and poured himself another drink, immersed in thought. What kids we were, Olivia, what asinine kids. I suppose we had to do our growing separately, though. Together we would have destroyed each other. He lifted his glass to me, for the first time; and then went back to rejoin his wife on the sofa.

Philip and Auriol listened together in her room at home. When it was over they said nothing for a while. Finally Philip spoke. "They changed it a lot."

"It's still got the point, though," said Auriol.

"Funny—she wrote it nearly eight years ago, but it still fits. I wonder," Philip went on, "if the Senator recognizes himself."

"What Senator?"

"Don't be dumb. Any one of those guys who spout about democracy and don't know what it means. The capital is full of them: the People's Choice—small-souled stupid men who couldn't pass a third-grade test; fat flabby old men with corrupt baby mouths; crooked politicians who use the American flag as a slip-cover for their venality!"

"My! My!" said Auriol. "Who's talking like Poppa now!"

"A little impersonal anger wouldn't do you any harm, Duse! All you get sore about is a broken nail!"

I left them bickering there to catch a brief and hazy glimpse of the living room, where Whitney and Elizabeth and another couple were playing bridge. There was a radio in the room but it was not turned on.

Elizabeth suddenly looked down at her watch, "Oh dear," she said. "How awful—we've missed the broadcast!"

"What broadcast?" said the woman guest.

"The broadcast of Olivia Baird's play," said Elizabeth in the low deferential tone she reserved for the dead. "We did so want to hear it."

"Pass," said Whitney, looking at his cards. He was angry at Elizabeth, angry at himself, and angry at me. It is impossible to be entirely free of her, he said. Everywhere I look, there is her book, everywhere I see her name, and now the air-waves are full of her. What did I miss, what was wrong, why does it seem as if I had never been married to her at all? Is it because she belonged to the world? Was I too narrow in my jealousies?

He looked across at Elizabeth, serene and lovely, and then at the other two. How she hated bridge, he said, how Olivia hated bridge. If there is no one worth talking to, echoed my words, I would rather be alone. Well, you are alone now, Olivia. And how do you like it there?

For what seemed a considerable time the publication of the book and the broadcast of the play had produced in Brian a negative state of being, as if he had been drained of me. I saw very little of him during that period and assumed again that he was too occupied with the living to be preoccupied with the dead.

My next sight of him bore out this assumption. He was sitting in his apartment smoking. A woman's voice, warm and vibrant, issued from the bedroom.

"I like your place, Brian," she said. "It's very much like you." I could see through the open door that she was walking slowly about looking at the pictures, at the books, at everything. She stopped at the photograph of me on the night-table.

"What a lovely face," she said. There was no word from Brian and the woman went on looking. "A sort of deathless face—" She came out of the bedroom then and paused in the doorway to look at Brian. He returned her gaze, but the expression in his face made her go to him and drop on her knees before him; a swift gesture of compassion, it seemed, that made her face and figure eloquent. She took one of his hands and held it gently and his fingers closed over hers.

"Brian—is that why you've never brought me here before?"

Brian took his pipe from his mouth and avoided her eyes. "Yes," he said. "I felt—I felt the place was—tenanted."

"Why didn't you tell me before?" said the woman. "I've wondered and wondered. I knew there was something—some reservation—some—well—some check in you. . . ."

Now Brian looked at her. "I meant to tell you before, Nora. But it's been locked up so long."

She settled herself on the floor, still holding his hand, her head sideways against his knees and leaning against them. For a while they remained silent.

"It has lasted ten years," he said, "and nearly eight without her. I suppose you might even call it an obsession . . ."

"Isn't love an obsession?" said the woman.

"I suppose so. This was." Brian paused a moment and then said, "Nora—"

"Yes, darling—"

"Nora—you know that I've never said the word—love—to you."

"I know—"

"It was . . . it was because in some way I felt it belonged to—her."

"I've never asked you for it, have I?" Her voice was barely audible.

Brian tightened his grip on her hand and put his other on her smooth hair. "No. That's what's so wonderful about you. You've asked for nothing."

"I've asked to love you, Brian."

He went on, stroking her hair. "You know—what you just said about her face—her deathless face—that's been the trouble, Nora. Until you came she's been living with me. Even now—sometimes . . ."

"Is there anything wrong—in that?"

"It's wrong toward you, Nora. I keep feeling that you're

getting the worst of the bargain. I'm not giving you what you're giving me."

"What am I giving you?"

Brian turned her head up toward him and looked directly at her.

"Everything I need, darling. Warmth—gayety—release—"

She rose to her knees again and faced him. "That's all I want," she said. "I don't want to usurp anything—cast anything out. There's only one thing—"

"Yes?"

"If you're always going to be in conflict because of me—if you keep feeling all the time that you're—that you're betraying her in some way—it won't be any good."

"I know—"

"We'll either have to accept it—or—"

"No. . . . I don't think I could face that—"

"Face what, darling?"

"Leaving you entirely."

Brian pulled her to her feet, rising as he did so, and held her tightly in his arms.

"Don't go. Don't ever go. I need you—badly."

They stood there closely embraced, their eyes shut, rocking slightly as Brian talked, softly and incoherently, as if the words were new and difficult for him, "I've been so lonely—I've held on to her, I couldn't let her go—I felt lost if I let her go—she was inside me—I talked to her, Nora, and she'd talk back. . . . We were together a lot—I couldn't tell anyone, I couldn't talk about her, I never could talk about her to anyone—but I needed to, terribly. Nora—darling—darling—don't let this hurt you— please don't—I have to tell you— It was so wonderful, what we had—so wonderful—even with all the separation, all the hopelessness—and then she died—and after that we became even closer—even closer. But all the while I felt I was slipping from life. I was only half alive. I thought I could never feel anything

again—never really give myself again. And then you came—
Nora—darling. . . . You came. . . ."

Her arms tightened around him, straining him toward her.

"Give me time, Nora. Give me a little time—we'll work it
out—we'll work it out." Then they turned toward each other
of one accord, his head bent and hers raised; and their meeting
mouths obliterated me.

The next time I saw Brian he was packing in his flat, putting
clothes in the large rawhide suitcase that had accompanied all
his travels since I had known him. My vision of him was not
as clear as usual: the outlines were blurred and it was difficult
for me to see the contours of the room. Only the area immediately about his person retained some degree of sharpness. The
suitcase was almost full when he turned to look at my photograph, still on his night-table, and tentatively put out his hand
toward it. Then he withdrew it, saying, No. Then, Olivia!

Yes?

Because I'm not taking your photograph doesn't mean that
you won't go with me. I need no images.

I know.

You know too why I am going, don't you?

Yes.

I never thought that I could start again.

You're alive, Brian.

Thank God, I am alive.

He closed the suitcase, pressed down the cover, and snapped
the locks.

Olivia—does it sound impossible to you that a man on the
eve of his honeymoon can say: I love you—I will always love
you?

No. I believe that.

Will you prove that to me? Will you do something for me
that I want, terribly?

What is that?

Will you come to our wedding? To Nora and me?

Are you sure you want me?

Yes!

And Nora?

She expects you to be there.

I was there. It was not in a romantic setting: the little hall in the Municipal Building was prosaic and bleak with its yellowed oak benches, its curtainless windows and the two dusty palms on either side of the platform.

Brian and Nora were standing side by side looking up at the clerk who was marrying them. There must have been something in the faces of these two, no longer young, no longer innocent, that affected the clerk, for his voice showed a gentleness and a feeling which could not have been as routine as his job. I would say it was a quality of humility and trust which made the scene poignant.

"Do you, Brian, take this woman, Nora, to be your wedded wife?"

Strong and clear, Brian's voice said, "I do!" Then he spoke to me: Olivia!

I'm here.

"Do you, Nora," said the clerk, "take this man, Brian, to be your wedded husband?"

"I do!" said Nora, and turned to look at Brian.

Look at her, Brian, go to her, I said. Give yourself to her wholly. It is part of our love.

Brian turned toward Nora and they smiled at each other. As they left the room, Nora said, "Brian—I think she was there."

"I know she was there."

"I don't think she minded, Brian. I felt nothing but peace."

"She wanted it," said Brian. "She understands."

Hand in hand they walked into the roaring street as I withdrew. But let me dispel here any illusions about my nobility in this scene, any thought of sacrifice. What I said to Brian happened to be the truth, at last wholly recognized by me. I was part of their love, part of any love, part of the creative spirit engendered by such love, part of that affirmation which is the core of existence. The final transmutation had taken place.

After a year of close involvement with the living, after a year of visitation and observance, of succor and guidance, of examination and trial, I was being released.

The silence returned, the moving geometry about me reasserted itself. Once more I had become a beat, a point, an element in some cosmic pulsation as pure and as ordered as the architecture of a fugue. I would now exist, not as myself, but as a single atom in the imperishable dust of creation. There was no end.

Suddenly the moving molecular pattern about me started a strange reassemblage, as if a multitude of dancers in a stadium had formed themselves out of a whirring mass into a recognizable design—a word, a flag, a symbol. And then, in a blinding kaleidoscope of imagery and sound, in a flash of inner vision that could only be revelation, I recognized these things which I must try to describe. Or rather, because I no longer presumably could see, I became these things; of which I was given a flash and a foretaste on the immediate moment of my death and which I could not then understand.

But how can they be described, when they are impalpable? Of no time and of all time, having existed and having yet to exist, of long past years and of days still to come?

What was the language of translation? There were human beings who had indeed pulled revelation out of matter and made it visible to human eyes, audible to human ears, comprehensible to human hearts. But what was the basic key? Love? Compassion? How convey these flashes of apocalypse other

than say that at this time, at the moment of my release from
identity, I became these things and a thousand more and a
thousand more than these: The gaze of the mother at her child
asleep . . . the temple of notes in the young Mozart's head
. . . the secret curves of the chambered nautilus . . . the
humble retina of the painter . . . the delicate feet of the doe
stepping on moss . . . the self-obliterative passion of lovers
. . . the shadow of a cloud of fields . . . ? These and a million
more?

Whatever the melody, the basic chord was affirmation: the
affirmation so longed for in life, so often concealed, so often
denied because of the material evidence against its existence,
and yet—so often, equally—proven. The final word was Yes.
There was no end.

The end of the flesh was no more the end of life than the
transmutation of fire into smoke and smoke into air was the
death of fire.

It was only Self that died. And if that is no comfort to you,
Philip, Auriol, Brian, all those who remember me for whatever
reasons, then remember your moments of greatest happiness; and
you will remember when you lost yourselves. You will then
understand the splendor of this anonymity and this participa-
tion; and be content to call it heaven.

Do not demand that the dead retain their contours and their
names. That is for your comfort, not for ours. I know you wish
I could tell you about the other dead, about my mother and
father, about a recognizable host. But that is not what happens.
Nor will you want it to happen when you come this far.

This I say and testify; but it is only the testimony of one.
Others who die may tell you other things, when they have
found a way to speak and you a way to listen.

All I can say is that what I have told I know; because it
has occurred.